The Road to Golden

a novel by

Dale M. DeVoss

ISBN-13 978-1-60145-270-2
ISBN-10 1-60145-270-5

Printed in the United States of America.

Booklocker.com, Inc.
2007

Library of Congress Control Number: TXu1-162-478

For Debbie & Daphne, Forever.

Acknowledgments

I wish to thank Brad Schreiber for his tireless devotion to this project and support he has provided me in seeing this to publication.

Also I wish to thank Dick Cote, and Bill Appel for the professional editorial help to get my novel to the publishable level.

One light, light that is one, though the lamps be many....

-Traditional Saying-

Chapter 1

It was Johnny who started everything. I don't know what kind of life I would have had without him.

It was Johnny who got me the job on the potato farm. It was Saturday and we were rumbling down in the early morning light to the farm in his '62 Ford pickup. In four years, it looked like it had been through a war. It was plain brown, no frills, the kind of truck that you get for your first mode of transportation and are damned happy to have. To us, it was the most beautiful truck that there ever was, because it represented our freedom. Johnny was a wise sixteen years old and I was his fifteen-year-old acolyte. He held the steering wheel with one hand while pointing out the vast country side with the other one.

"You know, someday this will all be nothing but stores and sub-divisions." And with this sad pronunciation, he shook his head from side to side, realizing the full impact of the inevitable.

The last couple of miles of road were like an asphalt patchwork quilt, the kind you usually come across in the countryside, and you had to be very careful to stay on the road. Hitting a pothole could send a roaring pickup careening off the road into a ditch. I never worried with Johnny though, because he had been driving since he was ten years old and seemed to have a sixth sense behind the wheel.

It was late autumn and the Michigan countryside had a general brownish tint to it, with occasional fields still throwing off a golden hue. It reminded me of one time, also in the fall, when Johnny was looking out the window as he drove and said that the fields reminded him of a painting by Van Gogh. I had asked Johnny who "this Van Gogh guy" was and he went on and on about the painter, as he would do about so many artists that he knew about. I would always enjoy these lengthy talks and I learned to be a good listener. It was Johnny who got me started reading poetry from the library.

We were on the final stretch of road now, and the big farm loomed in the distance. It was on twelve hundred acres in all. We worked out of the big barn, just off the road, with the large farm house just to the right of it. Actually, it made me feel as if I was going to my real home, every time we arrived. It was always a beehive of activity, with dogs barking, people going this way and that, chickens scurrying. There would be energy everywhere you looked.

Johnny wheeled into his spot as he always did, as though he was in a hurry to get there, even though we were always fifteen minutes early. He liked to get to the farm before our shift and have a cup of coffee with Mr. or Mrs. Petersen who ran the farm. I didn't care much for coffee, but I loved listening to the chatter that preceded our workday. It was the kind of talk that you would hear in small towns everywhere.

"Little cold today, but I don't think the ground will be hard enough where we can't plow it," Mr. Petersen might say.

He reminded me a little of Andy Griffith, who I watched on TV, a kind, soft-spoken gentleman farmer of the great American landscape. Once the afternoon group heard him or his wife make some statement about the quality of the sky or the soil or the time of year or the harvest, we allowed for a long pause, and then, out of the silence, the foreman bellowed, "Let's go," and the work commenced.

With that statement, the foreman took his seat in a moving chair way above the floor layout in the barn. Everyone scrambled to get into position. I had a spot right in front of the machine that automatically bagged the potatoes. I placed the plastic bags up on clamps that opened up and grabbed the bag. If I wasn't careful, the bags would slip off and potatoes would spill on the floor.

This happened rarely but was always an awkward moment, for when it did, the foreman gave me the evil eye. I had just four seconds until the next clamp came along and in these four seconds I had to take the bag and put it through a staple machine and then drop it on a conveyor. This automated process didn't allow for any pause on my part. I had to be just as quick as the system and if I got out of sync, the whole process shut down. On these occasions, the foreman would swing over to where I was and give me a verbal thrashing. I’d just smile as I picked up the loose potatoes.

I really didn’t mind the foreman, whose name was Leonard. He was all business during working hours but after, he cut loose and joked around, usually snapping someone with a rag. Leonard had stopped going to school after the third grade. He had a squarish head which sloped toward a pronounced brow, and huge, ape-like arms. His thumbs pointed straight out at the first joint, almost to a ninety degree angle. Leonard talked to you out of the side of his mouth, even when he looked at you straight in the face. He often ate raw potatoes from the wash line as if they were apples. Sometimes he spied a rat or a mouse and hurled his potato at it as quick as most people spit, and continued talking without missing a beat.

Johnny had the job of fork lift driver and as with all machinery, cars and trucks, he operated it with the utmost skill and dexterity. He usually was so quick that in between loads, he could be found puffing on a cigarette, waiting for the rest of us to do our end of the cycle. The potatoes never stopped coming in, the never ending process of dump, wash, inspect, wash again, inspect again, and then finally, into the bags and loaded on the trucks.

Despite the repetition of the job, I felt I belonged to something, perhaps just part of the history of farming, as well as being part of a unit, something functional, workable, of benefit to others. As with most farm life, there were always the rich, enticing smells issuing from the farmhouse kitchen. Mrs. Petersen was in there all day cooking, answering the phone, taking care of all who came to the door. And forever, she had that same, sweet patient demeanor about her. I wandered into the kitchen from time to time just to say hello and Mrs. Petersen greeted me with a welcoming smile, and some fruit cobbler, or an ear of corn dipped in butter, or still warm peanut butter cookies.

One night, I sat in the strange yet beautiful twilight, the workday over. The sun had set on the farm and made the great expanse of land shrink down to just the twinkling lights of the barn and farmhouse, fine jewels in a vast darkness. Often Johnny and I would stay for twenty minutes or so just to join everyone and chat. The older workers would sit down with glasses of beer which they made themselves and the rest of us would have a pop. I was busy watching the lock up, enjoying the last moments on the farm before heading home for supper. Johnny broke my reverie.

"Eddie, you want to go with me tonight to the bar?" By this he meant the place where his girlfriend Missy was a go-go dancer. By 1966 standards, Mary "Missy" Springer was a bad girl who wore "wicked outfits" and shook it up for farm hands. To make it even more sordid, Missy told them she was eighteen when in reality she was only sixteen. I thought Johnny was extraordinarily fortunate.

"Sure, yeah, I'd love to go Johnny." It was a reason to leave my house early and another chance to talk to Missy's friend Pamela. We said our goodbyes to the Petersens, to Leonard, to the other farmhands.

They waved and called out good-natured warnings, like "Don't let Johnny drive too fast" and "Not too much booze" and "Make sure you can still get up in the morning." We returned their chuckles and headed to Johnny's truck, reluctant in a way to leave but still heading off to our own separate dinners, and then on to our mutual adventure for the night.

***

The clutter of my room was welcome chaos: my guitar, the songs I'd written, my records, my favorite books. My father poked his head in on occasion, and would remark "What a pig sty!" and, if I was lucky, went on his way. Sometimes, he took belongings of mine and hurled them against the walls, complaining about what I read or listened to or had decorating the walls of my room. I watched him vent, silent, not afraid but more confused by his utter disgust. I wondered what made him so furious. Surely, selling used cars for years in the same small town, no matter how many times you were rejected, did not amount to this much bitterness. He seemed like an outsider to me, someone who I didn't belong to.

But my mother, in marked contrast, could stand in the doorway of my room and talk with me without once remarking about the state of disarray. She noticed when I put up a new poster or picked up a book of poems by William Blake or one of the Beat poets. She knew how much the poetry meant to me, how I tried to create songs which captured the same feelings I had when read those poems.

My mother and father both knew that Johnny pointed me to the books, to other artists and writers. My father did not like that I read more than most kids. To him, reading was another opportunity to avoid work. But my mother, whose only indulgence was the touch-up of her platinum blonde hair she had done each week at the beauty parlor, knew how much I needed music and poetry to survive life in Romeo, Michigan.

Johnny had dropped me off at home and promised to be back in an hour. I washed up, put on black shirt and black jeans and black socks, in preparation for the evening's activities. This style of dress was known as the "greaseball" or "greaser" look and Johnny and I were proud members of that fraternity, whenever we were not working on the farm.

I lay across my bed, the smells of pot roast and green beans wafting in from the kitchen where my mother labored. In those few moments when I found myself alone, I either wrote songs or read, and now, I stretched my lean body out to the night stand to bring out, if not the poems of John Keats, then the book that served that function for me.

Johnny had given me the collected poems of John Keats. He had purchased it at a book sale sponsored by the local library. He read it and one day and simply handed it to me with the curious half-smile which often crept over his face.

His only words about its contents were, "This is rock and roll from another time."

Its worn, black cover, which went so nicely with my greaser outfit, was pebbled and I liked running my fingertips across its surface before opening it, inhaling its musty, comforting smell. On the first page were the words "Hyperion by John Keats (1795-1821)." It was poetry about poetry, a dream about having dreams, and on the first page, I had underlined one of many passages: "*Who alive can say, 'Thou art no Poet–may'st not tell thy dreams?*'" My father could say it. But I didn't have to believe it.

***

I looked at the clock and brushed my hair. Entering the kitchen, I took one of the three plates laid on the pale blue cloth and walked over to the stove to serve myself.

"Eddie," my mother murmured, in a sweet, sad tone. "Please have dinner with your father and me."

I helped myself to some meat and vegetables.

“Smells great, mom,” I complimented her, as I sat down and dug in, powerfully hungry and in a hurry. There were no sounds but the alternate chomping of food and guzzling of milk.

She wiped her hands, studied them to be sure they were clean and then stood behind me, gently placing them on my shoulders. “I wish you would at least wait until your father comes home, say hello, and then go out with Johnny.”

I chewed the food in my mouth, which gave me more time to consider my answer. “I would, Ma, if he could just limit it to hello.”

She walked around the table and sat facing me. I made noises to suggest how tasty the meal was. She smiled.

“What do I have to do to get you to have dinner with us every once in a while?” she asked, but there was no anger in her voice.

I looked up into her eyes and the feeling of guilt that washed over me became strong, too strong to meet her gaze head-on. I glanced past her shoulder into the living room, to the piano which sat against a far wall.

“Promise me you’ll play the piano for me tonight and I’ll stay home.” She shook her head, smiling ruefully.

“You know your father doesn’t like piano playing when he’s around.”

I shoveled the last of the green beans into my mouth and got up, walking over to the sink.

"Then play something for me, right now," I called over my shoulder. I had asked many times before, and always, she had claimed an excuse, either that my father wouldn't like it or, if she had used that in the recent past, that she didn't feel in the mood.

I turned on the hot water in the sink, let a bit of cooler water mix with it and tried to remember the last piece of music I had heard her play. Was it one of the Chopin etudes? Or perhaps it was one those old standards, like "What's New?" There was the time we were alone in the house and I sang The Beatles songs while she good-naturedly played them. She actually giggled while I sang "Drive My Car," and twisted and writhed, as if performing in front of thousands. But it took a turn when I showed her the sheet music for "In My Life." I sang it softly, as it was written, put my all into the line, "In my life, I've loved them all." And then she had stopped, her eyes misty. But willing back the tears, she continued and I finished the song, the last one of the night. But that was long ago and I knew she wouldn't remember the last song she played. I knew that it would hurt her to ask, so I didn't. Instead, I scrubbed the dish with a vengeance.

"You can leave that. I'll wash it."

"No, no, I got it." I brushed the gravy and bits of gristle off the plate, watched it mix with the water flow and slowly circle toward the drain. I jammed the plate and my cup into the dish drainer. It clattered loudly. My mother looked over, to see if anything had broken.

"Sorry, ma," I said. And then the lights of Johnny's truck appeared coming toward us. We both turned slightly in its direction, as we had done night after night, before my father had come home from the car lot.

"You're going to play again for me one day, aren't you?" I asked. I was not sure I wanted to hear her answer.

"You go, now," she replied, patting my shoulder. "Have a good time. You're only young once."

***

Johnny had a perfectly fine radio in the truck but being the master of all things mechanical and electrical, he had a record player hooked up to the wiring under the dashboard. As we blasted down the road, I glanced through the stack of forty-five RPM records he had chosen for the soundtrack of our drive. I knew what the first one was. Every night together began with the same song, Johnny Rivers lamenting about life on the "Poor Side of Town." This song seemed too personal, like Romeo Michigan was in the middle of nowhere. I felt cut off from the world, from the possibilities of my own life.

"Hey, DJ," Johnny shouted, breaking up my thoughts, "next song. You think I want to hear the crackle at the end of song for a half hour?"

I lifted the tone arm and put it aside. I couldn't tell what the next song would be because Johnny always mixed up the stack after Johnny Rivers. There was only the faintest light from the dashboard and Johnny's cigarette for illumination. I wondered if the phonograph was pulling juice off the electrical system of the truck to such a degree that it dimmed the lights. It didn't matter. We were dressed in greaser black, driving in a barely lit truck across a night road with no lights, and it fit the black, despondent mood I was in.

I put the unidentified 45 on the record player and lowered the tone arm, hoping for the surge of power I might feel from a hard driving song, the boost from the screech of an amplified guitar, the lyrics of wild abandon that could make me want to French-kiss the first cute girl I spied. Instead of any of that, Roy Orbison began wailing "Only the Lonely."

"Man, in just a while, I will be looking up at Missy, and her body and that face, God, that face, and she'll be gyrating in front of all those guys and then throw me a wink like she always does. And it will send me to Heaven. Whoooooeeee!"

He was tapping on the steering wheel, and as I listened to Roy Orbison, all I could see in my mind was my father yelling at my mother while he ate, and her scurrying between the table and kitchen, to bring him whatever he asked for. I saw him asking for one thing and another so that by time she began to eat her own dinner, it was cold.

"Man, I need to hear something more upbeat, something that will rock me senseless."

Johnny looked at me surprise, not only for the tone of my voice but for assertion that somehow the songs we had listened to over and over on many nights with great gusto now no longer were worth hearing.

"What's with you?" he asked.

"I want a rock chord to tear through my stomach and pull out my innards and swing them around my head like a rope!"

I rolled down the window on my side and pushed half of my body out the window, staring out into the black countryside. I screamed a high shriek of disgust, a trapped animal. I battled the roar of wind but I kept shouting. When I felt the rage dissipate a little, I pulled my body back inside the truck.

Johnny looked over me with his half-smile. "Exactly," was all he said.

Chapter 2

The drive out from the farmland into the town was always a chance for us to "cruise by" what we considered the hot spots to see if we recognized anyone who was hanging out. A good night involved seeing two cars racing side by side, or a couple of guys thrashing each other in a parking lot over some girl they both wanted, or even a rumble between the rival gangs which roamed the area. As was usually the case, the mundane world of adults, their business, shopping and farming ruled by day, while the hormonal, bored, overly energized kids of those adults ruled by night.

As we sidled up to the neon glow of the A& W Root Beer restaurant, we spotted Gino Titale's hot rod, gleaming, metallic red, chrome insanely reflecting back the light of the sign. No one was parked next to it and for good reason. Everyone in the night world of Romeo knew who Gino was, that he was a teen carved out of granite with a hair trigger temper. If you hadn't seen Gino snap and flash his fists into the face or knife into the stomach of a potential adversary, then by all means you had heard about it from a number of bystanders.

Like I said, no one parked next to Gino's car. Johnny and I were eating at the A&W the night someone new to town pulled up next to Gino's car. Gino was making out with one of his revolving door girlfriends at the time and he immediately got out of his car, approached the unsuspecting victim and blocked the door to the restaurant before the poor bastard could slam closed his own car door.

"You're crowding my car there, pal."

The visitor took one look at Gino's flat, dead eyes and blank stare and knew instantly he picked the wrong place for a cheeseburger. He quickly apologized and moved his car. Such was Gino's power that those inside the parked cars had fallen silent and held their breath.

Johnny eased his truck one space away from Gino's car. Tonight, Gino had a blonde with dark roots hanging on him, nuzzling his cheek. Gino turned in slow motion toward us. Luckily, he liked us. He had seen our band The Caretakers playing a gig. Afterward, he walked right up to Johnny, who was still sitting behind his drum kit.

"You drum loud. I like that." He nodded slightly to Johnny, then to me, ignored the two other players in our band, and then walked off with whatever girl he happened to be with that night.

People came up to us and murmured in amazed tones how great it was that Gino liked us. I was just relieved he hadn't impaled me with the neck of my own guitar.

"Hey, Gino, check this out!" Johnny called out.

Not even members of Gino's gang shouted to him. You never spoke to Gino unless he acknowledged you first, with a word or a gesture. But Johnny felt the power and status of Gino's acceptance and pushed it. He wanted to be like Gino. This puzzled me. I thought it would have been more than enough to be Johnny.

Gino blew an impossibly long stream of cigarette smoke into the air as he surveyed Johnny, who tested the limits of his speakers with a song by The Byrds. Gino stopped to listen. The blonde stopped to look at Gino, to see his reaction to the music. He stared up into the night sky for a few moments and then gradually shifted his gaze back to us with the slightest nod, indicating his approval.

"The Byrds. Pretty cool, huh?" Johnny smiled.

"Yeah," I agreed, looking at Gino, almost talking directly to him. "Byrds are great."

The blonde, relieved that Gino was pleased, leaned her head on one of his massive shoulders and we listened to the song, one car parking spot apart. When it was over, Gino looked over at us again.

"When you guys play again?"

"Two weeks," replied Johnny loudly.

Gino nodded and then turned to his female companion, to kiss her and officially notify us that our conversation was over. Johnny flashed the headlights a couple times and one of the carhops came out and hooked a tray on the half-rolled down window on Johnny's side. He flashed her a dazzling smile and she returned it, in mild, unspoken flirtation. I never stopped marveling how confident Johnny seemed to be in everything he did or said. He probably could have asked the carhop to hop in the back of the truck with him and have her seriously consider it. We ordered two root beers and as she wrote it down, a series of screeches sounded in the night air. Three cars came fishtailing into the parking lot. They stopped, side by side by side, their lights on, their engines rumbling.

"Oh, no. It's Bobby Jones's gang," the carhop gulped. She headed back into the restaurant without even asking us what we wanted to eat. Gino's girl had glanced over a couple times at the cars but he directed her face back to him, as cool as can be. For a couple minutes, despite the presence of the cars, nothing happened and we waited for them to leave. These stand-offs sometimes occurred and since Gino's gang was not with him, it seemed Bobby and his boys were merely making their presence known, trying to spook Gino. There was a loud, exhaust-filled period of inactivity. The people both inside and outside of the A&W looked tense, wondering if Bobby's gang would attack Gino without the defense of his guys. In fact, the only one who didn't seem at all concerned was Gino.

Then, Bobby exited one of the cars with a nervous-looking girl who he walked a few feet toward us. Bobby put his arm around the girl, who looked to be growing tinier by the moment, as if she was trying to will herself into a puff of smoke, disappearing from the parking lot, and possibly Romeo, forever.

"Hey Gino," Bobby called out and all conversation stopped. "Cheryl over here says that you're a worthless slime ball and treated her bad, man. What's the matter with you? Don't you know shit how to treat a woman?" He was shouting so loud, there was no way Gino could pretend he didn't hear it.

Gino had gone out with Cheryl for a while, and, she not only decided to leave him, she had caused further insult by taking up with Bobby, the person Gino most despised. This was a mounting insult, carefully chosen at a moment when Gino would be most humiliated and least able to do anything violent.

Gino, who was known for an explosive temper, appeared cool for the moment. He got out of his car, leaving the door open, walked around to the back and leaned on the trunk, sizing up Bobby and Cheryl. Johnny and I looked at each other, wondering what would happen, whether we would have to come to Gino's defense in front of Bobby's thick-browed, excessively mean goons.

"Cheryl," Gino called back, forcing her to take an unconscious step backward.

Bobby gripped her arm, preventing her from fleeing the scene.

"Cheryl," he shouted again, this time with an amused tone, "I know you don't got much brains, but what are you doing with a guy who needs you and his pathetic gang to back him up just to talk to me?"

Bobby shoved Cheryl away from him and took a few steps toward Gino. Some of his thugs opened their car doors, at the ready.

"Fuck ass dago shit, don't talk to her! I'm talking to you! If you knew the first thing about satisfying a woman, she wouldn't have left you." As an additional comment, Bobby raised his middle finger to Gino.

Now, the veins were starting to protrude from Gino's neck. In the past, this had been an indication, if you saw it, that you were about to have your ass handed to you. It was a road map to his fury. We saw it before, when he had lashed out and put some kid into the hospital. But yards away, across the parking lot asphalt, Bobby and his gang could not see it.

After a few moments, Gino smirked and shook his head, as if amused. He looked back at his car, the girl in it, her face drained of blood, and then to us, looking as if we expected to be rushed and sliced open by Bobby's horde. He headed back to the car.

"You're chickenshit!" Bobby hurled one last epithet, hoping to goad Gino into a self-destructive, angry rush toward his own doom.

Gino reached the car and lazily turned back to his potential assailant. "Hey, Bobby. Your class is in your ass. When you don't have your gang and your girl protecting you, I'll be happy to take you on, any time."

He got into the car and turned up the radio loud, preventing Bobby from saying anything in response. Bobby did shout something we could not hear, pointed in a menacing fashion and his armada of cars revved up and roared off.

We drank our sodas and bid goodbye to Gino, who invited us to a barn dance, if we felt like it, later that night. He casually dismissed us with a gesture that was almost a wave and Johnny fired up the truck and got us moving again.

"Gino could have mopped the parking lot with Bobby," Johnny claimed.

"It's a good thing he didn't try," I mused. I listened to the whooshing of air and squeaking of springs on the truck as we tore down the dark country roads of farmland America. “Why do you think Gino likes us?”

As Johnny often did, he tilted his head back, his cigarette dangling from his mouth, and replied out of the side of his mouth.

"Music,” he said. “He likes our music. It’s one way of communicating. If they like the words you write and sing, and the music I write and play, they don’t have to know who we are. They’ll either like us and the music, or they won’t.”

***

I thought about this as we bounced up and down in our seats as we drove across the gravel of the parking lot of the bar where Missy was a dancer. But I had no time to ponder the mystery of music, for Johnny wheeled the truck to a parking space, spitting up the crushed rocks into the air.

“In just a few minutes, I’ll see my baby’s face. And she’ll dance for me...”

He paused. The part of my mind that created lyrics unconsciously snapped to attention.

“In a tender embrace.”

“Nah,” Johnny offered, “I was going to say, ‘eternal embrace.’”

"I don't like eternal embrace," I countered. "It sounds too much...."

"Like what?"

"Like a tombstone."

Johnny nodded agreement with my logic, threw the truck into park, turned it off and was out the door in one fluid motion. As always, I was trailing him, trying to catch up as he let the smoke of his cigarette curl around his head, standing in the back door of the bar. His eyes scanned the darkness of the interior, finally settling on his intended target: Gus. His stare gained the attention of Gus, who beamed and walked over to us, shaking our hands and ushering us to the niche he saved for us in the kitchen. Pounding music was issuing forth and we heard the yelpings and howlings of the patrons, as a girl in a bikini gyrated on a small stage to blaring music which pushed the capabilities of the bar's speakers.

"That little lady of yours is next," Gus yelled into Johnny's ear.

Gus was much older than us, perhaps even in his thirties but he seemed to understand Johnny's gyrating free-spiritedness and swagger, and treated Johnny in a way I often wish my father treated me: as a pal, one glad to see me whenever I happened by and not too nosy about the details of my life.We didn't know that much about Gus. He had been single all his life, and spent some years traveling the world in the Merchant Marines. We never saw him making a move on any of the girls who danced there. Maybe that's why they hired him.

From our underage vantage point of the kitchen counter, we could not see the announcer who informed the crowd that Missy was taking the stage. A raucous cheer went up, suggesting she had some followers in addition to Johnny. Missy was cute all right. Her jet black hair was piled up alluringly, with tendrils, giving her a somewhat Spanish style, complemented by a rose slipped through a knot. Her body was petite but still curvaceous and she had a single swirl of hair that came down perfectly situated between her perfectly shaped, milk-white breasts. The dress she usually wore, and had on that night was the go-go style, very short, pale yellow with glossy white vinyl boots. The dress had sparkles on it and refracted the strobe light that bounced off her, as The Beatles's "I Want to Hold Your Hand" blared.

When she finished, Missy looked in our direction and blew a kiss to Johnny who immediately returned it. You couldn't see the patrons very well because of the lighting, but that was okay with us and it allowed us to hang out without getting into trouble with the owners. Most of the guys there, Gus had told us, were usually just frustrated farmer hands and local business folk, who were escaping for a couple of hours from the pressures of their world. Who would deny them a peek at clothed young women flashing limited views of their supple thighs and breasts to the steady beat of the best rock and roll had to offer at the time?

I felt a little guilty being there, having led my mother to believe I was at teen club for the night. But before I could think back to her entrapment in our home, Johnny's loud hooting distracted me from the guilt. He was watching the next girl on stage, who danced listlessly, with no energy. The audience was clearly quieter than when Missy was performing.

"Come on," Johnny shouted. "Shake it! Do something up there!"

A couple patrons turned their heads sideways, not really making the effort to see who had shouted, but showing they had heard the catcall.

"What are you doing?" I asked in a hushed tone.

"She's a lousy dancer. Can you believe they pay for this?"

"We didn't pay anything," I reminded him. "So, just let it go."

"Eddie, you got to live life with a passion or there's no point to it."

Again, he turned his attention to the rather tired looking blonde girl, who barely seemed to have the energy to lift her arms past shoulder height.

"Fucking hell," he yelled, louder than before, "will you dance or get off the goddamn stage!"

Now, despite the lack of lighting, I saw heads turn completely around and look in the direction of the kitchen. A couple of voices told us to shut the hell up.

"Quit it," I warned in an insistent, low voice but Johnny never heard it. He was now responding to not only the dancer but those voices that had told him to stop.

"Don't yell at me. The girl can't even dance!"

Johnny lifted his middle finger in an obscene gesture to unseen opponents in a darkened room. I pushed his arm down, despite the fact that probably no one saw it. He yanked his arm away from me, annoyed that I was trying to control his behavior. A dark shadow descended on us. A tightness came to the pit of my stomach. I thought it might be an angry customer, ready to slam his fist into the face of the rude visitor who had belittled his favorite dancer, perhaps even his girlfriend. It came toward Johnny and me and I wondered if I might be mistaken for the intruder and suddenly feel the crunch of bone on bone, flesh smacking flesh. The outline of the shape became clear. It was Gus, and his face was taut with anger as he stared at Johnny.

"What the hell is wrong with you?" Gus hissed, in a very untypical tone of voice. "I risk my job getting you guys in here and this is what you do? Are you out of your mind?"

In quieter voice, which I barely heard over the still blaring rock music, Johnny blithely said, "Not my fault if she's a lousy dancer."

Gus, who had always been kind to us, now shouldered me to the side as he stood in between Johnny and me. "You know what; you better get out of here before someone else comes over."

"What are you talking about?" was Johnny's reply.

"Right now," Gus insisted and Johnny headed for the back door.

I started to go around Gus to follow him but he restrained me by my arm and steered me toward the door but not outside. I looked out to see if I could spot Johnny but by this time, he was undoubtedly half way to the truck.

Gus looked intently at me, placed his hands on my shoulders and gave me a bit of a shake.

"Look here, kid," Gus began, and thought a moment, obviously not sure how to say what he had on his mind. His look softened as he finally felt the words come to him. "Johnny, well, he's older than you, and he is already wrapped up in his life, does what he wants to and doesn't always think about the consequences. Even though you're younger than him, you think about things."

Mild applause came from the room after the music had stopped. But I did not look away. I had no idea what Gus was trying to say, but the way he said it kept me still, entranced, wondering. As if realizing the intensity of this lecture, Gus looked down to his shoes and then back up at me, with a wry smile.

"Well, anyway, what I'm trying to say here is, well, you're a good kid. Johnny's a good kid, too, but he's not the kind who listens to advice. And I don't want to see you messing up your life, Eddie, you know?"

The announcer presented the next dancer and the next song began. It shook me out of my speechlessness.

"It's okay, Gus. I know what I'm doing. Johnny and I are tight, but I have my own mind."

Gus smiled. "So, if he jumped off a building, you wouldn't do it too, right?"

"He's my friend," I explained. "I don't worship him."

Gus, apparently pleased by my response, gave me a big bear hug, lifting me slightly off the floor. But as I looked back, walking through the back door, Gus was still watching me, with a look of doubt crossing his usually cheery features.

Chapter 3

Johnny and I rode in bumpy silence, away from the club, a bare sliver of a moon little help in illuminating us. Johnny expertly lighted another cigarette while temporarily steering the truck with his knees. It was odd about Johnny's outrageousness and Gus's sudden expression of concern about me. But I said nothing about it. It was Johnny's adventurous nature that took me far away from my home life, which had created our band, and, with his seemingly unlimited charm, brought women constantly into our circle. He considered Missy his girlfriend and the other girls he often found himself in bed with were in a different category. That, too, was something we never spoke about.

I knew this meant that we would go somewhere for about two hours until Missy would be getting off work. Then, we would head over to her parents house, both of whom worked the night shift. This thought was always a blessing for me because it meant there was a possibility of romance ahead. Missy often came back with another girlfriend and while Johnny and Missy were off in a bedroom, I had a chance at physical bliss, if the conditions were right, the girl was in the mood and I wasn't feeling too shy.

The sudden illumination of the barn where the dance was being held broke the mood in the truck and Johnny and I exchanged a smile of expectation. The weathered building had lights bouncing off of three of its sides, as if a Hollywood movie was about to premiere in the middle of a Michigan farm. Wild music poured forth from the barn. We heard the shouts of the dancers inside, and as we approached, saw the shadows of those dancing projected largely on the barn walls.

Inside, we immediately spotted Gino, standing by the beer cooler with two girls wrapped around his arms. Neither was the one who had been with him at the A&W. They were a pair of little schoolgirl kittens, purring and rubbing up against Gino, trying to engage his affections. He just stood there stoic, rock solid, like a statue of John Wayne or some real-life hero of the Old West.

Johnny and I eased our way through the bodies. I kept my eye on Gino, who was staring back at me, holding my attention. Johnny, however, was being Johnny, smiling at every woman whose attention he could pull, whether she was alone, with a girl or with a boy. Then, all of a sudden, the strangest thing happened. Gino was wiggling his index finger at me to come over to him. There was no expression on his face. I stood there, at first totally confused by the gesture, for Gino would only talk to those people he thought were important to him and I never felt myself in that category. I turned to Johnny to see if he was reacting to Gino's summons, but Johnny was already moving through the dancers toward a woman who had returned his dazzling smile with one of her own.

I began to walk over to Gino and had the feeling of watching myself walk in a movie, seeing my tentative approach toward Gino from various camera angles, the music roaring. I felt myself inching towards him but not aware that my feet were moving. The lights inside shifted colors, unlike the all-white lights set up outside. It was eerie and at the same time very familiar to me. I had just seen Gino not long before, yet my knees were somewhat wobbly and I wished I could take a few minutes to have a beer, look over the action, before having to speak to him on my own.

Gino was slouched now, one leg resting on a bale of hay beneath him, the other leg keeping time to the music. His left arm was around one of the girls and the right was clutching a beer. His gaze, now that he saw I was coming, was directed over the heads of everyone else, as though he was seeing something that the rest of us couldn't. Now he looked right at me. I was almost right on top of him. He gave a signal to stop with the hand that had the beer in it.

“Okay, not so close, sonny. You’s crowding my space here, huh?" Then he took a swig from his beer. He wiped his mouth with his right arm and then looked at me intently.

“Look, kid, I like you, you know, and well, I don't want you to get hurt or nuttin’. But you know that gang at the drive-in tonight?” Here he paused for effect.

I realized he was expecting me to say something. First, I bobbed my head up and down. Realizing that must have looked stupid, I tried to talk but my voice was dry and brittle.

"Yeah, you really told them, Gino. It was great.”

He continued, "Well they ain't done with us yet, see? They'll be here later tonight and try and straighten things out. Know what I’m saying here?” Now, his head tipped down from his bale of hay throne and looked me right in the eyes.

I was speechless for what seemed like hours and then finally muscled up the courage to say,

"Johnny and I ain't scared, Gino. We'll help you fight those guys."

Gino burst into a great roar of laughter that sent chills down my back.

"Oh, whooee, did you hear that?" The girls giggled a little. "The kid wants to fight for me, ain't that somethin'?"

He raised his head up, looked at the barn's rafters and let out another blood curdling laugh. Even with the music blasting, some people nearby glanced over at us. Gino regained his composure, leaned in toward me again but now, his voice was like a loud whisper, more confidential, not at all glib.

"Look, kid, I appreciate your courage and all, but these guys, see they'll be coming with guns and knifes and brass knuckles and all. My guys and their guys are going to go at it, probably back of the barn. It's no place for a kid, and besides if the goons (the word he used for cops), come, my ass will be cooked if they knew I had such a young kid on my side, *capiche*?"

He then tapped me on my shoulder a couple of times in a fatherly fashion and I knew that there would be nothing more to discuss. I raised my head up and thanked Gino for being so kind and he gave me a wink and I turned and left.

I had to go find Johnny now and that would be no easy task. I cruised through the dancers. I took a quick look outside. I had to wait in line to get a beer. The thought occurred to me that it was odd our band was named The Caretakers. That term, for a professional who dealt with the` sick and dead, seemed strange, even funny. How much care can you take with a stiff who can't feel anything any more? But now, I was trying to find Johnny, trying to take care of him. It was not one-sided. By having me as his friend, in his band, he took care of me too. But after the lectures from Gus and Gino, I was seeing a different way of interpreting our band name.

***

Outside again, I was walking past long lines of parked cars. Out of frustration, I headed back to the truck and sure enough, from inside it, I could hear moaning and groaning. Now what? I gently leaned against the back of the truck and I looked up into the sky and I could see all of the constellations whose names Johnny had told me about, standing out in bolder relief because of a slice of a moon that was afraid to shine. But I couldn't concentrate on its beauty because the sounds of animal lust confined me to earth. I knew that we had to get the hell out of there, and fast. If the other gang didn't beat the crap out of us, then Gino would.

I moved away from the truck a few yards and started calling out Johnny's name, as if I was still looking for him. Johnny stuck his head out of the passenger's side window, his hair tousled, his eyes wild, and yelled,

"For Christ's sakes, Eddie, what in the hell are you doing out here?"

Now Johnny loved Missy, in his fashion, but I came to the conclusion that Johnny was addicted to sex, to chasing, entrancing, enveloping the opposite sex and in turn, girls seemed to cling to him as well. Both Gino and Johnny had it, whatever "it" was and I just had to live with the fact the indefinable "it" was something that had evaded me. Missy herself would sometimes have other guys and that was the type of relationship they had. They couldn't live without each other, but when they couldn't be with each other, they simply found someone else.

"Johnny, we've got to get out of here, Gino pulled me aside and said there's going to be a rumble out here tonight and he wants us to get out of here." There was a moment of silence and then Johnny pounded the metal ceiling of the truck three times.

"Shit! All right, man, give us a minute to get dressed."

I politely moved toward the tailgate of the truck as, in the cab, arms and legs and clothes flailed about, making the truck rock a bit, back and forth, although with considerably less exertion than it had a few minutes before. Johnny fired up the engine, I hopped in and in a swirl of gravel, we were off again.

It was a comical sight, the three of us in the truck. The girl that Johnny latched onto at the party was all over him. He had a new cigarette dangling from his mouth. The smell of the smoke had not yet erased the scent of their bodies which clung to the worn vinyl seats. I avoided looking at them and did my job, to sort out the records for the player, pretending that I was nothing more than a disc jockey that had somehow been transported into their truck but still had to play music for all those tuning in.

"This here is the Eternal Energy Machine," Johnny said to the girl, slapping his left palm on the outside of his door. "And this is my best friend," he said, looking at me. Hearing the words, all the annoyance I had felt vanished.

"Eddie, this is Carla."

"Carlene," corrected the shapely, blonde girl, but she didn't seem at all upset.

I guess I was Johnny's best friend because I knew him better than anyone and put up with him more than anyone. And I knew what Johnny was going to do. He was driving to some remote spot to park the truck and make love to this lady he met. This meant that I would have to fend for myself. I didn't really mind. It wasn't the first time.

When Johnny pulled off the road, I said, as if on cue, "I'm going to take a walk." I got out of the truck and reached behind the seat, finding another copy of Keats's poems and a pen flashlight.

Carlene picked up immediately how accommodating I was being and purred a sweet thank you to me as I nodded and walked toward a small grove of nearby trees. Behind me, I heard the door slam and Carlene squeal and giggle.

To the squeaking of the truck, the gasps of the young lovers, the dim sounds of rock from the radio, I turned back to "Hyperion," and entered its world again, seeing the visions of it in my mind:

> "*Methought I stood where trees of every clime,*
> *Palm, myrtle, oak, and sycamore and beech,*
> *With plantain, and spice-blossoms, made a*

> *screen, In neighborhood of fountains, by the noise, Soft-showering in my ears, and, by the touch Of scent, not far from roses."*

I knew that we would be heading out soon enough, because we would have to be back in town to go to Missy's place.

The panting and heavy breathing of Johnny and his new friend could be heard in between notes but I found it no trouble to focus on Keats, on his tale of beauty and truth and aging and the cycles of life and death. It brought me comfort, even though I did admit to myself that I could not know the meaning of every phrase he wrote and desperately wanted to. But then, I thought about rock and roll, how some groups so moved people that they sang the songs when they played on the radio, on a record player and when they were lucky enough to see the group in person.

What was it, I asked myself, about the restless youth of night that they should have all these yearnings and sweaty aspirations anyway? Why couldn't they be content with going to school, working on a potato farm, playing the occasional gig, eventually to find a girl and settle down in the same town, and take over the family business? Was I destined for a holy path, a special destiny, out here in the woods reading Keats, with my companions only the occasional skunk or possum? If there was to be another truck full of kids coming down the road, they might be looking for a rumble, and then what? Could I fend them off with my book of poems? If they attacked and killed me, as I tried to defend the naked Johnny and Carlene, how would it change the rest of his life? What would I have missed if I died at this age?

Anyway, Johnny broke my train of thought, shouting out,

"Come on, Eddie, get in the truck. We're moving out."

As he drove, Johnny was all hyped up and talking a blue streak, like he often did after making love to some girl.

“Now we're going to go into town and check out the Blue Note, see if Little Leon and his Caravan are playing. If they are, we're going to go in and catch some of that sweet soul music that'll tingle us right down to our love bones."

Carlene laughed her face flush with the radiance of sexual satisfaction.

***

The Blue Note was where all the greasers in town hung out, and the bands that played there were all in the vein of Motown artists. Little Leon was very similar to Little Anthony and the Imperials, a terrific performer. The only problem that I could see in going there was the fact that Johnny’s many women often hung out there. There had been more than one confrontation. Johnny took it in stride.

Inside The Blue Note, the guys had their hair slicked up in greaser fashion and the girls teased their hair toward the ceiling with lots of hair spray. Guys were required to do a sort of strut that showed coolness, often accompanied by light shoving and playful punching. Usually you didn't see any knives or brass knuckles, it being so dark and all, but you knew they were there.

This scene definitely took you back in evolution a couple hundred of years.

The Blue Note was an old movie theater that was gutted out for dances. You had to be very careful how you walked about in the utter darkness. There were usually couples making out in various spots and you didn't want to bump into them and get the guys mad. I don't recall ever seeing anyone that resembled a manager or guard there. No doubt, they feared for their well-being. This is not to say that the police wouldn't drop in from time to time, just to let you know they were close by, listen to a song or two, and keep an eye on former convicts who were out to find some trouble

.

When Little Leon and the Caravan hit the stage, there was much confusion everywhere. I had wandered off on my own now as Johnny and Carlene had found one of the dark corners to make out in. After the band belted out a couple of blues numbers, Johnny found me, with Carlene literally hanging onto him. He hugged her goodbye.

“But where are you going, Johnny?” Carlene asked coyly.

“Now, sweetie, you know I have to go pick up my sister at my stepfather’s house, and we've all ready been through all this.”

In fact, Johnny and I had been through it more times than I wanted to remember. Sometimes, the story was about his mom being ill or his sister needing a ride or his stepfather being mad at him or the homework he didn’t do. Johnny would take a deep drag of his cigarette, blow smoke rings in the air to show how nonchalant he was and then, after an embrace, be out the door, with me mumbling goodbye to the girl and trailing after him.

"Just think, Eddie, me boy," he said over the roar of the truck's engine, once again, "in about five minutes, I'll be hugging my sweetheart and she'll be wearing the smallest of small nightgowns that she always wears for me."

"What she wears for me," I said, thinking of a rhyme, "to draw stares for me."

"Good one," he laughed, gunning the engine in approval.

***

Just as we got to Missy's house, Johnny brought out his flask of brandy and we took a couple pokes. We pulled up in a field adjacent to Missy's house so we could sneak in the back door, like thieves in the night, while her parents were working the night shift. We used our usual commando skill to sneak past the neighbors' lights, not slip on their slick, recently watered lawn

and dash to the back door before their dogs could sniff us or, if the dogs barked, be out of sight when someone popped a head outside a window.

I heard music playing already as we entered. It was Missy's favorite song, "Cherish," by The Association. She ran into Johnny's arms, wearing her little gown and as this song played over and over, she and Johnny did their ritual dance. The room was filled with candlelight and Johnny pushed his groin into hers as they moved to "Cherish."

Johnny had told me that Missy was a "nymphomaniac" but she and her friend Pamela, who hung back in the shadows, also wearing a negligee, both liked to be known as "sex kittens."

"Did you bring the Spanish Fly?" Missy purred and Johnny nodded. In fact, he couldn't find it so he had bought a muscle relaxer, figuring correctly Missy didn't know the difference.

"Do you want to dance?" was the first words out of Pamela's mouth.

Pamela was okay, but not physically my type of girl. She was about five foot two, full bodied, with very large breasts. But, what the heck, I was there, and she was there, and the candles were going, the music playing, and she was ready for romance.

"Yeah, sure, we can dance. But first, how about a beer. I'm thirsty as hell."

"Oh yeah, how rude of me, I'll go get one out of the fridge." She quickly ran off to the kitchen.

I could see that Johnny and Missy wouldn't be with us much longer as already they were deep into the throes of their "sex dance." Just as I had made my decision, Pamela came in with my cold beer.

I thanked her and went to grab for the beer, but Pamela pulled it away at the last moment and said, "First, you must do something for me," She stood there with that look in her eyes that women get when they know they have the upper hand. She asked me if I could get her one of "those Spanish Flys" from Johnny. I explained I would try and she smiled with dreamy eyes that invited me to places I had rarely been.

I approached Johnny about the supposed Spanish fly. He actually gave me a wink when I asked him about it. Missy was pulling him toward the bedroom and he leaned over to me and whispered, "We have to be out of here in an hour and a half, lover boy."

Pamela and I started to dance and within minutes we were French kissing. Her tongue darted furiously through my mouth, sometimes taking my breath away. I didn't have to embarrassingly request she slow down. She stopped on her own.

Shelly, Missy's younger sister, who was eight years old, was peeking out of her bedroom door. Missy had assured us Shelly would never tell on us and she never had, but every once in a while, she spied on us. I made a hand motion for Shelly to go back inside her room, which she did and then I returned to Pamela, kissing her neck. I slowly moved my passion to her ear lobe and then the time was right.

"Let's go off to the bedroom, Pamela." She didn't put up a fight.

We kissed all the way down the hallway and just before we got to the target bedroom, I pinned her up against the wall. Now, I was licking the outer part of her ear and occasionally humming a few bars of one of our songs into it. This actually made her so weak in the knees that I had to catch her and pick her up. I made a mental note to remember the song but in the heat of the moment, it would eventually escape me.

I then carried her off into the bedroom, threw both of us onto the bed and we both laughed giddily.

"I've been waiting to do this to you for a while. Did you bring little Mr. Raincoat?" she asked as she giggled.

I informed her that indeed I did bring the little guy and suggested that she put it on. I always thought it was more erotic for the woman to attempt this usually clumsy act. Even if she had trouble with it, it would feel pretty good.

Then came the act of tearing one another's clothes off, which in Pamela's' case was easy because she was just wearing the small negligee. When I was removing her panties, I slid them ever so slowly down her legs, taking little breaks at certain times to rub our bodies together. Now, with all the musician sensitivity I could muster, I positioned my face between the thighs of Miss Pamela. I imagined my tongue as the neck of a guitar, swooping through the air as it was played by an expert rock guitarist. I gained more confidence as Pamela responded with an increased bucking of her hips. She was apparently a great lover of music.

We were making love for what seemed like a long time to me. But I did not want to ask what time it was, for fear she would get upset and all our pleasure would stop. She was on top now and I had already had an orgasm, but Pamela seemed to be still working up toward that momentous event. My manhood had worked itself back into a military salute, and I was trying everything I could think of, using every appendage I had, to stimulate Pamela. We rocked wildly, feverishly, and Pamela began moaning loudly. Her fingers dug deeply into my skin and Pamela collapsed on top me with a final surrendering gasp of joy. Lying there, I felt pleased that I had persevered, that I had found an unpredictable rhythm, angle and flow that made Pamela happy. But the sounds of our heavy breathing did not last long in the darkened room. There was a loud knock at our door.

"Eddie, quick!" Johnny appeared in the doorway, half dressed, his eyes wild. "Put your clothes on. Missy's old lady's home. Better leave through the window. You won't have time for anything else. I'll meet you outside by the bridge."

I thought my performance with Pamela had been fairly impressive but I doubted it had been an hour and a half. As I rapidly dressed, I whispered to Pamela to block the door. At the very worst, I could always dive under the bed. We heard faint voices in the hallway, then a door closed.

"Good night, dear," said Missy's mom.

It sounded promising enough to make a break for it, and I quietly slipped out of the bedroom window, giving Pamela a good night kiss before I jumped down. It felt like a scene from Romeo and Juliet, sneaking out before the dawn, avoiding parents and all. Johnny told me all about the plays of Shakespeare. He told me that if I were to read all of Shakespeare's works, I would know all there is to know about human folly, greed and love. Well, he hadn't read them all and neither had I, but Romeo and Juliet seemed to say everything there was to say about deep, true love. I wondered what it would be like to see the play done, maybe with rock music in the background.

These were my thoughts when I got to the mowed field but then the dogs started to bark. Then, a spotlight was turned on. It was the kind of light that cops use on their cruisers. A voice shattered my progress.

“Stop or I'll shoot! I know you're out there and the cops are on their way.”

It must have been Missy’s father. And he must have thought I had been with Missy. I began to tiptoe but the crunch of some leaves gave away my general position. There were shots fired in the air. Other houses in the distance began turning on lights. If I die tonight, I thought to myself, at least I will have died after making love.

It was a fast crawl that took me to middle of the field. Then, I stood and ran as fast I could to where Johnny’s truck would be–or should have been. It was gone. But then I heard the engine gunned maybe thirty yards away. Johnny had anticipated a quick getaway and had already had the truck ready to take off. I started running. Another gun shot split the air but Missy’s father was firing in frustration. The truck was slowly pulling away as the right side door flew open, I jumped in, slammed it and Johnny floored it.

***

As we tore down the main drag, we could see that the cops were coming down from the other side. Johnny, as usual, had this all figured out and headed for a two lane dirt road that ran along the main creek in town. About five hundred feet down this trail he cut the engine, and we rolled down a little valley which led to a small dumping ground.

We were quite secluded now. Johnny pulled out the flask of brandy and we drank to friendship and the bonding effect of near-death experiences.

"I'll tell you Eddie," he sighed, "why is it a guy can't even see the girl he loves without the whole world coming unglued." He shook his head from side to side. I took another hit from the brandy and knew that Johnny was asking this question and didn't expect an answer.

After quite a long silence, Johnny asked, "So, how was it with Pamela?"

I was glad it was dark. I felt like I was blushing. "Fine."

"Fine, huh?"

"Yeah, you know. It was great. I don't talk about it like you do. It's not my thing."

Johnny let that sink in. Then, he chuckled. "Shit, Eddie, you must have looked pretty funny running across that field, like some kind of jack rabbit who has the hound dog on his ass." We both looked a t each other and burst out laughing.

It seemed as though we had enough adventure for one night and were more than satisfied to head home. The very fact that it would be dawn in a couple of hours seemed to help solidify this feeling. I asked Johnny what he planned on doing about Carlene, who undoubtedly expected to see him again, if not later that night, then another night.

Johnny didn't look at me but pulled real hard on his cigarette.

"Eddie, me boy, you have to understand that some things are just understood. She knows deep down inside that there never was going to be a later meeting. Yet, there will be another meeting between us. We both knew that when I left her at The Blue Note, she would just follow whoever to wherever and would be okay."

With this pronouncement, he blew his cigarette smoke out of the window, and that was that. I wondered if Pamela felt that way about me. I wasn't sure what I felt. I wanted to be like Johnny but knew I was different in so many ways. How could one battle his own nature?

***

The jumbled evening and confused feelings had deeply exhausted me and I feel quickly asleep when I finally, quietly, snuck into my room and slipped under the covers. I was hoping to sleep in a little bit in the morning, sleep off the drinking and making love and running through the fields.But the bursting open of my door in the early morning light told me that I was going to catch extra winks another time. My father stood in the doorway, his eyes ablaze and I propped myself up on one elbow and rubbed my eyes, trying to get ready for yet another confrontation

.

"I went to bed at midnight, boy, and you weren't here. I want to know right now where you were and who you were with." My father was now standing over me, dressed to go to work, his fists clenched, his face flushed with anger.

"Went out with Johnny," my voice croaked, and just the sound alone made me sound guilty somehow.

"You were playing music again, weren't you?" he yelled. "I told you, I won't have you playing music—"

"I was listening to music. I wasn't playing it," I interrupted him. "You don't let me play, you don't let Mom play. Do you mind if I just listen to someone else play? Or does everyone have to be miserable in this house?"

I might have been all right if I had left off the last sentence. But now, I was fully awake and getting angrier. His efforts to ensure we had no joy had now extended to the precious moments I was away from him.

"It's my house," he growled, "and you can live on the damn potato farm or with your worthless friend Johnny if you don't like it here."

With that, he began rummaging through my belongings, searching behind books, under furniture, scavenging. I knew what he wanted but I asked anyway. He didn't answer me, just kept on, occasionally hurling paper or books in one direction or another. When he stopped suddenly, I knew it was a bad sign. He reached under some papers and found a reel of audio tape

"That's not new," I protested. "It's some old songs Johnny and I"—

He was at me so suddenly; I didn't have time to protect myself. My father had the tape in one hand and a fist full of my hair in the other, dragging me out of bed and then flinging me to the floor.

"I can give you an honest profession, one in which you do something of value. I offered you the chance to work with me. If you want to throw your life away with Johnny, drinking and playing that stupid rock and roll, then you're headed for a horrible future and no one will be able to help you."

I had hit the floor hard and rubbed my back and side where I landed. I looked up at him, with contempt, but also pity, because I knew his life must have been very unhappy, which is why it bothered him that I had any pleasure at all.

"I'm not going to spend my whole life with Johnny," I said. "But I'm also not going to spend my whole life selling cars. You decided your own life. I have a right to decide mine."

"Not while you live with me you don't!" He looked at me, smashed the reel on the floor and then turned away, in disgust. I heard him storm outside and the front door thundered closed. I picked up the broken reel and rewound the tape that had started to unravel.

My mother peeked in. “Are you all right?” she asked in a quiet and pained voice.

“I’m fine,” I said, sitting on the floor. “Nothing’s stronger than poetry and music.”

Chapter 4

While I pondered such weighty issues as my music, poetry, truth, beauty and how to avoid any more confrontations with my father, my parents went about a life I neither understood nor cared about. My mother seemed to have no other joy than to go to the beauty salon every week, just prior to the weekend with her neighbor and friend Alma. Together, they would dye their hair Marilyn Monroe blond.

As kind as my mother was to me, and as quietly as she suffered the life she found herself caught in, it annoyed me that she did not want something more, didn't demand it. She had left music behind for no other reason than her husband insisted upon it, without an explanation. He had made a pronouncement that there was to be no more music when he was around, like a crazed minister who thought that Elvis or Beatles records were the work of the Devil and urged his parishioners to burn them in a big bonfire.

My father had not yet dared to actually burn or break or throw out my records or books. It was almost as if he knew that was a boundary that even he could not cross, without consequences which were unpredictable. I had finally surpassed him in height, if not in weight, and while he never acted fearful of me, he felt content to occasionally plough into my room, throw things around, shout, knock me around if he felt specially imbued with righteousness and then tromp out.

While I can't say he behaved like most fathers would have in 1960s Romeo, he certainly looked like a lot of other men. There was apparently some tacit agreement among middle aged men of the time to cultivate the look of slick lounge singer Vic

Damone. To prevent them from having a complete breakdown regarding the emptiness of their lives, many of the parents in our little community, the Vic Damone and Marilyn Monroe stand-ins, would go out on the weekend to whatever glamour spot they could find in farm country, generally a dumpy, poorly lit restaurant where the waiters looked like they came out of a crypt to serve for the evening.

Just because their lives were swirling down a sinkhole, I felt, was no reason I had to give up. I continued with The Caretakers, despite my father's admonitions, and tried to stay out of the house as much as possible. Between school, the potato farm and running around with Johnny, I hoped that there would be time for fewer inquisitions. I had heard my mother also remind my father, after one of his tirades, that I was an honor roll student. Very rarely, when he was exceptionally enraged and she was feeling disgusted and brave, I heard her say, from another part of the house,

"Stop it. We've already lost one child."

Being that it was Saturday, and it had been a late and memorably out of control Friday, I was sleeping in. When I awoke it was almost noon and after I shook the clouds out of my head and surveyed the damage to my room that my father had provided, my first coherent thought drifted to the rehearsal we were supposed to have in a matter of minutes at Johnny's house.

I scrambled around the room, trying to dress while at the same time, I gathered together lyrics, Keats's "Hyperion," and my guitar. I tiptoed down the stairs, but to my great relief, I found the house empty. My mother had left me some breakfast on the table. I guzzled the juice and devoured the cinnamon roll and took the apple with me as I jettisoned out the door.

I often hitchhiked to Johnny's house for rehearsals. I didn't mind that it was out in the country. I felt a certain kind of comfort, leaving the suburban area where I lived, the carefully paved, tree-lined, overly planned streets of my neighborhood, and heading for the countryside, with the vast pastures and the grazing animals. Toting my guitar, I walked down to the highway near our house and put out my thumb, seeing what the wind would bring me in the way of transportation. I rarely found it difficult to catch a ride in those days. Perhaps, drivers felt I had an honest face. Perhaps, they saw the guitar and in picking me up, felt, as I did, an affinity with the roots of all folk music, felt as if they were helping a wandering minstrel in his chosen profession.

It took me fifteen minutes to get a ride from a guy I knew from junior high school. He dropped me off at the winding dirt road that led up to Johnny's house. I walked uphill past the birch and poplar trees that bordered either side of the bumpy road. Johnny's father would plow the half mile or so every year to make it passable in winter.

But the walk up to the house was always pleasurable for me. The dogs they owned would always come barking down the road to see who the intruder might be. But these were not the dogs that so tried and failed to guard the long-lost virginity of Missy. When Johnny's dogs finally got close enough to recognize me, they stopped barking and wagged their tails in delight. I would lay my guitar down and start hugging and petting them, scratching them behind the ears vigorously. There were three of them and they would always knock me down with their joy.

Despite my writing ability, I could never have written or verbally explained to my parents how much the ritual of walking up the road to Johnny's house meant to me. Probably, if I did, it would have hurt them. But after Skipper, Jojo and Mack had licked me and playfully pushed me this way and that with their front paws, the four of us would head toward the Janowski house. Johnny's mother, Magda, was seemingly always there to greet us, her broad, doughy face beaming in welcome. On this Saturday afternoon, she was wiping her hands on the apron stretched across her wide hips.

"Eddie, Eddie, is so good to see you," she said in her thick Polish accent, patting me on the back as I entered the house. It had a warm, salty smell coming from the kitchen. I sniffed it, savoring it.

"Come, come into the house and have some lentil soup. I have been making a pot all day."

She always had something on the stove. I heard Johnny and the guys upstairs playing one of the songs we did. She didn't seem to mind the noise at all.

"I'd love to, Mrs. Janowski. Maybe we could have some as soon as we take our first break."

She laughed heartily, as if I had made a hilarious joke. "You boys always excited about the music. To you, more important than food or air!" She patted me again on the back and extended a hand, showing me to the stairway I had ascended so many times.

Up the stairs I went racing and when I got to Johnny's room, there he was wailing away on the drums, as our bass player, Tommy, and our rhythm guitarist, Bobby, supported him. Tommy and Bobby were both kind of silent partners. Tommy was solidly built with a thick shock of black, curly hair. Bobby was thin, red-haired and often had a nod or a smirk in place of a comment. They both noticed me and nodded but Johnny was in another world. His foot was pumping hard on the bass drum and beating the snare and cymbals in syncopation. His head was bent down and occasionally nodded up and down when he was particularly pleased with a beat he had created. This lasted a number of minutes before he actually looked up and noticed that I was standing there. The final crash of the snare drum announced my official arrival and he comically tossed the drumsticks through the air.

Johnny sat back for a second as though trying to get back down to earth. He then looked at me and screamed, “Well, c'mon Eddie!”

“What?” I asked, totally lost.

“Plug in that damn guitar and let’s go before I lose all this built up energy and the wild beasts in my head.”

I just smiled; I plugged into an amplifier he had for me and started blasting out some shimmering chords. After Johnny, Bobby and Tommy watched me expectantly for a while, I finally looked over at them.

"Feeling kind of hung over today."

"Yeah, nice of you to show up at all," Johnny joked.

"How about 'House of the Rising Sun' for starters?" I offered.

Johnny liked the suggestion, and his voice growled and wailed, the bluesy quality coming from his belly, up through his chest and throat, into the mike attached to a stand hovering over his head. I was swept up in that energy, and took a solo that flowed out of my fingertips. It seemed to elongate and after bar after bar, I looked over at the guys, realizing how long it had gone on. No one seemed disturbed.

Johnny finished the song, jolting us with the power of his voice.

We faded and let the last note hang in the air of the bedroom.

"Nice solo," Tommy murmured.

"Yeah, real good," Bobby agreed.

Johnny popped up from behind the drum kit.

"Yeah, it was. You should stay out too late more often, I guess."

I thanked them and began looking through my lyrics to find a song I had been developing for The Caretakers. But

Johnny was overcome with enthusiasm and yanked on my arm, pulling my attention away from the songs I had brought along.

"Guys, dig what I'm about to lay down on you."

Johnny lit and puffed on a cigarette before he spoke again.

"I got this call this morning from that manager, Byron Orr, who saw us last time. He says if we sign with him, we'll make a demo. And then, he knows this promoter in the Grand Rapids area. And they've got a statewide battle of the bands going on that we can enter. Now dig this." He knew he had our full attention and milked it for all it was worth, the monster.

"The first prize is…" And now Johnny lightly drummed his fingertips on the snare, as if a firing squad was about to commence.

"Would you just tell us?" I interrupted.

He smacked the high hat with his palm and blurted out, "Five thousand dollars annnnd..... a record contract to record the winning band and $3,000 dollars and a record contract for second place." Now Johnny let loose with a big "hallelujah" and threw his arms up into the air, as if we had already competed, won and were basking in the applause of an adoring crowd.

The usually low-key Tommy smiled so widely, we could actually see his teeth, a vision that we had not been treated to in some time.

"That's pretty damn cool," he agreed. Bobby only nodded, but did so with more energy than usual.

I was excited too but I also tended to be a bit more cautious than Johnny. "This Orr guy. He wants to manage us for sure?"

"Yes, yes," Johnny waved off my concern with his arms, hopping around his bedroom excitedly. "He's going to set up our recording a demo at a studio in Ann Arbor. We sign and then, my boys, we are on our way."

"This battle of the bands," I asked him. "They want original songs, right?"

Johnny heard me but he barely seemed to notice the three of us. He jumped on his bed and sprang up and down, paced the limited floor space, walked out into the hall, came back into his room and looked through albums.

"Johnny." I was trying to get an answer and he looked up, annoyed, as if I had interrupted him from important work which could not be disturbed.

"What? What?"

"We're going to do some songs I wrote for the battle of the bands, right?"

He hesitated and in that moment, I had a flash of fear, a momentary thought that Johnny was not happy with the songs I wrote, that they were too obscure or poetic or didn't rock hard enough or something he had yet to tell me.

Johnny got up from his crouching position in front of a stack of albums, came over to me and put both hands on my shoulders, looking at me like a puppy who had wet the carpeting once too often.

"Man, this is not the battle of the cover bands! This is a search for new material, new groups, the groups of tomorrow. This is our chance to cut out of this town and see the world, see what's going down in this big, wide country of ours."

I relaxed, let out a breath of air. Tommy plunked away idly on the bass and Bobby fidgeted with his amp as Johnny and I sat on his bed and looked through some of the songs I had brought. With high spirits, we debated their relative merits, enjoyably tried to find the magic combination of rock power and lyrical sweep to knock those judges on their asses.

***

The ride back from the rehearsal, in the Eternal Energy Machine, was filled, not too surprisingly, with Johnny chattering away about the band, what the record we would eventually record would have on the cover, going to Hollywood to record, what the women there would look like, what bands we could see perform on the West Coast, what others might think of our music in the rock world. He saw only the possibilities of the moment. I saw only the obstacles.

It wasn't that I was afraid of going, of succeeding. But I had more to overcome than Johnny, in order to just go to the competition.

"My father is not going to want me to skip school for a few days and go to Grand Rapids. You know how he feels about me playing music." And here, I looked a bit sheepishly at Johnny and he glanced over from his driving to read the expression on my face. "And you know how he feels about you."

Johnny smirked and shook his head in disgust. "Listen, I don't want to say anything about your family, Eddie," he began cautiously, "but I think you should tell your dad to stick it up his ass."

"You don't have to live with him," I replied, staring at the farmland whizzing by, wondering, just for the moment, in a bittersweet haze, how exciting it might be to travel with the band, to actually visit and record and play in L.A.

"You want me to tell him?" Johnny smacked the steering wheel. "I'll tell him what we're doing and that–"

"That's my job," I cut him off.

We drove in silence, except for the engine noise and the occasional rattling of the Eternal Energy Machine. It had all been leading to this. My father's recent brutality, my efforts to get my mother to play music again, my own hard work in crafting song after song, even ones we had never performed publicly before. This was what it was for, to compete, to win, record and tour, to see the respect of others for what we did, to feel some satisfaction in creating music that went out into the world, not just into the dank air of small clubs in the small towns of Michigan.

And it was Johnny who had been the driving force, who had led us to this opportunity, which could change all our lives.

"I want to do it," I said. "I want *us* to do it."

The urgency in the word "us" made Johnny look over at me for a few seconds longer than was truly safe while driving a vehicle, even with his skills. His head slowly returned to the road.

"We will. You know I couldn't do it without you."

And as fearful as I was about the future, about the pact we had just made, I was elated too. The jumble of emotions made my skin tingle but it also made my stomach tighten into a progressively larger knot.

That knot grew considerably larger as Johnny wheeled the truck up to my house. From where we sat, we saw the front door open and my father come outside, waiting for me, eying Johnny's truck with loathing.

"Pretty soon," Johnny said, trying to sound reassuring, "you're not going to have to deal with him. We're going to be on the road and he won't have any say about it."

"Yeah," I agreed half-heartedly, "but I have to live with him until that happens."

"So, what's the worst that could happen?" Johnny asked.

"Oh, I don't know," I drawled. "Knock me around, like he did recently."

The smile slid off Johnny's face and he looked through the windshield at my father, his hands on his hips, unmoving, his jaw and eyes set.

"The son of a bitch," Johnny fumed. "I'd like to punch his lights out."

"Thanks but that's not going to help."

"Come on. We're going to have a talk with him." Johnny quickly popped out of the truck before I could say a word. I leaped out after him and put a restraining hand on his shoulder.

"Listen, this won't help."

"Let's just see his face when there are two of us against his one." Johnny fearlessly walked ahead. Again, as always, I was trailing Johnny. I caught up, double-stepping, and whispered in his ear, "Okay, but we were just hanging out. No music."

We walked up to my father and then the three of us just stood there, like in an Old West stare down, waiting for the other to make a move. Finally, tiring of the staring contest, Johnny, in an exaggerated, cheerful voice, said,

"How you doing, Mr. Defoe?"

"I told you," my father said, his eyes burning into me, "I don't want you two playing music."

"We didn't," I lied. "His mom made some soup and we just hung out there."

"You're going to amount to nothing," my father began his tirade, but Johnny couldn't hold his tongue any longer.

"You know, Mr. Defoe, a lot of people would say the way your talking in front of me is very rude."

My father walked up to Johnny, almost nose to nose with him. Johnny didn't flinch. I knew that Johnny would not hesitate to throw a punch if provoked, so I tried to separate them. My father pushed me away.

"You want to hit somebody, Mr. Defoe? Is that it? Tell you what. Why don't you hit me? You can have the first punch. But then when I get through with you, you won't be punching anybody for a long time."

"Get off my property," my father growled.

Johnny stood his ground, not moving an inch.

"You see why I tell you to stay away from him?" My father backed off, now turning his attention back to me. "He's going to be nothing but trouble his whole life. You want to mess up your life too?"

Johnny turned and began to walk away but whirled around with a last thought. "We're just young and having fun, Mr. Defoe. I guess that must make you miserable. See you later, Eddie."

"See you," I called back, wanting to thank him, to tell him how much his standing up to my father had meant to me in that moment.

"Get in the house," my father ordered.

But I just watched Johnny get in the Eternal Energy Machine, nod at me, and screech his tires as loudly as possible, as he made a U-turn and tore out. When I went inside, my father was waiting for me. My mother was in the kitchen, staying out of the way, as, no doubt, he had demanded her to do.

"He's my friend!" I yelled, anticipating his fury and deciding to get in a few words before having to hear his monologue. "I have a right to spend time with him."

"You have no rights," my father shot back. "You live here, you're a minor and you do as I say."

My mother puttered about the kitchen, pretending to be busy, despite the fact it was spotless. She quickly threw a glance of concern at me and then looked away, not wanting to be caught looking at me and showing the concern that was so evident on her face. The feeling of seeing her in distress made me change my approach, lower my voice.

"I'm not a failure, Dad. I'm not going to be like anybody except who I'm supposed to be. And wanting to play music? There's something wrong with not wanting to play music? It's like saying; I don't want you to be happy."

I took the stairs two at a time. "You come back down here!" he shouted but I was headed for my room and the sanctuary of a locked door. He knew it and followed me up, shoving the door open before I could lock it.

"What do you want from me?"

"I want you to stop throwing your life away with Johnny and make something of yourself."

"I'm not you. I'm not going to be like you. I like music. You can beat me up all you want but you're not going to make me stop loving music, like you did with Mom."

His face contorted with rage. I didn't know what he would do and as the seconds went by and he did not attack or throw anything around, I thought I had a chance to actually talk with him this time. I sat on my bed, hung my head, murmured into my own chest but loud enough for him to hear.

"Dad, please."

A pause, followed by his angry but somewhat subdued voice. "What?"

"Do you hate me, Dad?"

"Don't talk stupid."

"No, I mean it. Do you want me to go? Do you not want me here? I try and stay away from you as best I can. I know you hate Johnny and you hate my music but except for that, I'm doing well in school, they like me at work and Mom and I get along great. I want you to be happy, Dad. But do I have to sacrifice my own happiness to do that?"

"You don't know about sacrifice, Eddie," he said and now, his voice was surprisingly plaintive. "You and your sister have always done just what you want and your attitude is, if you don't like it, I'll just run away. I'll just leave. Like your sister did."

"My sister–"

"I'm not finished," he interrupted, his voice getting louder again.

"Go ahead," I said quietly. "I'm listening."

He looked like he wanted to sit, maybe on the chair in my room, maybe even on the bed next to me. But he didn't. His concession to the waning of his rage was to lean against the door jam with one arm, peering at me, as if trying to figure out what I was.

"Sacrifice isn't just doing what someone tells you to do," he said. "It's doing it and admitting that, even though you don't like it, it's what's right. I worked a whole hell of a lot harder than you, when I was your age and I didn't fight my father. I accepted his ways. And then I went out into the world when it was my time and made more sacrifices. It doesn't mean you're never happy. It means you learn discipline and respect. You may not like it now but when you're out in the world on your own, you're going to find out it serves you a lot more than just doing whatever the hell you want."

He stopped and I had nothing to say that would make the situation any better. I could argue, I could apologize, but he knew and I knew that we would never agree.

"Can I just ask you one question and not have you get mad?"

He eyed me warily, finally nodding although his expression seemed to expect something bad, possibly infuriating. I hesitated. "Go on," he said, now annoyed at my hesitation.

"We all used to listen to music, as a family. Don't you like any kind of music, any more?"

He exhaled heavily and pushed off on the door jamb, straightening up his body and giving me one final look of evaluation, filled with disappointment. "There are times when music is the last thing you want to hear." He quietly closed the door and I knew there was no hope for us. I felt there was always time for music and that there were times when conversation was the last thing I wanted to hear.

Chapter 5

Byron Orr wore a blazer, jeans and open necked, button-down shirt and while this would seem fairly casual in most places, it was definitely overdressed in Liquid Sounds, the small, four-track recording studio that The Caretakers assembled in. Liquid Sounds was in Ann Arbor and it was a small storefront, with a sign hand-lettered in psychedelic script, reminiscent of the posters being created for Bill Graham's concerts in Northern California.

Mushroom Bob was the proprietor and engineer of the studio, and his hair, unlike our own, hung far down on his back, with a droopy moustache also headed in the same direction.

"Mushroom Bob, huh?" asked Johnny, as we carried our gear into the studio.

"Shrooms, man. I can get you a great price on them, if you want." Johnny nodded, although he was not entirely sure what our engineer meant.

"Listen; let's get this demo done for The Caretakers before we get them whacked out of their skulls on magic mushrooms, okay?"

Byron was smiling, as he always seemed to be, but the more I was around him, the more I realized that he always seemed to be both in the present and somewhere else. His eyes darted around like a hummingbird, his hands flapped to support his speech, or point at someone to get something done or gently push someone in a certain direction or pat them on the shoulder to convince them they were all right or that they should agree with him.

"You guys got everything? Johnny, is there anything still in the truck?"

As we set up and plugged in, I thought about my conversation with my father, just the weekend before. I wondered if hearing any of my music played on a radio would change his mind about the importance of it, even if he most certainly didn't like the sound.

"You okay?" Johnny asked, now standing next to me, as Bobby and Tommy whispered to each other, glancing around, taking in their first professional recording studio. "You're looking kind of out there, man."

"I'm okay," I assured him, plugging in and hitting a few chords, pretending to tune up even though I was already in tune. I didn't want Johnny to worry about me, about my distractions. I had to focus. This had to work. This had to happen for us.

"This Is Your Chance," boomed the enthusiastic voice of Byron. "Boy, I can't think of a more appropriate title for a band's first single." He surveyed Johnny, then me. "You write all the lyrics, Eddie, or you guys trade off?"

"I write the lyrics; Johnny and I do the music. Sometimes just him. Sometimes just me."

"Well, 'This Is Your Chance' really rocks, man." Byron turned to Bobby and Tommy, so they would not feel excluded from his limitless optimism.

"What do you say, Caretakers? Let's make a hit and start a career for you guys."

Byron got what he wanted, a chorus of laughs and loud shouts of approval, bringing up the energy of the room. He started toward the door of the dingy studio, which had not only egg cartons pasted on the wall but ugly, gray carpeting hanging on the walls.

"Um, Byron?" He turned to me, his eyes filled with expectation.

"After we record 'This Is Your Chance,' well, Johnny and I were talking, and we have this ballad I wrote. It's called 'What You Cannot Know,' and it would be great if we could record it too."

Byron immediately patted me on the shoulder. "We'll see if we have time Eddie. First, let's get the kickass demo down, and then, you'll have a whole album to fill. I'll be in the booth with Mr. Mushroom." He gave us all a wink and raised a fist in the air. "You do what you did when I saw you at the club, and you'll be just fine." Byron walked out and the studio door closed with a solid, definitive thud.

We all waited until we could see both Mushroom Bob and Byron through the small glass window which separated us from the booth. Mushroom Bob pressed a button and his voice came into the studio, high-pitched and metallic. "Okay. 'This Is Our Chance.' Take one."

"This Is *Your* Chance, '" corrected Johnny, annoyed.

We saw Mushroom Bob turn in the recording booth to Byron, who flapped his hands, as he explained something and then gently laid a hand on Mushroom Bob's shoulder. Mushroom Bob nodded and pressed the button again, leaning down to speak into a microphone. "'This Is Your Chance.' Take one."

"This Is Your Last Chance," said Johnny and we all chuckled.

He looked at the three of us, as if he was a proud parent, seeing his children about to perform for the first time at a school play. No words. Just four guys from a small town, looking at each other, feeling, for the first time in their lives, the possibilities, the tense, delicious joy of being in a unique position for success and trying to be calm and not screw it up.

I hit the opening chords. Johnny came in with the drums. Bobby and Tommy simultaneously let the rhythm and bass guitars join and I moved about six inches from the mike, closed my eyes and pushed everything out of my mind but the song I had written about love on the rocks, even though I had never known that kind of love yet in my relatively sheltered life.

After we had finished, they played back the song through the speakers in the studio. Then, Byron spoke to us from the booth. His voice was a bit more distorted than Mushroom Bob's, because he was speaking louder and closer to the mike.

"Good. Sounds real good, guys. Let's do another one, just to be sure."

"Do you want it different in some way?" Johnny asked.

"Nope. That was fine. Just do it the same way."

We finished the song and as the last pluck of a string from my guitar faded from the room, Mushroom Bob invited us into his booth, which turned out to be pretty small for two people and ridiculous for six. "Sounds better in here," he said, casually brushing a long patch of hair out of his face and playing with some knobs on the board.

There was no place to sit, since our manager and engineer had the only two seats in the booth, which reeked of cigarette smoke and imitation butter on stale popcorn. Despite that, we listened with great interest to our music through a mixing console for the first time.

"Can you bring up the rhythm guitar a little bit?" asked Byron of Mushroom Bob and then turned to us, to be sure we had the illusion we were being consulted. "It sounds a little thin with the rhythm guitar so far back in the mix."

"Aren't they generally?" Johnny asked. He was the only one who thought of protesting the idea.

When we heard the playback with Bobby's guitar more present, though, it inspired more confidence in Byron because it did balance the music better and we listened to it with the slightest tapping of fingers and nodding of heads, enjoying it but not sure if it was cool to show how much we liked our own work.

“I think that’s it,” pronounced Byron. “Gentlemen, unless there are specific questions about that mix, let’s have Master Mushroom Bob make a master of that. I will get us a demo record pressed and get you on the air and into the Battle of the Bands. And from there, it’s California, boys, the land of your dreams.”

Byron shook hands with Mushroom Bob, exchanging business cards and discussing when to pick up the tape. Johnny started to ask Mushroom Bob some questions about his studio but Byron was hustling us out the door, like a group of overly frisky dogs hopping on the guests.

“Let’s go, guys. Lunch’s on me. We’ve got business to attend to and so does Mushroom Bob.”

We carted our equipment out of the studio and locked it up in a van Tommy had borrowed. Byron led us into a local luncheonette and we ordered food.

“That went pretty fast,” I said.

“Sure did,” agreed Johnny.

“Well, I can’t help it if you guys are good and have great studio chops.” Byron looked up and caught the attention of the waitress, asking her how the lunch order was going.

"It's going as fast as it can go," she answered with a tight smile and went to help other customers.

"So, what other bands have you worked with?" I asked.

"I've got three or four, mostly around Ann Arbor, Grand Rapids."

"Anybody we've heard of?" asked Bobby, timidly.

"I don't know. You ever hear of Chocolate Fire?" We shook our heads, in unison. "How about The Sacred Brain Trust?" Again, we had to profess our ignorance. "Well, the idea is, we all get big together. And with your music and lyrics, guys, I really believe it's going to happen for us.

The waitress brought our food and as she set the dishes down on the table, Byron pulled some contracts out of a satchel, along with some pens. With our mouths full, we looked them over.

"Fifty per cent to you," Johnny mumbled out loud. "That seems like a lot."

"It's a standard deal. You've got to figure, I'm fronting the money for the studio time, the mastering, the demos. If you guys go nowhere, I'm out all that money."

"I thought we were destined for greatness," I kidded. Byron gave me an intense look.

"We're in this together, no matter what. You guys are going to make plenty of money. What do you do for a living now?"

Johnny and I looked at each other. "We work on a potato farm," Johnny said.

Byron's eyes opened wide and he stifled a laugh. "Well, you're going to make enough bread to buy that whole goddamn potato farm."

"We don't care about making millions of dollars," I said, an edge in my voice. "We want to make music and make a living at it and reach a lot of people. That's what we want."

Johnny, the band, and especially Byron, were surprised by my anger. He folded his hands and looked a little sheepish. "No offense. I'm going to guarantee I get you into the Battle of the Bands in Grand Rapids. If I don't, mark my word, we tear up this contract and go our separate ways. And if you guys hit it big, then we'll renegotiate the terms. What do you say? Are we a team?"

There was another moment, much like in the studio, when we simply looked at each other and considered the moment and what our future might possibly be. It culminated with Johnny staring at me. I gave him a smile that doubled as a smirk.

"Okay," said Johnny, picking up a pen with a flourish and signing. The rest of us signed. Byron counter-signed them and raised his Coke. We held aloft our soft drinks.

"I'm going to take you to the top, Caretakers."

I raised my glass a little higher than the others and said, "Here's to the caretaker of The Caretakers."

We laughed and talked with food in our mouths. The waitress who minutes before had given Byron a look of consternation now looked over at us, smiling. I felt happier than I had ever been since my sister left home. I was happy for her, to get away and start a new life down in New Orleans.

***

In addition to a popular childhood disease, The Mumps was a small club where we had played before. Byron had talked to the owner, explaining he was our new manager and that we were looking around for new opportunities. The owner, sensing he was going to lose a band that was on the way up, increased our pay. It was not enough money to allow Johnny and me to quit the potato farm but it gave us a boost of encouragement, in ourselves and in the still untested Byron Orr.

As we sat in the concrete back room, which served as the "dressing room" for The Mumps, I realized that if Byron could get us more money for one of our usual gigs, then a lot of things could really change. Johnny was his typical, high energy self, humming, rattling his drumsticks on the walls, double- and triple-checking our set list, giving us all his free-spirited, anything-can-happen vibe. Tommy and Bobby were their introverted selves and in fact, my own personality was turning inward on this night.

I felt stuck, in between what my life was and what my life could be, and the comfort of what it was battled the disappointment of how I existed. Yes, if The Caretakers actually became a working band, I could leave Romeo and my father far behind, but that would also mean leaving my mother alone to live with my father in their tiny, smothered existence. If we went on the road, I could drop out of school. I never cared much about school but did well in it. And the reason I had exploded when Byron made fun of the potato farm was that even though it was hard work, I looked forward to it.

I doubted if I could explain it to someone like Byron, who had dollar signs for eyes and ball point pens for fingers. I looked forward to joking with the farm guys, of seeing the result of working with my hands, of sweating alongside Johnny and the other workers. They had become a big part of my life. Now, The Caretakers might replace that group of friends. Of course, it seemed preferable, but I knew what to expect on the farm. I had no idea what a life with the band would be like. I had no idea what Byron was really like and I had no idea if it would change Johnny.

Plunking at the strings on my unplugged guitar in the bunker that was the artists' retreat in The Mumps, half-listening to Johnny half-talking to himself, saying,

"This could be our last gig here, boys. This could be our stairway to the stars, man."

I had a thought that truly chilled me: that Johnny, who was the focal point of my life, could be leading us to a place I was not willing to go and that, even worse, could turn into someone I was not willing to be with.

I looked at him and the glow of excitement, the utter fire of confidence in his eyes, wiped the thought from my mind. I smiled widely at him. His happiness had overtaken me.

He smiled back. "You're feeling it, too, aren't you, Eddie? This all is a turning point. This is our goodbye to The Mumps, man. Don't you feel it?"

I didn't want to lie to him. I didn't want to take away any of the energy he felt. So, I stayed as close as I could to the truth of the moment. "I'm feeling a lot of things at the same time."

"That's what excitement is, man," Johnny enthused. "It's a jumble of feelings. It's, oh, man, I'm happy but wait, what about *this* thing? And what if *that* happens? But hey, if it does, then I can do *that*. That's what's going on for us. We've got more possibilities. Isn't it cool?"

Bobby and Tommy said, in their low-key ways, how cool they thought it was. Johnny turned to me for my confirmation. I didn't have to lie. Byron opened the door to the airless little room.

"Caretakers, it's time to rock this little place like you've never rocked it before."

He held the door open as we filed out and wound our way past boxes of bottles of pop and onto the two-foot high stage which barely had enough room to hold all four of us. Most nights we played The Mumps, we wandered onstage and the crowd drank and talked among themselves until we began playing. But there was a different vibe entirely in the crowd. I didn't know if the word had circulated that Byron was managing us, or , some rumor had spread about our venturing out into the big, wide world, perhaps never to come back, but there was a hush in the crowd, one which made us a little self-conscious as we plugged in and tuned up. It was unnerving, having that much quiet in the club before starting. Johnny and I glanced at each other and then out at the crowd.

Despite the lights on us, we could see it was a full house. Gino sat at the back of the house with yet another woman hanging onto him for dear life. Johnny was going to call out to him but feeling the eyes of so many on him, he just nodded his appreciation to Gino for being there. I did the same, as Bobby and Tommy fidgeted behind me.

Gino simply gave a magisterial nod in our direction, with the slightest effort, as if a cool breeze has just blown in from the parking lot and slightly made his head bob. Johnny tested out the drum kit a bit, and then leaned forward and spoke into his mike.

"Test. Test Testing. Ahem, well, and a good evening to all our old friends here at The Mumps." There was a light, polite applause from the crowd.

"You know," Johnny continued, "you know, there's no other place we'd prefer to play than right here. But folks got to make a living. So, we may be knocking around the country a bit, but it will always be a pleasure to come back home and get a dose of The Mumps."

Now, the audience applauded more heartily, getting the sense that this was a special gig, even though I personally had no idea how I would arrange to go away to the Battle of the

Bands with the battle of wills between my father and me. But there was no time to dwell on that now. We launched into our first number and the crowded now hooted and cheered, recognizing it and appreciating it.

It's funny what you think about when your perform songs you've played many times over. It isn't that you play without feeling. And in fact, The Caretakers, I could tell from the opening, were giving it our all. But I personally, while giving as good a show as I could, felt my mind wander even while hitting all the notes, the pauses, the ebb and flow of loudness and the variation in tone.

I thought about how I got angry at Byron about the potato farm and how much something simple and comfortable like working alongside those guys meant. And naturally, my mind drifted back to The Mumps, to the owner who we had known for years, to all the gigs we had done there. The band felt it was like a headquarters, or maybe a touchstone, some place you knew you would always return to and feel good about, and would always have a warm reception.

The audience gave us a nice round of applause and we went into a ballad I had written, influenced in no small degree by Keats. "The Journey Never Taken" was a song about a man who falls in love with a woman but never has the courage to tell her and they stay friends until she falls in love and moves away, breaking his heart. The fact that I read "Hyperion" all the time showed that besides being obsessive, I was moved by the idea of a great adventure, which also was terrifying.

And as we played "The Journey Never Taken," I thought about the people in The Mumps and wondered how many of them would spend their entire lives in the area and never travel anywhere or live anywhere else. Relying on the familiarity of your surroundings was both a comfort and a torture. It annoyed me that I was so conflicted. If Johnny knew, he would feel like I was betraying him and the band. I would have to work hard to hide it.

The third song we did was one I didn't write. It was Johnny's lyrics and music, a hard-driving rocker called "What You Don't Know." It was an angry love song, about a guy who felt his girl was cheating on him so he cheats on her. I didn't think a whole lot of Johnny's simplistic lyrics but it was a fun number to play and the emotion of the song always brought out a wildness in me, prompting me to thrash the strings of the guitar at times, emphasizing the resentment of the guy in the song.

Usually, "What You Don't Know," got my blood pumping pretty good on stage and tonight was no different. I felt the sweat building on my forehead and somehow, the lights seemed to grow increasingly hot. But I knew this could not be. We were still in the first half of this set and the fatigue that was overtaking me was very odd. As the song continued and we hit the instrumental bridge, I was now the focus of the band, not Johnny's singing, and as I played my solo, I felt a wave of nausea pour over me. My head hurt and the music rang in my ears, almost as if it was feeding back slightly.

I looked over at the band, to see if they sensed anything wrong with the sound. But they were involved in their instruments. The hot flushed feeling increased and when I finished the solo, I stepped out of the spot that was on me, trying to get through the song, as Johnny sang the remainder of it. I felt my stomach heave and I bit down on my lip, trying to hold back the contents that threatened to explode out of me. I guess my playing was now out of tempo because the guys were throwing me quick looks of concern.

Johnny's voice faded as he belted out the last note and I finished with a flourish. The audience began to applaud and I already had the guitar strap over my head and laid the instrument in a stand, dashing off the stage. I knew I couldn't fight my way through the crowd in order to get to the bathrooms in front, so I headed toward the back door.

Johnny, ever the fast thinker, joked into his mike, "Hey, Eddie, the set list is right here!"

I ran past the concrete bunker dressing room, out the back door, into the night air, over to the dumpster and a torrent of food and fluids burst from my throat onto the pavement. I gasped, my stomach propelled the remainder of its contents out and I spit what remained in my mouth angrily onto the asphalt.

What had happened? I had never felt so suddenly sick in my whole life and it had happened while I was onstage, at what was possibly our farewell gig at The Mumps. I was furious with myself and kicked the dumpster, hearing its metallic clanging complaint. I took a couple deep breaths, felt better and went back inside.

I hadn't been gone very long, so when I got back up on stage, the audience didn't seem too concerned. But Johnny did.

He motioned me over to him with a drum stick and as I picked up my guitar again, I leaned through the kit to whisper to him.

"What's going on?" he asked.

"I don't know. I felt sick, all of a sudden. And the music, was it feeding back? It didn't sound right."

"It sounded fine until you fell behind the beat," Johnny said. But he looked at me, the paleness of my skin and his voice immediately softened.

"Can you play?" I nodded. He looked down at his watch. "It's nine thirty. We can do one longer set, skip a second set, get out of here early."

"Fine, I'm fine," I assured him. My throat burned from the vomiting. I leaned into my mike and asked, "Anybody here at The Mumps got a coke for an awful thirsty guitarist?"

Three people in the first row instantly offered me their cokes and I took one that looked mostly full and thanked the young woman who had offered it. I took a long slug and it felt soothing. I breathed deeply again and felt somewhat revived. The band was waiting for me to give them a signal that we should continue.

"Some people say home is where the heart is," I said, "but home is also where the most people offer you a drink." I held up the drink in thanks to the audience. They roared their approval. I took another quick slug, set it down, nodded to Johnny and we were off into the next tune.

We did a couple extended jams and finished, about forty-five minutes later, to a tumultuous reception. Johnny, playing up the rock star attitude, jokingly threw his drumsticks into the audience.

"Come on," Johnny said as we made our way offstage toward the concrete bunker, "I'm buying the band a round."

I put my guitar in my case. "Listen, guys," I said to the band, "I'm feeling kind of wrecked. You hang out and have some fun. I got to get home and get some sleep."

"I'll drive you," Johnny offered and Bobby and Tommy chimed in, insisting they would do so instead of Johnny, since they both had wheels too.

"No," I told them all, "you stay. Hang out with the crowd. I'll get a ride."

"You got one," said the low, deep authoritative voice, and we turned to see it belonged to Gino. His new girlfriend stood a couple paces behind him, smiling at us all but not seeming to want to talk to anyone. "Good show," Gino said. Johnny thanked him for coming and I followed him and his unnamed blonde girlfriend. Many of the people in the crowd patted me on the back or shook my hand, wishing me well and I sadly explained, over and over, I was feeling tired but thanked them over and over.

Byron, who was busy talking to the owner, didn't even notice as I was escorted by Gino and his newest girlfriend out of The Mumps and into his cherried-out dragster, heading fast, but for me, not fast enough, back to my house.

Chapter 6

I rode in the back, the windows opened, the air whipping about everyone's hair, as Gino's street machine ripped down the highway. Only Ginger, his current main squeeze, seemed ill at ease with the gusts, trying to hold her beehive hairdo in place.

"You feeling any better back there?" Gino bellowed against the howl.

"Yeah, yeah, a lot better." I watched Ginger's futile attempt to prevent her hair from becoming a bird's nest and felt bad for her. "You can roll up the windows." Ginger looked to Gino for permission and he nodded. When both had been rolled up halfway, Gino began to talk.

"You're lucky," Gino said. "You got everything on your side. You're young, you got this band happening, your whole future ahead of you."

"Yeah, your band was really great," Ginger said, her eyes sparkling with appreciation, whether it was for the music or for my suggestion they roll up the windows.

"The rest of us around here," Gino continued, "we don't know what's going to happen with our lives. We got no idea. I could get drafted and go to 'Nam. I could kill one of those frigging idiots from Bobby Jones's gang who get in my way and boom; I'm in jail for life." He turned his body around so he could meet my eyes for a moment, as if merely catching my gaze in the rear view mirror was not enough. Then, he returned his attention to the double yellow line and his headlights.

"You know what I'm saying here? *Capiche*?"

I wasn't sure that a guy in his early twenties was supposed to be so fatalistic about life. Even as a minor, I had the sense that it was wrong. But I was not about to tell Gino I disagreed with his general philosophy. He could break me in half and leave me miles from home. So I tried to show that I *capiched.*

"Yeah, Gino. It's about feeling you have no choices, no options, right?"

"That's what I'm saying. I don't. But you do. You stay with Johnny and the band. I think it's going to take you places."

***

When I arrived home, I snuck in like a thief, but set down in the kitchen and had my usual cookies and milk before turning in. As I was sitting at the kitchen table I heard the creaking of the floorboards in the hallway. The footsteps were too quiet to be my father, which made me relax a bit. I turned toward the hallway and illuminated by a small hall light came my mother, wearing a satin robe with faded red and purple flowers on it.

"Eddie, is that you?" she said with a faraway and timid voice.

"Yeah, Ma, it's me. I know it's late but I'm okay. So you can go back to bed."

She sat down at the kitchen table, wringing her hands, her face twisted with concern, marring her loveliness.

“Eddie, your father isn't home yet. He hasn't called either. I'm really worried about him.” Her eyes were red, giving away the fact that she had been crying.

I got up and went over to comfort her.

“Ah, Ma, you know Dad. Sometimes he has to work late, and you know, he probably just had to unwind with the guys. I’m sure he'll be walking in the door any minute now.”

I put my arm around her and rubbed her neck, trying to relax her. I thought about the times she had done the same thing for me, when there had been fighting in the house, between my father and my sister, and more recently, between my father and me. It made me feel small, helpless to see her unhappy and I wanted to erase the doubts she had.

“Imagine Dad getting home later than me,” I joked. It went over rather badly as a joke. She started crying quietly.

“I'm so worried that something's wrong,” and as she said this, the phone rang and I gently stopped rubbing her and let go of her.

“See that's him calling right now, saying he'll be home soon.”

When my mother answered the phone she turned pale. Her words were very weak, coming from her quivering lips.

“Yesss, I am Mrs. Defoe,” and she was trembling so bad it looked as though she was about to faint. I sat her down and took the receiver from her shaky hands.

"Hello, this is Mrs. Defoe's son." There was a long pause at the other end and then a female voice spoke.

"Ah, yes we are calling to advise you that Mr. Defoe has been in a car accident and he is in the intensive care unit at the Critteton Hospital. Is it possible that you could come down right away?" Now I was at a loss for words for a moment and then offered a weak reply.

"An accident? Uh, he's in intensive care, you say? We'll be right down." There was a quick and official "thank you" from the other end.

Now so many things were swimming through my head at this moment but I knew that I had to be clear-headed, because my mother looked up at me with lost, pleading eyes. I was going to have to be in control.

"Now mom, you'll have to get dressed we have to go to the hospital, okay? Everything is going to be fine, but we have to go as soon as possible."

Even though I was trying to be as reassuring as possible, my mother still clung to me, speechless. I walked her down the hall to her bedroom. But I could see she was not about to change clothes herself so I put on her long coat and boots for her. Even though I was too young to have a license, I knew that I would have to be the one to drive us to the hospital. This wasn't that big of a deal as I had many lessons from Johnny and it was only five miles and on back roads.

My mother was still in a trance and moved her hands like she was washing them, as I drove. I glanced over at her and had the distinct thought that now that I needed to talk to her calmly, simply, that now, I had to become the parent and make her feel comfortable or the world would come apart for both of us.

"Now Mom," I said in a soothing voice, "we both need to be strong now, for Dad. He's going to need us to be in control here, okay. Mom? He might need us to make some decisions for him."

She was rocking back and forth. I knew I just needed to keep talking until we got to the hospital. I had no idea what news would greet us there and I also didn't know how my mother might react. You go through so much of your life with expectations, relying on things. My father had been a source of fear. My mother had been the rock of support that brought me through it. Now, my father was clinging to life in a hospital and my mother seemed incapable of communication. Things had changed and changed again, until I felt I had nothing to hold onto, no sense of direction. Hours before, I was debating with myself how I might convince my father to let me go to compete for a music award or whether I would just go and ignore his wishes. Now, I couldn't even ponder that possibility seriously.

I drove fast, faster than Gino had, taking me home. I saw a hazy reflection of myself in the windshield. It was like looking into an empty mirror. I had no distinct reflection. I wasn't anyone, anymore. Part of my mind wondered if this was some kind of punishment for starting to believe that things might be different for me, that I had options, like Gino seemed to think I had.

I offered some more words of comfort to my mother but she was elsewhere. I doubted she could even hear me. My mind moved to Johnny, how much a part of my life he had been, how often we experienced things together. And yet, here I was in a crisis, feeling more alone than I had ever felt.

I knew it wasn't fair to resent Johnny not being there and that I had to be a man, even as a young man, and learn to do things on my own. But he had been behind me. I remembered the last time I had seen my father, how Johnny had stood up to my father, how he would have literally fought my father in order to gain me some level of freedom from him.

I was now on the street that led to the hospital, zooming through red lights, not at all concerned about being stopped, wondering if my father was still alive. Despite what I had been through with him, including the last time he struck me, I desperately wanted to see him, to talk with him in the same reassuring way I had been doing with my mother. I could not bear the thought that I would not have another conversation with him. So, I put the thought out of my mind and screeched into the emergency entrance parking lot to the hospital.

I got out of the car in the same way Johnny always seemed to leap out of his truck. But my mother was frozen in her seat. I had to actually pull her from the seat and lead her all the way into the building. When we arrived at the main desk, there were all kinds of activity. People talking to each other, to doctors, signing papers, asking questions. It was a large, bright, white, clean, antiseptic mess. The clerk behind the desk was doing some paperwork and then looked up at me and politely spoke.

"Yes, may I help you?"

I thought it sounded unbearably casual. I was holding my mother upright, wondering if my father was still alive and here was a stock phrase, uttered in a simple, straightforward way and yet, it disturbed me. I wanted someone to show some concern. This was the emergency section. Did that mean they dealt with emergencies so often that they no longer meant anything to them? I realized I still hadn't answered. It took me a few more seconds to compose myself to respond appropriately.

"Um, we are here to see my father, uh, Mr. Defoe. I am his son and this is my mother."

I don't really know why I felt as if I had been sent to the principal's office. I think it was the cold, clinical feeling I had standing there, dealing with a strictly businesslike clerk. It was a combination of feeling I was being punished and I was being forced to see others' pain as an additional punishment. The clerk gave me a room number and a direction to walk in and I thanked her, as flatly as she had spoken to me.

We went down the long hallway together; my mother and I, and the feeling of going to school came back to me, only this time, I was the mother taking the fearful child to the first day of class. We were in the intensive care unit now, and I heard moans from one area, heavy, raspy breathing from another. I did not dare look into those rooms. My mother looked straight ahead, leaning on me, using me as a cane. Her face spoke of knowing what was ahead, and I am sure she saw the hospital as a waking, living nightmare.

There was a nurse at a station who accompanied us to my father's bed. Tubes were stuck in him, giving him the appearance of a machine, not a human being. His body had cuts all over it and was bloated almost to the point of being unrecognizable. I felt all the air go out of my body. My mother suddenly sprang to the bed and threw herself onto my father's body. She was torn between sobbing uncontrollably and stroking my father's hand. The nurse and I comforted her, while pulling her off of him. I refused to cry, to cave into what I was feeling. I didn't feel I could afford to indulge my feelings. I needed to know more of what the future would be.

I went over to the nurse and walked out of the room with her. When we were enough distance from the room, I asked her if she knew what the diagnosis was. She turned her head from me, as if looking at me in that moment would be more than even she could bear. In an almost inaudible tone, she answered,

"I'm afraid you'll have to talk to the doctor." I looked at her, my eyes demanding more of an explanation.

"All I can tell you," she went on, "is that your father is in a critical stage right now and we are doing everything we can to upgrade his condition." She looked into my eyes with genuine concern and I thanked her and asked where I might find the doctor.

"Well, he's with another patient right now, but I can page him and leave a message for him, if you would like."

"Yes, that would be fine. Thank you very much." She left to go leave a message for the doctor. She seemed to be like an angel of mercy to me right now.

I walked back into the room, back to the scene of my mother bending over my father's body. She was weeping, hanging on to his hands and rocking back and forth. The phrase that came to mind was "the child is father to the man." I had never fully comprehended the meaning of it, sometimes thinking it meant children have much to teach adults but then sometimes wondered if it meant that children have to eventually become adults, sometimes too quickly. Was it about children becoming adults and being parents but still being children in some way, never fully growing up, despite the responsibilities? I didn't know. But in that horrible, glaring light and terribly lonely image of my parents stuck together over a hospital bed, the phrase, which I repeated to myself, inside my head, made me feel stronger.

I took my mother by the shoulders and told her I would talk to the doctor that she would be all right here with the nurse. She didn't respond but I could tell that she understood. The nurse shortly returned and informed me to go to the nurse's station and the doctor would meet up with me there.

One day, a man is at the peak of his powers and the next, too weak to move, struggling to hold onto life itself. The pain of seeing the dying is also the pain of remembering that we face that moment, too, and not knowing when it comes, or how painfully. Having an opportunity to travel with a band, truly a dream and then have it seemingly swept away by this horrible turn of events, made me wonder about the purpose of my life.

I slumped down on a chair and exhausted, stretched my legs out over a couple of them, staring up at the ceiling. I thought, then, of John Keats and all of the inspiration that he had given me. I thought about reading about his life in the library, after Johnny had given me a copy of "Hyperion," about how surprised I was to learn he was just twenty-four when he died and was sick most of his life to boot; yet he gave the world so much in that brief time. I remembered a particularly pain-filled passage of my favorite poem:

> "*Meanwhile in other realms big tears were shed,*
> *More sorrow like to this, and such like woe,*
> *Too huge for mortal tongue or pen of scribe.*"

Then, a wave of dizziness came over and I began to sweat. I lay down across the chairs, alone in the waiting area. I remembered being on stage only hours ago, suddenly overtaken with these symptoms. It was almost like a premonition of something bad to come, a preparation for what had happened to my father. With my skin feeling feverish, I wanted desperately a drink of cool water but I tried to sit up and found that I couldn't.

With great exertion, I pushed myself up off my elbows, slightly raising my torso but the dizziness was so acute, I fell back, looking up at the ceiling, feeling myself slipping into unconsciousness. I closed my eyes, not wanting to pass out, wanting to be there to help my mother through this terrible night. I breathed deeply and opened my eyes again. But instead of the garish light of the hospital, all was muted, dull, as if the light came from some other, unseen source. The periphery of my vision was hazy and then, like a star going supernova, a burst of light appeared and I squinted, too worn to even raise my hands to shield my eyes.

Then out of the brightness came a beautiful face, and I couldn't quite tell if it was a man or woman, but the gentleness of its effeminate appearance, ringed with short, golden curls, somehow comforted me. The intensity of the light changed to a glow and I couldn't take my eyes off the face. It looked at me and as it did, I felt a warmth that began in my stomach and progressed up into my chest, bringing me relaxation. The fever cooled. The vertigo abated. There was no voice to be heard but the face that peered back at me, without ever changing its expression, communicated to me that whatever happened next, I would find a way to continue, to find some kind of happiness, to find a meaning in what I did with my life. I tried to understand what was happening and couldn't but the eyes that looked down on me held me in place, not allowing me to move until I somehow acknowledged the message. I thought how thankful I was to have this moment, to be given this strength, even if I couldn't comprehend it. And as soon as I had that thought, the vision was gone. The hospital ceiling reappeared.

I sat up, groggy but feeling better. I slowly got to my feet and found I was no longer dizzy. I proceeded to the nurse's station. When I approached the desk, I noticed there was a doctor in his early forties poring over some charts with a nurse. I then introduced myself, and he introduced himself as Doctor Rubell. Then, he took me aside, carrying his charts, a stethoscope hanging around his neck. He appeared to be very weary, and when he looked me in the eyes and I could sense the impending bad news coming.

"I'm afraid your father is in very bad shape. He has multiple internal injuries, and when we operated on him he went into cardiac arrest." Here, he paused as if to let me absorb what he had told me already.

"Your father was clinically dead for five minutes. He was very oxygen-starved during some critical moments prior to his arrival. I can't rule out the possibility that even if he is to survive, with all that has happened to him, that he won't have some brain damage. He is in a coma state right now."

"A coma," I repeated, still feeling half awake from my visitation moments before.

"Yes," Doctor Rubell continued. "Sometimes, patients will break out of a coma in a few days, and some patients remain in it for a very long time. Right now we have him on life support systems and are monitoring his vital signs. I will need to explain these things to your mother now. Please follow me."

And the words clattered like empty shells on a sidewalk, newly fired from a warmed gun barrel. And the numbness I felt was then broken as I had to experience the words again, as he told my devastated mother. She completely fell apart. She fell on me and broke down and wailed in the room as I had never heard her before.

Doctor Rubell apologized for having to tell us and left us alone.

My weeping mother, next to my comatose father, had wiped away all the negative thoughts I had harbored, for so long, toward my father. Gone were the moments of hatred, of fear, of wanting to understand how he could order my sister away, could insist his own wife not play piano. Here was my father, the man who gave me life, tossed a ball with a very young version of me, held me tight when I was afraid, when I had a bad dream, needed comforting. Now, in front of me was a maimed image of him, kept alive in twilight, unable to talk or move, unable to die, unable to give last minute confessions or handle final preparations before his departure. It was the special cruelty of being in limbo. I wasn't sure it was better than assured eternal blackness.

The overwhelming sense of helplessness, though, was shifting, as I turned my attention back to my mother. If I concentrated on her, I felt I could get through the night and then, the next and the next, no matter what came.

My mother sat next to my father and was holding his hand. She was looking into his face and shaking her head back and forth, not wanting to accept that the person beside her was her partner in life, her love.

"That a life of trying to build dreams could come to this," she said, in a sob-choked voice.

I walked over to her and all I could do was to stand over her and rest my hands on her shoulders. She patted my hands with hers and we both silently stood there and looked upon my father, her husband, and this time, we both rocked back and forth, back and forth.

I couldn't bear to stare at him any more. I closed my eyes and saw the time I was lost at the carnival, and went crying through the dark masses of people in search of a familiar face, only to come across stranger after stranger, until at last my father came rushing out of the crowd and grabbed me by the hand.

I saw one of the Christmases when my sister and I painted snowflakes on the windows, while my father, who then loved music as much as any of us, sang along to Nat King Cole, "Have Yourself a Merry Little Christmas," his favorite. These memories came rushing now at rapid speed, some of them just a word or two from him, or a look or my recall of watching him as he read the newspaper or showed someone a new car on the lot. Small moments, ones I never would have expected to remember, were replaying themselves, in no order, with no particular meaning except the reminder of loss.

I opened my eyes. My mother was bent over my father, as though she was asleep. She looked up at me with red-rimmed, hopeless eyes. “Call your sister,” she mumbled.

“Um, I don’t know her number.” She recited it to me. She had memorized it, although my father had forbade her from calling.

I had not spoken with Michelle in over a year myself and the surreal horror of the whole night seemed to be continuing without end. I found a pay phone and called the operator, asking to make a collect call to New Orleans and repeating the number.

The phone rang many times before her sleepy, throaty voice answered. The operator asked if she would accept the charges from me and after a long pause, she realized who it was and said yes, three times.

“Michelle, it’s Eddie. I’m sorry I’m waking you up but...” and now that I did not have to be strong in front of my mother, the tears burned, the sobs choked my voice box.

“What is it, Eddie?” The sleepiness in her voice was now gone and the tone of concern, something I fondly remembered from so far in the past took over. It reminded me how long it had been since I’d seen her and it made me cry harder.

I finally pulled myself together and told her, including the fact that there was no sense of how long our father would be in a coma. I promised we would let her know of any changes.

"I'm sorry it's been so long, Eddie."

"I know. I'll talk to you soon."

"I'll see you soon," she replied.

"I miss you."

"I miss you too. But I'll see you again soon."

There was nothing more to say and we both hung up at the same time. I wiped my eyes with my sleeve and glancing up, I caught Doctor Rubell looking at me from the nurse's station. He quickly looked down and I immediately walked over to him.

"Doctor, I don't even know what happened to him."

Doctor Rubell cleared his throat and then spoke in a quiet tone, his jaw tense.

"He had apparently been working late with some associates. His car went off the road, struck a tree. He went through the windshield. I'm sorry."

Doctor Rubell started to walk away, not out of callousness, I knew, but out of protecting himself from the pain he encountered every day. I could tell from his face, he cared. I could tell by catching him looking at me while I was on the phone.

I caught his sleeve with my hand. “I’m sorry, but just one other thing.”

“Of course,” he said, sympathetically.

“I know this will sound odd but I have a good reason for asking.”

“Go ahead.”

“What time was the accident reported?”

Looking through some paperwork at the station, Doctor Rubell scanned with his fingers, his tired eyes darting back and forth, flipping through the handwriting on the pages.

“Here it is,” he said. The driver who witnessed it said it had happened about five minutes before he got to a phone. Nine thirty-five was the call. So, that puts the accident at about nine thirty.”

I nodded. He patted my arm and went to help others.

I went back to the chairs in the waiting room where the face had appeared. I stared at the ceiling, not expecting to see anything but thinking, considering, about its meaning, about my mother’s sense that something was wrong, about the sudden wave of nausea and dizziness that drove me from the stage at The Mumps, at nine thirty that night.

Chapter 7

After one month in the hospital, my father, as it is said, "shed off his mortal coil". During the four weeks that my father's life hung in the balance, my mother spent most nights alone in her room. I could hear her crying in between the low rumblings of her prayers. Neither my mother nor my father were churchgoing folks, but my mother came from a very religious family. Her strong faith, indoctrinated when she was a girl, helped her deal with this tragedy in a way. But the fact that our own family had not been observant, in another way, created guilt and a confusion that really undercut her ability to recover from the loss, to find the will to carry on, and fully live life.

The bizarre parallel was this: My father had been in limbo in terms of his consciousness, of being alive. After he died, she was in a limbo of spirituality.

A very different life, of course, had been forged for me as well. My job at the potato farm, which up to now just brought me a few dollars to spend on the weekend, was going into the pot to help our family. My father's insurance policy from the dealership paid us only ten thousand dollars, of which one-fourth went to funeral expenses. The house we were living in was now going to cost more than we could pay. My mother had little experience in the world of working.

But while my mother had brought these topics up after my father died, we were all too consumed with the funeral arrangements to deeply pursue them. Michelle arrived by bus, and when my mother and I saw her walking up to our front door, we ran to meet her and the three of us hugged a long time, saying nothing, just making sniffling and muffled sounds.

Michelle made me forget the pain for a while. I had been waiting so anxiously to see her since my phone call to her from the hospital and she was more beautiful than I had remembered, her dark, wavy hair now cascading farther down her back, her shimmering eyes holding secret stories and pleasures of her new life in New Orleans.

***

The preacher at the funeral in the town cemetery spoke in general terms and I wondered how much he really knew about my father. He said he had bought a car from him and judged him to be a decent man. I had an oddly humorous thought: would his opinion of my father have changed if the car was a lemon?

The eulogy took up the topic of my father's place in the community and as the preacher intoned, the word "community" came up a few more times. But community is different to all people. I had a family that had not felt like a community and now, my father was gone and suddenly, my sister was next to me, holding my hand, giving me a courage I hadn't felt in the longest month of my life. And yet, how would the shift in my family community affect me in my community at the potato farm and the community of my band and the community of those who I interacted with in Romeo. I had not spent any appreciable time thinking about it until now, in the moment of having my sister and my mother at my side, now watching the casket lowered into the ground, now tossing a handful of dirt onto the box and hearing it hit the wood with a soft thud.

The gathering at our house after the funeral was filled with soft voices, offers of help, presents of food. Some of our visitors did not know how to talk to Michelle, for she and my father had fought terribly and it had been a subject of gossip when she angrily left and went to create music as a guitarist in New Orleans. My mother was surrounded with support from those who came but I kept an eye out for my sister, going to her side whenever I noticed she was alone, sometimes just holding her hand, saying nothing, until someone approached us, to give condolences.

The most distinct memory I have during the wake was when Johnny and his father and mother said goodbye to me. Mister Jankowski, like his wife, a full-bodied farmer type, pumped my hand and Mrs. Jankowski, who had herself brought enough food to feed us for a week, hugged me ferociously and said,

"You be sure to come by soon for music and food."

"They're kind of the same thing," I smiled and walked them out. Johnny's parents instinctively walked to their car, to let Johnny have a few moments alone with me.

"I'm sorry, Eddie. I know he treated you rough but I'm sure it hurts a lot."

"It does," I mumbled.

"I tell you what." Johnny was clearly struggling to find something positive to say. "We're going to win that Battle of the Bands and everything is going to be a whole lot better, man. You and me. Together."

I nodded but then found myself shaking my head. "Johnny, I really want to."

"Want to?" Johnny looked stunned. "It's all set. Byron set it up."

"I don't know, but now I'm going to have to work extra at the farm to help out my mom."

"What about Michelle?"

"I don't know. I don't know if she's staying."

Johnny walked around nervously, sent a quick look over at his parents, waiting in the car. "Eddie, Eddie," he sighed, "this is not the time to talk about this. This is a bad, bad day." He gently punched me on the arm. "It's going to be okay. You'll see."

I nodded again, not believing anything was going to be okay, and thanked him and he jogged over to the car and they drove away.

When the last guest had reluctantly retreated from a house filled with foodstuffs and sadness, my mother excused herself and went up to what was now just her room and rested. Michelle and I tidied up the living room, gathering silverware and plates.

"What was the last time like between you and Dad?"

I looked at her surprised she had just come out with the question but then, relieved to have permission to talk about it with her, knowing I could be safe, that no one, not even my mother, would hear about it. I told her of both the episode of him knocking me down and of the last time we spoke, when I asked him about the lack of music in the house.

"Sounds like a replay of me leaving," she said, starting to wash dishes.

"Let me do that," I insisted, wanting to do something with my hands. She let me and apparently she felt the same way, because she began rearranging the food in the refrigerator.

"What about you?" I asked over the steamy water and clattering of plates. "Did you ever talk to him by phone or write him a letter after you left?"

"Nope. I called on occasion during days when I knew only Mom would be home. I think I caught you home one day, cutting school."

"I remember that call." I smiled sheepishly. "I had stayed out too late with Johnny drinking after a gig."

She smiled sadly and I was overcome with the feeling that my father had driven my family apart and that even with him gone, it would never be back together again.

"Michelle, why did he have to push you away?"

"I know, but the thing is, I love New Orleans. I barely make enough to survive, playing on the street and a couple gigs here and there. But I've got all these great friends. They're wonderful musicians. I split the rent with two friends and we help each other out. You have to come down there."

She had said it. "You have to come down there." Any idea of her staying in Romeo was gone, like a puff of exhaust fouling the air from an old car.

"Can't you stay here for a while?" My voice was choked and I hated myself for hearing the words come out in such a way. I bent to my task, scrubbing at a stain on a casserole. Michelle leaned her head against my arm.

"I can stay here for a while, Eddie," she said, so softly, I almost didn't hear it. "We can get to know each other again, spend time with Mom. It'll be nice. But I have a life down there. I was scared when he told me to get the hell out but in some weird way, he did me a favor."

"I don't feel that way," I said bitterly. "He threw you out and Mom stopped playing music and I had to hide playing music and for what?" I turned off the water, now getting angry. "For what, Michelle? Because he was angry, he had to ruin the lives of everyone else?"

"It's not ruined. You can still do what you want. You and Johnny have your band."

"Yeah, I'm just going to leave school and Mom and go off and be in a rock band. I can't even go to this Battle of the Bands contest our manager set up."

Michelle took a dishcloth and instead of handing it to me, she dried my hands, like I was very little and could not do it myself.

"Dad was angry at me because I wanted to go out with boys and play music and I refused do what he wanted. I did what I needed to do and now, you have to do what you need to do. He may have never realized it but he gave me a new life. And I'm telling you, Eddie, you're going to the Battle of the Bands. I'll be here, helping out Mom. Do you hear me Eddie; *I'm* giving *you* a new life."

My eyes filled with tears and I hugged her with all my might, leaving wet handprints on the back of her dress.

***

At the potato farm, everyone was sympathetic to what I was going through and offered any help they could possibly give. Even Leonard, the often gruff foreman, took me aside and told me,

"You ever need extra hours or less hours, whatever, you just let me know, Eddie. We'll make your schedule flexible, from here on out."

I had always felt I was one of their fold. Most kids my age would never feel that way, let alone sometimes actually look forward to going to work. Now, they were more than ever part of my foundation, an anchor in a sea of worldly troubles.

I often worked for ten hours a day and always volunteered for Saturday work. Even though this made the cash flow in greater amounts, it was still barely enough to make ends meet. I had little time to hang out with friends, no time for reading or writing songs and The Caretakers would have to be fitted in where I could. Johnny emphasized how good we needed to be for the competition and in order to make some of these rehearsals, I sometimes skipped school. This was another problem that was creeping in at the time, a grade point average which had always been a source of pride. It began to suffer and I knew my mother was displeased, but she kindly let it go, not wanting to put more pressure on me.

The money that we received from my father's life insurance policy was not going to carry us very far, and to give us a little breathing room, my mother insisted on getting a job herself. It was going to be the first job she held since she was married. She went to a school to learn typing so that she could get a clerical job somewhere. She told me that the money that was coming in now would help to pay for my education, which meant college after I graduated from high school. College was to me a luxury that looked pretty unlikely in our situation but I never stepped on her dreams for me to pursue a higher education.

I told her about the Battle of the Bands and Michelle must have already mentioned it, to prepare her, because she did not seem too surprised. She sat me down on the sofa in the living room and held my hand and looked me square in the eyes.

"I know how hard you've been working," she admitted. "You go play with the band and do well. I know you've had some disappointments, Eddie." She brushed some hair out of my eyes. “Do you remember when you were running track? You were setting local records for the 440, wasn’t it?”

“Yeah, until I blew out my knee.”

“But you made me very proud, Eddie. It made your father proud, too, even though he probably didn’t say much to you about it.”

“I don’t think he said anything to me about it.”

“But I’m telling you now,” my mother said, an insistence in her voice, an energy that had all but disappeared since the accident. “I am proud of you. You’re good at so many things, like track and guitar and writing songs and I want you to do all the things that appeal to you. But I just don’t want you to be too downhearted if they don’t work out. Like with track. Life is unpredictable and it never goes the way we plan it.”

***

The night before I went to Grand Rapids, for the competition with the band, I had this dream that upset me. It started in a peaceful and serene field of tall grasses and wild flowers. The afternoon sun was gently pouring down on me and there was a slight breeze blowing. I was sitting next to a still pond and could see the various forms of life moving about. The blue sky and clouds were also reflecting in the surface of the pond. I couldn't take my eyes off the water. It mesmerized me.

Then, all of a sudden an object appeared in the reflection. At first, it seemed to be a bird's shadow crossing over, but then it became clearer, an airplane, slowly flying overhead. I didn't look up, somehow frozen in position by the pond's reflection, but I could hear the sputtering of the plane's engine.

Now in the pond I could see flames coming from the plane. The plane then began to fall from the sky. Everything was in slow motion now in the reflection. I turned to look up at the sky, directly at the plane. It seemed to be impossibly close to me. I could somehow see the faces of the passengers inside and all their faces were stretched out of shape with looks of terror. There was nothing I could do but watch as they fell to the earth. I was totally helpless to do anything for them. There was a huge fireball as the plane hit the earth's surface, just a few dozen yards away from me, and I threw myself to the ground and covered up for protection.

As the sound of the explosion receded, I looked up. There was a huge glowing orb surrounding the plane. It was almost blinding me but I had to keep looking towards it. There were forms of smoky light floating about the plane, some type of energy that was of this earth, yet somehow different. It was actually a beautiful sight to behold, but just as that thought came to me, the orb came over to me and I stood paralyzed. It didn't speak but it was somehow communicating to me. In my mind, I heard the following words:

“Few have seen the other side. You have been chosen to calm the waters in these turbulent times. Do not take this gift lightly. You will have more visions come to you and you will need the wisdom of all times so that those in need will listen."

I woke up from the dream, my heart pounding, and sat upright in bed. I looked at the clock in my room. It was just after seven a.m., time to prepare for my musical destiny.

Johnny had arranged to borrow a van from his uncle to tote us and all the gear up to the Battle. As we passed by all the little towns along the way, knowing the fact that we were supposed to be in school, the four of us felt an incredible sense of total freedom. Conversations began, shifted quickly, splitting between the four of us in different configurations, with new topics popping up with rapidity and frequency. It was apparent from the happy disjointedness of our chatter how much we were excited about the opportunity before us.

Bobby and Tommy were playing riffs on their guitars in the back of the van. I held their notes in my head while, at the same time, hearing Bob Dylan's "Blowin' in the Wind." Somehow, three different lines of music went together in some absurdly happy, dreamlike way.

"Man, can you belieeeeve this," Johnny smiled, puffing on his cigarette after drawing out the syllable to emphasize his giddy mood. "We're really doing it. Wow."

"Wouldn't have even gotten this far without you," I said.

We pulled into the little town of Webberville for our first stop. We filled up with gas, used the bathrooms and grabbed some candy bars for the remainder of the ride ahead.

As we were walking out of the gas station and were heading to the van, we saw two girls standing by it. When we were closer, the girl with brown hair offered a small "hello" and we returned the favor.

She asked, "Where y'all headed?"

This was the perfect cue for swaggering, swashbuckling Johnny.

"Why we're heading up to Grand Rapids, honey, to play in a Battle of the Bands."

"Wow, we thought you were in a band," admitted her blonde companion.

We chatted a bit, found out they were Linda and Kim, in order of speech, introduced ourselves, talked about our band a bit, explaining who did what and then, suddenly, Linda burst out with "Can we go with you?" Just like that, they were ready to jump in the van with us and be our groupies. The idea of being a working musician was looking more attractive to me by the minute.

Johnny, with both joy and apprehension, due to the fact that the girls seemed to be so young, tried to negotiate the sensitive topic of age.

"Um, you see, now , we're going to be gone for a few days, and won't it be kind of strange to just take off like that? I mean, won't your parents be worried and all?"

Linda stared right back at Johnny, who blew a smoke ring trying to look cool. "Naw, man, you see, me and Kim here, well, we're running away anyway."

Kim chimed in, “We've just been hitching rides to go to Saugatuck to stay with my brother. We've been gone two days already and having a blast, man.”

Johnny took all this in. He wasn’t one to pass up a chance at a lovely young girl but was also good at thinking on his feet. “Yeah, but don't you think the cops will be looking for you? Don't you think your parents will have a bulletin out for you?”

Linda answered with assurance, “Naw, man, my dad ran away with another woman. And my mother is living with a drunk in a trailer park and they could both give a shit where I am, man.”

With this information, Johnny gave us a look and apparently our communal look back was filled with lust and excitement. He proclaimed, “Well, all right then, come aboard. What would any decent band be without their women, anyway?”

Linda took the passenger seat and I joined the others in the back. As we got moving on the highway again, Kim whipped out a bag of pot and immediately began to roll a joint.

Up in front, Johnny had Linda to match his gift of gab and they chatted amiably and nonstop. The rest of us were smoking pot and playing our instruments in the back of the van. It was a great scene and as we found songs they knew well, the girls started to sing along with us. Johnny, our pilot, nodding and smiling, taking the occasional hit off the joint, confidently smiling as if this had all been planned from the beginning.

We made Grand Rapids in no time at all. The one thing that none of us thought of though was where we were going to hole up for the night.

It wasn't a very big concern for Johnny however. "Man, we can all just camp out in the van in the park if we have to."

I knew that of course everything would be okay, but with the six of us it might be a little cramped, not to mention a little bit cold, being on the west side of the state. I mentioned this and Johnny calmed everyone down with, "Hey, we'll just go over to the site of the gig and find out what everybody else is doing."

Byron had not given us the exact address before we left and so, we trudged on to find the spot of the Battle of the Bands and the promoter of the gig.

Grand Rapids, in the mid-sixties, was a quiet, religious community nestled on the shores of Lake Michigan. The townsfolk were less than excited that a bunch of rock and rollers were invading their peaceful burg. We made frequent stops to ask people on the street but nobody seemed to know, or wanted us to know, where the Battle was being held. We decided that we would go get something to eat and regroup.

The minute we made this decision, another joint was lit up, which added nothing to aid our endeavors. As usual though, Johnny was in control and in no way did we lose our faith in him, driving around, checking out the area

.

We ended up at a place just outside of the city limits called Edna's Eats. This had all the markings of a movie set. The big trucks were all lined up outside and the diner itself was the old style, a metallic Twinkie with an awning on it. We were all extremely hungry, or at least that's what our pot-induced minds led us to believe.

The layout of Edna's was such that you could see all the customers and tables in one glance but the place had a good feeling to it. The folks in the diner were too busy talking or eating to care about the motley crew of young, stoned, tired rockers shuffling in the door. We all moved in unison towards a big booth by the window, a naugahyde semicircle of comfort. We pressed together and giggled and whispered.

Our waitress was young, slightly older than us, which was good, because we definitely didn't want to get stuck with a disgruntled waitress that long ago gave up hope for anything better in life and would ruin our high with the evil eye.

Her cheery hello was all Johnny needed to tell her how hungry we were and that we were part of the Battle.

"Oh, yeah, man everyone's excited about it."

We were glad she was. The other people we'd met hadn't been too thrilled. Someone yelled something from the kitchen to her and she turned her head and yelled back a response.

"I'll be right back to take your order and tell you where the place is. God, this is so exciting."

When she brought our food, she also had written down the location of the Battle and said she and a friend would look for us there. "What's the name of your band?"

"Caretakers," said four guys, excitedly, with food in their mouths.

Chapter 8

We followed the hastily drawn map that our waitress had sketched for us, between serving tables at Edna's Eats. When we pulled up to the spot, we were greeted by a large mailbox in the shape of a castle. There were two huge pines on either side of a driveway that led back into the hills. The long drive curved past a small stand of trees on either side and through the hilly landscape, leading us to a clearing. There we could see a huge house sitting way atop a hill. It was a large version of the mailbox castle.

The sight seemed almost unreal to the six of us in the van. Don Miller's home was set up on a great bluff that overlooked Lake Michigan. In the twilight, the scene was so distant and barely visible; it was almost as if it was painted, not really there.

Johnny took the lead and started to stride confidently towards the house. We all followed right behind him. There were already about ten cars and vans parked up by the house. Johnny reached the giant double doors at the front and knocked with eager anticipation, seeming almost ready to spring out of his shoes.

We waited patiently. Outside lights came on. To our surprise, the man who greeted us did not appear to be a promoter or anyone who actually worked at anything. A long haired guy, in tee shirt and bell bottoms, his eyes slightly glazed, strolled outside of the doors and checked us over.

Johnny, somewhat surprised that a freak would answer the door, blurted out, "We're here for the gig, man."

"Oh wow, all right, the party keeps growing." He seemed as though we were friends of his friends who had got lost on the way to a big party. "You're going to want to talk to Don, man. He's the guy that owns the place and is putting on the happening. Just go upstairs and turn left, first door on your right, man."

"Yeaaaah," Johnny almost sighed and turned back to us, those he was caretaking. "Let's go, everyone."

The place inside was huge, bigger than any house any of us had ever been in, without a doubt; we didn't need to ask or tell each other. The walls were lined with paintings. Statues stood in seemingly every room. It was one of those mansions you see in the movies, only this one was sans butlers and filled with rockers. There were sounds bouncing around the house in every direction. Some bands were already rehearsing. Johnny looked around, taking in all the sights and sounds and while I was not worried, I couldn't help but notice it was the first time Johnny seemed to be out of his element, unable to process the information, sum up the situation. I didn't blame him. We were all knocked out by the mansion and the doings in each room.

When we finally arrived upstairs, the chaos was different but just as present. Upstairs served as the area for communications and the press. There were microphones thrust in the faces of various people in the rooms, even in the hall, cameras taking pictures, flashes going off, with people trying to talk coherently, despite the distractions and whatever they had ingested during the day.

A man in his early forties, dressed casual chic, was now coming over our way. He stuck out his hand and introduces himself as Don Miller. He asked us if we were here to play in the event. Johnny composed himself and introduced the band, leaving out of the names of Linda and Kim. Johnny realized Don still didn't know the name of our band.

"We're The Caretakers.'' He thrust his hand toward Don again.

"Ah, yes, I seem to recall the name from the roster. Please come in and have a seat."

We all walked into a huge living room area, with a fireplace and Oriental rugs lining the floor. He recognized we were weary travelers and told us we could help ourselves to food and drink in the kitchen, after we registered for the Battle. We then walked over to the sign-in sheet and Don kindly asked us who the leader of the group was. We all pointed to Johnny. Don turned to Johnny and asked politely if he would sign in all the members of the band. Johnny got a crooked grin of pride on his face as he turned to us and bent to his task.

Don went on to tell us more about the Battle and general rules and scheduling. When we inquired about lodgings for the night, he looked at us and then gave out a great big belly laugh.

"Well, most of the bands so far have decided that they want to camp out on the land. We have over fifty acres here. Did you bring a tent with you?"

This last question only brought blank looks on all of our faces.

"Well, don't worry guys. We have plenty of equipment here you can use. We'll set you up in no time."

The girls were very excited about the whole thing and it looked like we were in for a hell of a weekend. Don was enthusiastic himself, telling us he had twenty bands from all over signed up for the event. Ticket sales were already going through the roof. He went on to tell us that we would be paid five hundred dollars, regardless of ticket sales, as long as we played our set. We felt like kids on Christmas morning.

Don wished us luck and turned to attend to other business, as a young woman from the event committee came to collect us and tell us where we would be camping out. As she led us outside Johnny couldn't hold in his happiness. He pulled me aside and whispered excitedly,

"Eddie, can you believe all this? This Don guy is great, isn't he? Even if we don't win, which I'm sure that we will, we will be five hundred dollars richer. Not only that, my dear Eddie, but can't you see that we are on our way?"

Once we got our tent up and our sleeping arrangements were out of the way, we began to mingle with all the other bands. Johnny led the way, always about twenty feet ahead of the rest of us, stopping in at this campfire and that jam, to listen, to introduce himself or whichever one of the band was near him. Bursting with excitement, he would cheerfully promise to see the new acquaintances later and then move on, finding the next group of musical vagabonds on the property. I had a perpetual smile plastered on my face. Everyone seemed happy to meet others, sharing whatever food, drink or drugs they had. I wondered how many of them came from small towns, like us, and thought, until the invitation to the Battle, that they never would have a chance at the big time, a ticket out of a locked, familiar room.

As night descended and the chilly winds from the lake started to blow over us, there seemed to be a migration to a spot where a towering bonfire was in progress. Johnny came over to me as if he had some important news to tell me. He got close to me and whispered that he had scored some mescaline from one of the bands and asked me if I would like some. I had never taken any chemical drugs at this point yet and I was a little bit apprehensive.

Johnny quickly assured me, "It's cool, man. This place is great and I'll be here to keep an eye on you." It felt the most natural place in the world to try this drug and with all the good vibes going on, I couldn't resist it.

Kim, the girl who had rolled joints and said so little during much of our trip decided that she would accompany me. She seemed more at ease. I finally had the first rush of mescaline in my blood, and the faces and sounds came at me in pleasing blurs. The giant bonfire helped to give me a sense a communal feeling and I started talking about music as a means of entering the spirit world, of creating communication, even without words. Kim enjoyed my spacey verbal meanderings, even linking her arm in mine. Johnny and the others had floated out of our range.

Other bands were assembling around the bonfire, bringing their instruments into a large, ritual jam to celebrate the Battle and all the good will it had brought together. Kim snuggled next to me, as we listened for a while and then, much to my surprise, ironically asked if I had any mescaline. I told her I didn't have any but that we should try to find Johnny and he could probably score for us.

It wasn't an easy task finding Johnny, however. We spent a few minutes wandering about the bonfire celebrants and then, my head spinning from the psychedelic, I paused, stared into the fire and had my instincts tell me to look first in our tent.

Sure enough, when Kim and I got close enough to the tent, I could hear sounds issuing forth, very much like two people making love. This would, no doubt, be Johnny and some girl he had just met. I waited a few minutes until there was a lull inside and then made my request from outside the tent. His head popped out of the little zipper opening, his hair askew in one direction and in my high state, I began to laugh uncontrollably and had a hard time getting out my full request. This of course was not to Johnny's liking because I was dampening the mood of his lovemaking. I obtained a couple of hits of mescaline from Johnny, and Kim and I went on our way.

I put the mescaline on her tongue and she seductively took my finger in her mouth and sucked on it. She thanked me. We stared at each other. Sounds of passion welled out of the tent. I took her face in my hands and kissed her gently on the mouth. It felt so free, but so completely natural and she returned the kiss, suggesting the same feeling.

We walked back toward the bonfire, checking out the dancers, the musicians and their friends, the screamers, the clappers, the hooters and nodders, until Kim turned to me. "I can feel the rushes coming on Eddie. I'm starting to see trails."

She went on to tell me that she had taken mescaline a few times before. “One time,” Kim admitted, “a friend and I took a hit, waited awhile, nothing happened so we both went to bed. The next thing, my friend woke up, screaming and I felt panicked. We had to call another friend at three a.m. to come get us and talk us down.”

“I’m sorry.”

“It’s okay. The other trips were great.” She smiled warmly at me. “So much of drugs, I think, is being with people you like.”

We decided to go up to the house and see what was happening. While there were still some people wandering about, the house was less crowded and we settled into a comfortable couch in front of a roaring fire in the living room.

“This is our living room,” Kim said and we both chuckled.

“Well, then let’s make ourselves at home,” I said and we wrapped ourselves around each other, touching each other.

The moment seized us in a somewhat awkward way. Our minds were laced with mescaline and we were just getting to know each other but we felt the special ness of the time and place and her kisses reassured me whenever my mind raced.

Someone sat down nearby and began talking with a friend.

“How do you feel?” I asked, wanting to make sure she was not unwell.

"I'm feeling like I want to be alone with you, but not here."

We then decided that it might be more comfortable for us upstairs in one of the bedrooms. We fell into one of the beds and held each other and talked for awhile. Kim told me all about her own small-town past, about how she, like Linda, had suffered some rough turns in her young life. We talked about how life was changing for the better for both of us, and that perhaps there was something happening in the whole country that was creating more awareness on the part of people, whether it was drugs or music or protest against the Vietnam War or even something we couldn't yet understand.

The stereo in the room was playing the Bee Gees and songs like "Holiday" and "1941 New York Mining Disaster" fit the mood of our talk. When the record ended, we looked at each other, heard the faint sounds from the bonfire celebration on the property far in the distance and then, together, without a word, took off our clothes and began to make love.

I seemed to have eight hands all of a sudden and Linda responded so passionately to my touch and my movements that all noise, all light simply disappeared, caved in to the two of us. That is probably why I didn't hear the doorknob being turned. But I sure heard the knob hit the wall as it was flung open. The climax of our beautiful moment together had been interrupted by another couple who had come in, arms around each other.

Kim and I covered ourselves with the blanket and held onto each other on the bed and turned to the intruders. The couple seemed to be somewhat embarrassed, but not so much so that they immediately left. In fact, they didn't seem to be planning to leave at all. We waited for an apology.

"Uh, we're sorry for breaking in on you like this, but Don told us this is where we were going to crash tonight."

Once we all gained our composure, we introduced ourselves. It turned out that this guy was Rick Rosten, from one of the hottest rock groups in Michigan at the time, G Factor. I told him it was an honor to meet him, that I had seen his band live and the next thing I knew, he lit a joint and handed it to Kim, who pulled the blanket up around her breasts with one hand and happily reached for it with the other. Rick's girlfriend went over to the stereo and put on The Moody Blues' "Days of Future Past" album. Their rock sound and the London Symphony Orchestra along with the smoke complimented our mescaline high quite nicely.

Rick exhaled a long stream of smoke and asked me if I was in one of the bands that was playing this weekend. When I told him a bit about The Caretakers, he became very animated and started talking about the gig and music in general.

There was a lull in his monologue and I asked if they wanted us to give them their bed for the night.

"Hell, no," Rick laughed. "Now, I'm all geared up." He turned to his girlfriend. "Let's go back to the bonfire." And back to us, "You want to come?"

They stepped outside and gave us a couple minutes to throw our clothes back on. We laughed and kissed. "Hold that thought," Linda said and we opened the door to join our new friends.

To our surprise, when we finally reached the bonfire, there was Don playing a wild, primitive beat on a conga, which everyone seemed to be enjoying. People leaped and gyrated all over as if they were possessed by demons. It was a strange scene, but very infectious. While I couldn't see Johnny, Tommy or Bobby in the crowd, I realized they were off having adventures and all would be fine tomorrow.

Rick grabbed a guitar and started to play along with the beat, feverishly strumming, bringing quivering excitement to more limbs, more feet. Kim and I danced for about an hour, and then, she fell into my arms, sweaty, smiling and put her tongue in my ear.

"I want to be alone with you," she said and we headed back to our oasis of love, our awaiting tent.

When we reached the tent, thankfully nobody was around. We located some candles, lit them and carefully put them inside the tent. We took off our clothes again and snuggled in the sleeping bag Don had loaned us. Kim crawled on top of me and in the sixty-nine position; we took turns caressing each other with our tongues. The mescaline was still toying with our heads and time seemed to be a long, sticky, dripping spoon of honey, never ending.

And when it did end, for both of us, together, our muffled cries of pleasure co-mingled in a night filled with howling, songs, instruments played with wild abandon. We were like hot air balloons, our tie ropes finally cut to send us adrift to the skies.

When we finally came back down to earth, we began to laugh and tell funny stories about our small town lives. We were in our own little world when all of a sudden, the zipper to the tent went singing open. In popped the head of Johnny.

"Hey guys, what're you all doing?" Our chuckling was his answer, as if he really required one. "Come on," he asked good-naturedly. "Join in on the fun outside. You won't believe what's going on, man."

"Oh, we'd believe just about anything at this point," I replied.

"No, really. That wild guy Don's got us all worked up into a frenzy. Everybody's taking off their clothes. It's like a bucket of bees out here, man." Johnny was gone as suddenly as he appeared.

In retrospect, it was pretty absurd but we got dressed in expectation of possibly taking off our clothes again. When we got to the fire, it was just as Johnny said. There were about eight guys and the same amount of girls all dancing around the fire naked. I caught a glimpse of Johnny and Linda, beginning to disrobe and join the rest of the bunch. Kim and I looked at each other and once again, on cue, took off our clothes. We began dancing to the night rhythms. And now a small circle of naked dancers, apart from the other revelers, formed around the fire, led by Don.

The organizer and promoter of the Battle of the Bands yelled, in a most professional manner,

"Swimming pool! Last one ins a rotten egg!" He began to scramble for the house and we all followed behind, howling with laughter. I could see Johnny up ahead of us rocking his head back and forth like a dog enjoying a blast of air out of the window of a moving car.

I held Kim's hand as we ran naked back to the house. It felt as though the night would just never end, that no matter where you were or who you were with, there would be friendship, fun, passion, utter freedom. It was so powerful and even with the mescaline in me, part of my brain was thinking what a tonic this first night was, how it seemed like a positive omen for the complete alteration of my life.

We reached the pool and all jumped in. There, the sounds of splashing, laughing, yelling all echoed into the night, as the pool was situated on a cliff. Far below, you could make out the waters of the big lake and up above, the stars illuminated our frenzy.

Kim pressed her body against mine in the water and I instantly felt myself getting aroused again. She smiled wickedly at me, as if daring me to do something to her in the middle of the pool.

"I want to bottle this whole night, like wine, and just sip it forever," I said and we kissed in the warm, roiling water, ignoring the shouting and playing around us. But then, Johnny, who had just dived underwater, emerged in front of us and gave us a great shot of water in the face. He and Linda laughed at us and the water in our eyes and the dim lighting made everything appear to be filtered through a lava lamp.

I don't know what drug Don was on, but it was either giving him waves of energy or it was his entrepreneurial spirit that kept things moving. He now wanted everyone to go up to the master bedroom of his house.

We ran inside and clambered up the stairs. The master bedroom was the size of an average person's house. It was actually three rooms in one. There was the bedroom, which was about the length of a football field. There was a living room area with yet another fireplace, and then there was an area with a hot tub, steam room, sauna and shower and, to top it all off, a tremendous balcony overlooking the grounds.

Everyone ran in all directions. Kim and I decided to head for the sauna-hot tub area. Don, being the perfect psychedelic happening host, had laid out about fifty towels and some robes. We chose our bath ware and headed for the hot tub. I only knew of these tubs from movies I had seen, set in rich homes and hotels in Hollywood. We climbed a small platform and were now looking down on the bubbling water. We both stuck toes in to test it out. It was plenty hot and we insinuated ourselves into the boiling cauldron, gradually becoming more and more immersed until all but our heads and part of our shoulders were under.

Once we were in and became acclimated, it was wonderful. Not long after we entered the tub, Rick and his girlfriend joined us. As we chatted, from my vantage point I could see into the living room area and there I caught a glimpse of Johnny. He seemed to be wrapped up with about ten other people in what looked to me like naked wrestling, but they were all giggling, like kids, not being sexual. We were exhausted from sensation.

Kim and I eventually bid good night and good morning to Rick and his girlfriend, donned our robes, floated down the stairs and out of the now-quiet mansion.

Outside, the dawn was fighting with the dark and a mist hung impossibly low over the grass. We wandered over sleepers in bags and blankets until we found the tent. Again, it was unoccupied. The sun was just starting to come up.

Kim and I crawled into the tent and slid into a bag, our legs and arms entwined.

"'*Voices of soft proclaim, and silver stir of strings in hollow shells; and there shall be beautiful things made new, for the surprise of the sky-children.*'" I recited it with my eyes closed, my voice dreamy.

"What is that?" Kim asked.

I opened my eyes. "A writer named Keats. He's helped me a lot."

"How?"

"He's given me the passion to survive the ruins of my life."

"I want to read him too," she smiled and we kissed one last time before sliding away to an unconscious world which, even if we had the most wondrous of dreams, could scarcely compete with our past night.

Chapter 9

"Come on, sleepy heads, breakfast is on the table, but it won't last long."

Johnny rattled the opening of our tent with his hand and seemed unbearably chipper. But as he retreated and I stretched awake, I realized I was really refreshed and ready for the day's activities. Kim said she would follow in a little bit but wasn't ready to join the masses just yet. It was a beautiful summer day outside and there was activity everywhere. Most of it seemed to be heading in the direction of the house.

The spread that Don laid out was fit for royalty. We were all seated in a main dining room with about twenty picnic tables to accommodate everyone. There seemed to be even more folks this morning than I had seen last night and there were still more straggling in. The media had started to arrive as well. There were cameras and floodlights strung everywhere. It was a musical media circus.

Don was energetic as usual, fielding questions from all the reporters, as he was taking in bites of food. One reporter had asked why he had organized this event.

"To have fun. To give two great bands the exposure they would never get otherwise. And to make some kick ass rock and roll happen." The roar of approval from those in attendance prevented the reporter from following up with another question.

Right after breakfast, our band joined together at the tent and we talked about the day's events, which were laid out on a program Don had printed up for everyone. Johnny took a bomber joint out of his pocket and we all smoked it. It was a good thing that Don had printed up an itinerary because after we smoked the joint, we were somewhat less than organized. What we were to do first was to bring our equipment down to the bandstand area to get checked in.

It was very organized down by the bandstand area. Nobody was getting high. Don had several people assigning numbers and location codes so that you could quickly locate and set up your equipment when the time was ready. Don also had a numbering system for when your band would play. As it turned out we were in about the middle of the pile.

Johnny, back in Romeo, had insisted on a small rehearsal before we competed. This was okay with everyone because we needed to ground ourselves a little bit after the night's wildness. We never sounded better and we actually had some folks gather around us to cheer us on. Johnny seemed to be possessed behind the drums and with his leadership abilities it seemed to inspire all of us. Also, I never heard Johnny's voice sound so good. It went a long way to lessening our nervousness about the Battle.

There was to be about ten thousand people in attendance. The judges were musicians, disc jockeys, music label execs, so it would seem fair to all the bands to be judged by one's peers. By our estimate, we would go on at about nine that night. There would be time for us to get ready mentally. We could already tell that most of the bands had divorced themselves from mingling, that they were off huddling, practicing, thinking about the competition to come. Johnny called

for a group meeting at six o'clock.

"I suggest you go off and relax, visualize winning, because that's what's going to happen, guys."

I decided to go down toward the lake with Kim, to walk through the woods and keep focused. She had become an important, calming influence on me. When I admitted that Johnny was more confident than the three of us, Kim said, in an assured voice,

"Eddie, I'm going to tell you something and you have to believe me. I'm not just saying this because I like you. When The Caretakers played earlier, at the sound check, you really sounded great. Didn't you see those people starting to gather around?" I nodded. "Those other bands are going to have a hard time beating you. You'll see."

I had never had a regular girlfriend, let alone one who gave me so much encouragement. I really liked it. Part of me knew that she was building my confidence but on the other hand, I took what she said to heart, even, later on, repeating the words in my head, in order to truly benefit from their strength.

Kim was sitting, leaning against a tree and I was lying with my head on her lap. We didn't talk for a long time. We both knew that there wasn't much that could be said until it was show time. It was a remarkably peaceful scene, sitting by a river that fed the big lake. A group of swans glided by, with a grace that was from another place, not of the world of bands and bonfires and making love inside candlelit tents in the middle of a field. I had a piece of grass in my mouth that I was chewing on, just looking up at the great expanse of blue sky overhead.

"Even if we don't win, the fact that this happened," I indicated with a sweep of my hand the environment, "the fact that we happened, that will be the prize."

"I love the way you talk," she said and bent down and kissed me.

I took her by the hand and we walked through the woods until we found a new path.

"Are you feeling adventuresome?" I asked and she answered by leading me down this new passage among the trees, lifting small branches to enter it.

The sun broke through the limbs in stripes of heat and light and we found a patch of grass and flowers that seemed to be there specifically for us. It made a soft cushion for us and we stroked and kissed each other, lazily taking off our clothes, not rushed at all, inhaling each other and the smell of the grass and air and flowers and becoming more passionately overcome by the minute. We embraced and rolled around the blanket of grass and it felt so good to be making love outdoors. It was something I had never done and it amazed me how I had missed such a pure, simple, rewarding pleasure. Both of our bodies shuddered with exquisite longing until we were spent, lying in the colorful patch, breathing heavily, feeling blissful.

"Now," panted Kim, smiling, "you're ready to win the Battle of the Bands."

The walk back to the stage area was quiet, pleasant, until we got nearer to the park where the performances would be held. Everyone was busy doing this or that on a perfectly sunny day. I noticed that there were a few dogs that were roaming around the place now. They seemed to be content, and I guess why they should be, what with this wide expanse of country to jump around in.

As we got back to the stage area, we saw there was a great hub of activity as bands were scrambling to get their show together. There was also quite a bit of partying going on already, groups drinking, smoking, trying to relax their pre-show jitters and I thought it kind of odd. I smiled to myself, thinking those that went on stage high might falter and give us a better chance. But I immediately wondered if there were bands so talented, that being a little high might help them, loosen them up, like one of Johnny's pep talks. I really had no idea what our chances were and had no sense of whether the dream would come true or not.

We gathered ourselves together and headed for the band shell. I knew Johnny would be anxious to get our practice set down. I was right. Johnny was there with Tommy and Bobby. Johnny was fiddling with his drumsticks. He called out, "All right, let's go," when he saw me approaching with Kim, who immediately went off with Linda to compare notes about their experiences so far. Johnny and I hadn't even had time to do this, and would not, for a while. Our exchange verified this.

"Man, I just heard this news from Don," he said. "Guess who is going to be in this Battle of the Bands here? " He looked at me as though I might guess who the mystery group might be.

"I really don't know Johnny. Tell me who it is. "

Johnny had a look on his face that was part astonishment, part respect. He then blurted out his answer.

"G Factor, man. Only the hottest group in the state. Man, they're just going to blow everyone away. We got to rehearse more, Eddie, if we want to be competitive."

I picked up my guitar and plugged in and switched on. "Yeah, I know G Factor is here."

"Who told you?" asked Bobby.

"Rick Rosten."

"You met Rick Rosten from G Factor?" asked Tommy.

"Yeah," I said, as nonchalantly as possible. "Actually, he walked in on me and Kim making love and we smoked a joint with him and his old lady."

"Yeah, very funny," replied Johnny, doubting me.

"He did. And then when we ran up to the mansion last night, they joined us in the hot tub."

The three of them looked at me, stunned. "He's a really cool guy," I told them.

Johnny finally had all this information sink into his head. He looked over at Linda and Kim, chatting animatedly some distance away and then back at me. "We'll discuss this later," he announced. "Let's practice."

We played the three songs that we had rehearsed for the gig. I thought we did pretty well on all of them. Johnny was a little bit more critical.

"Come on, guys, we got to get in better rhythm if we're going to beat these guys. We are up against the best in Michigan and who knows where else. We got to get it so we *feel* it."

We played for an hour or so until Johnny felt we had it. "Are you ready?" he asked, simply. We all nodded our heads yes. We were as ready as we'd ever be, I thought. It's either meant to be or it isn't.

We got off the stage and let the next band rehearse. It was a good thing that I had Linda along because she was so steady through all of this. Johnny, on the other hand, was utterly wired. He paced back and forth, running the songs through his head, humming, sometimes pantomiming his drumming to the unheard song. Linda tried for a while to be with him, but his furious pacing made it impossible. Instead, she came over to Kim and me and Tommy and Bobby and said,

"You guys are going to be great."

We milled about backstage, said hi to other bands who we had met, wished each other good luck, nibbled some food, had some water or coffee or juice to wet parched, expectant mouths. I watched the park fill with people gradually as the gates were open. Finally the announcement came over the public address system that the festivities were to begin. As to be expected, Don took first crack at the mike and received a huge applause from the crowd. Don was reading word for word from a three by five card, belying his confidence as host of the festivities but still, clearly, pleased by the ten thousand he had drawn to his property.

We were to play in the middle of the pack, which was good for us. We would be able to hear half of the groups play and get an idea of what we were up against. As Johnny and I stood together, backstage, watching group after group, his animated quality shifted to one of quiet intensity.

After a particularly successful group that got a tumultuous sendoff after their third and final song, Johnny leaned over to me and shouted in my ear,

"There are maybe two or three groups that might be better than us. But on any given night, some band can pull off the best sound they ever came up with. Tonight has to be our night, Eddie. I don't want to go back to living in Romeo, now."

"I don't either, Johnny."

"Then, we have to make it happen." Johnny saw Bobby walking over to us, curious as to what had been said. Johnny deftly patted him on the back and went to the refreshments table to get something to drink.

Kim drifted over to me and we listened to a group that was heavy into the R& B sound. They had a big band complete with the minimum daily adult requirement for horns. Their singer had a nice, strong, gravely voice. They sounded good. When they finished, Kim and I nodded, wordlessly recognizing that this was not going to be easy.

The next three groups were decent. They had a raw sound that came from a mixture of Motown & psychedelia. They were putting a lot of feedback and fuzz tone into their music, which was so popular then. Johnny liked the sound but for our band, had always made me use those effects sparingly, often telling me to "not overdo it."

Now, a stagehand told us we were next. There was no doubt we were all nervous but we refused to show it to each other. As Don started introducing us, Johnny pulled the four of us together.

"Okay, guys. We're as good as anybody who's here. You know it. I know it. Let's let them know it."

Johnny stuck out a fist and held it at belt height. We all put our fists on top of one another, just like we were going into a baseball game when we were in elementary school. During the first song, I thought we sounded better than any gig we had ever done, but then, the sound systems in and around Romeo could not compete with what Don Miller had set up for the crowd.

I could see Johnny sweating on every down stroke of the stick and I think it inspired us to take our songs to the limit. We were tight and in control. But it gradually came from the place all young musicians dream about but cannot understand, the crowd, an insistent clapping and nodding. We looked briefly out, each one of us noticing, within milliseconds of each other, that we had ten thousand people into our music. We were so green, it took us a few seconds to look back toward our own instruments and each other, so dumbfounded were we by the approval. Johnny flashed me a smile. We finished our second song and the applause that greeted us lasted longer than we thought it would be. I moved toward Johnny at the drums, waiting for the noise to die down.

"This Is Your Last Chance," he said, calling the name of the song we knew was next, we knew backwards and forwards and knew we had to play with some kind of newness or we wouldn't have a chance.

"Don't be so dramatic," I joked and Johnny laughed.

We launched into the song and as we played, and felt the audience with us, it made me feel different than I had ever felt at a gig. There had been some particularly good nights, together, when we were on, when a crowd in some smoky dive really got into us and we had a grand time. But playing "This Is Your Last Chance" at the Battle of the Bands, I think something happened, inside me. I had the fire in me that Johnny had. It wasn't just wanting to win, to leave Romeo. It wasn't just what I had claimed was my intention, to create music and have it appreciated. It was those things but something else.

It was feeling I belonged on that stage and stages that size, with Johnny and the guys. That this was what I was meant to do, not just what I hoped to do. And in that moment, when I hit the last chord and the crowd roared, and we took our bows and Johnny put his arm around me, I felt that for the first time, I understood what drove Johnny so hard, why he couldn't ever slow down.

"Let's see them beat that!" he yelled in my ear and we left the stage, still hearing the applause while we were backstage.

We had not seen G Factor yet that night, though, and they were the third to last band to perform. When they finally hit the stage, I marveled at Rick's fluidity on the guitar and the seemingly effortless power of their music. As Kim and I watched from the wings, Johnny was back to pacing.

"Johnny," I called out, "come over here."

He came but looked annoyed. "What?"

"Listen to these guys. They're amazing."

"I can't." He turned to walk away. I caught hold of his arm.

"We were great out there, Johnny. It felt like something else."

Johnny nodded. "Yeah, it felt great to me too."

"Don't worry, Johnny," I said, in a strangely calm voice. "It's going to happen for us. If not here, somewhere else."

Johnny smiled but it was a mixture of waning confidence and nerves, as well as an unquenchable pride, which was one of the reasons I loved being his best friend.

There were some groups that played after us that were good, but I felt that we had it over all of them based on the crowds' reaction. It was when G-Factor came on that everybody in the place was completely blown away. They not only nailed all of their songs note for note right on and in perfect harmony of each other, but they also had the audience completely going nuts.

I'll tell you one thing, when I saw the G-Factor do their set I knew we were in the midst of a great, great talent. They had the look, they had the sound, and, they had the audience in the palm of their hands. It was, for me, a great learning experience. I knew that we did great in our set, but these guys went that extra step that our band needed to be with the greats.

At a few minutes before eleven o'clock, the last group had performed and it was pins and needles time for us all until the judges sorted it all out.

The band and our new groupies huddled together. Don took center stage.

"First, I want to thank all the people who came and all the bands that played for us, all day and night. This had been the best weekend I've ever had. How about you?"

The crowd cheered in agreement. He reminded us all that the winner and runner-up got money and a recording contract. There was a drum roll and then, Don glanced down at a card he held.

"And the winner is... G-Factor." The crowd went crazy with this announcement. G-Factor came out onto the stage and Don waved for the crowd to be quiet. He got another drum roll and the audience was quieting, he yelled into the mike, "And the runners up are The Caretakers!"

There was a moment when everything stopped and I couldn't hear anything. I saw Johnny and he looked like someone had just struck him with a baseball bat on the back of the head. And then, that moment was gone and the noise came and Tommy and Bobby jumped on us and we ran out onto the stage and spotlights blinded us and the blood pounded in my temples. Johnny grabbed the check and shook Don's hand as I went over to Rick, offering my hand. Instead, he bear hugged me and the crowd loved that too.

***

After the gig, the newspaper and TV media were all over us. Johnny did most of the talking for the band. Kim ran into my arms, her eyes wet and happy, Linda gave Johnny a wet kiss after he was done with the press. A party of about fifty people made their way to Don's house.

It wasn't until we were at the party that we saw Byron, who hugged us all, telling us how he knew all the time we would do it. The record company exec, Joe Hersenson, cornered Johnny and me and Byron later at the party and set up a recording session in two weeks. Byron had already gone over the contract and we found Bobby and Tommy, pulled them away from attractive girls, and made them sign. The four of us posed for more photos, along with Rick and G Factor. Don told us he had set aside special guest rooms for us to stay in. I turned to Kim, who was looking at me with stars in her eyes, and kidded,

"Hopefully, we'll have it all to ourselves this time."

About fifteen minutes later, I bumped into Johnny at the victory party and mentioned the fact that we should enjoy ourselves tonight because it would be back to school on Monday. He waved me off with his hand.

"Not now Eddie, not now. Let's just have this moment now, man, and think about that tomorrow." So that was that and I did just that, let it go.

The next morning, Kim and Linda admitted they weren't going to go back home. They would hitch up north for a while. I gave Kim my address and she told me she would write me about her adventures on the road. Deep in my heart, I felt that we would never see each other again.

I kissed her goodbye and whispered in her ear, "You made this whole weekend amazing."

"No, you did," she smiled but the tears were starting to come and she quickly joined Linda who already was at the side of the road, with her thumb out.

The local paper back in Romeo got wind of what we accomplished at the festival and wanted to do a piece for the paper. This was the news that Johnny passed on when we first saw each other at school after the Battle.

"Well, if they do a story about us, they'll know we skipped school," I mentioned.

"Big deal," said Johnny with typical, devil-may-care bravado. "What are they going to do to us? Suspend us for three days? That'll be fine. More time to rehearse. Come on, boy. We're going into the big time now. Stop thinking little."

***

I wasn't thinking little. I was thinking of my family. Michelle and my mother were thrilled to hear of the check and the recording contract. But Michelle was not going to stay in Romeo for the rest of her life, and the prospect of leaving my mother alone especially so soon after losing my father, ate away at my conscience.

I was distracted from figuring this out by the reception we received from other students at school. We were welcomed as heroes. Well, perhaps not by the principal, who called each one of The Caretakers into his office separately, to lecture us about responsibility and rules and order. Johnny had it pegged. We got suspended for three days. This simply increased our aura of fame and newness

Apparently, Byron had been on the phones as soon as we returned. I was home when Johnny called me to say that Byron had already received a handful of offers to do gigs, and for more money than we had ever made at the places in the area.

While we mulled over those offers, we rehearsed at Johnny's place in preparation for making our first record. For two weeks after we got back, we tried a number of different songs. Finally, after a few heated arguments, we went with "This Is Your Last Chance," and a bluesy number I had written after being miserable right after another confrontation with my father. Byron agreed that we had picked two strong songs, showing we could both rock and do something with sad, deep conviction.

***

The recording studio was in downtown Detroit and Byron drove his car behind our van as we headed up to the city. It was wonderful to be in a big studio where so many great performers had passed through. Many pictures of the biggest Motown artists adorned the walls. I thought to myself, you're not even old enough to drive and you're in a studio where Marvin Gaye had recorded.

It took a long time for us to get everything down like we wanted to. Byron pushed us and to his credit, he wouldn't let us do a single that he didn't think was our best work. This was no one-take, get them in, get them out routine like with that bizarre Mushroom Bob character. The engineer was a grizzled looking vet who had been on staff for years and he just had the look of a guy who knew his job backwards and forwards. I tried to talk to him about some of the acts he had recorded, during one of our breaks, but Byron hustled me back into the studio for overdubs. I guess he was paying good money and didn't want to see one second of time go buy that wasn't being used.

When the final take was done on the B side blues number, the engineer played it back through the studio speakers. The sound was so rich, and the guitars blended so well, we were all knocked out. It was almost as if the music had not come from us.

Byron explained, as we packed our equipment back into the van at the end of the day, exhausted, that we were going to get local airplay and distribution, but if the song took off, it could go on to get national exposure. We couldn't even imagine what that would be like. Johnny was beside himself now and when we got outside the studio, onto the street, he grabbed me by the arm and had a wild look in his eyes.

"Your life will never be the same now, Eddie, never!"

With this he went into a wild laugh and started whooping and hollering as he ran down the street with a snare drum. Some of the black folks who were walking past turned and looked at him like he was out of his mind, which he was, at least in the moment. I watched him jump around and even Bobby and Tommy admitted to me they had never seen him quite like that before.

Chapter 10

The record slowly rose up on the local charts, and became a small hit for us. We were getting a modest ten percent commission from the sales, which was not about to allow us to retire in our teens. But on the other hand, we had more offers for gigs than we knew what to do with and Byron discussed them with Johnny and me, pondering which ones would pay the most, attract the most attention, help us grow.

We didn't need our jobs at the potato farm anymore. I told them on a separate day from Johnny. He thought it was an act of liberation and told the Petersens before I did. In fact, I dreaded going over there and informing them that I wouldn't be working there again. I got Bobby to give me a lift because I felt so confused and didn't want Johnny to see me. I knew he'd question my commitment to The Caretakers.

The irony of the goodbye was that everyone on the farm was very happy for me and gave us their blessings. Bobby waited in his car while I said a final farewell to Mrs. Petersen, in the kitchen, who handed me my last check.

"I hope you know," I said, my voice a harsh whisper, "that you've been better to me than my own father, you and Mr. Petersen. Especially after he died. I'll never forget that."

Then, Mrs. Petersen grabbed me and hugged me ferociously. When we separated, I could see the tears starting to form in her eyes.

"Now, don't go doing that," I said, reprimanding her gently. "Or I'll do it too and then Bobby over there will tell Johnny and I'll never hear the end of it."

She bit her lip and nodded, took a deep breath and then, recovered, gave me a look of kindliness, a look that was all about wanting the best for me, a look so pure, so filled with love, I wondered what else Mrs. Petersen might do with her life, with her bottomless kindness. I had been thinking a lot about destiny and wondered why a woman so full of kindness would do nothing more with her life than run a potato farm in a small town. And as if reading my mind, she spoke about life and one's direction in the world.

"Eddie, you are a wonderful boy and it's good that you leave us. We'll miss you but you have a life to lead, and many exciting things to experience as you become a man. You're starting off on a great adventure. We only ask you come back some time and tell us about it."

"You bet I will," I said, too loudly, too strongly. "I'll be back, Mrs. Petersen. I'll tell you about where we go and the people we meet. Thank you for everything."

She insisted I take some of her homemade bread. "It'll bring you good luck."

I waved as I walked back to Bobby's car, watching her stand on the porch, waving back, until I got into the car and then, she went back into the farmhouse.

"Mm, bread. Let me have some." I offered some to Bobby, who pulled off a hunk and began to chew. "Mm, great, it's still warm."

With a mouth of half-chewed bread, Bobby looked at me. I was still staring at the now empty porch. "Wha the mava wiv you?" he asked, his mouth filled.

"Just drive," I said, not looking at him.

Johnny dropped out of high school and Bobby and Tommy followed suit. I was not sure that was the right thing to do, not knowing what path The Caretakers would have and also, knowing my mother would disapprove.

Johnny did his best to convince me, telling me that music was our destiny and that was where we needed to focus right now. Of course, dropping out of school, even with a marginal student like Johnny, was frowned upon. Bobby and Tommy were the same age as him, seventeen at the time, and even though their parents were more excited about the future of the band than lost scholastic development, Johnny told me that the principal had given him the third degree, in front of his rather quiet parents.

Johnny had replied to the principal, "You think it's good advice to leave a career that will pay me thousands and thousands of dollars and that I love just so I can get a piece of paper from you?"

It takes youth to build such wonderful dreams around so little to hold onto.

My mother was trying hard to handle everything. I'm sure that it was hard on her to be so supportive and yet be a parent too. Michelle being at home made a great difference in my mother not trying to dissuade me from doing the band. She was not happy about the news of Johnny and the guys dropping out of school. But when Johnny would come by the house to pick me up to go somewhere in the Eternal Energy Machine, she never mentioned it, never gave him the impression she was displeased, as my father was, with our friendship. For that especially, I loved her. She was holding her own now that she had a steady job, doing seamstress work. The band would also enable me to add more money into the household pot. But her melancholy was clear to Michelle and me and we often went out of our way to cheer her or just stay out of her way, not annoy her, when she seemed particularly despondent.

Michelle and my mother and I were eating in silence one night, a night when my mother was off staring into space in the other room.

Michelle asked me, "Are you going out tonight?"

"There's a meeting with the band. Byron is planning a big record release party, so he can get national radio and an album deal for us."

"Way to go, little brother," Michelle smiled.

My mother suddenly snapped to attention, as if the words just registered. I felt immediately guilty.

"I can skip it if you want, Ma. It's just to tell us about this party he's organizing. No big decisions or anything."

My mother offered a sad smile as reassurance. "Go on, Eddie, I'll be all right, really."

Michelle touched my mother's arm and tried to cheer her. "Hey, how about I drive us into town and we watch a movie?"

"You go if you want," my mother replied. "I can manage on my own. You two don't have to watch after me."

But that was exactly the way we felt, that her lack of enthusiasm about anything anymore made us worry. Michelle and I had late night talks, hypothesizing whether she seemed capable of taking her own life or descending into such a deep depression that she wouldn't even be able to leave the house. We had no answers but the process of worrying about it together helped us both.

***

When Johnny and I arrived at the meeting, Byron was pacing around his apartment and Tommy and Bobby were reading music industry trades. Byron smacked his hands together, in anticipation of telling us about all his hard work and our bright future.

"Now, boys, let me get right to it. I figure that there will be roughly about 300 people at the party, and there will be reporters and record people too, so, it won't be all fun and games." With this, he looked us all over, like a football coach making sure his players knew what they were up against. "We will be performing about fifteen songs for everyone and I want us at our best. It's got to be a knockout!" When he said this, he took his index finger and waved it over us like it was a magic wand about to give us even more talent than we already possessed. He went on and on, actually diminishing our interest in what would be an important gig, another turning point. Byron kept saying "us" and "we" as though he was going to be up there with us, playing guitar.

He sensed the lack of energy in his living room. Byron readied us for the big news. "Now, I know you've been anxious to know where this party is going to be held. And after a lot of thought and discussion with clubs around here, I've lined up none other than..." He milked the moment for all it was worth.

"The Silver Bell Hideaway."

He smirked with satisfaction as Johnny shouted out spontaneously, "All right! The Silver Bell!"

Short of going into Ann Arbor or Grand Rapids, it was the nicest looking and best known club he could have chosen. We talked excitedly.

"The Silver Bell. I've seen some great gigs there."

"Their sound system is really happening, too."

"Hell, G Factor has played there a bunch of times."

Now, Byron had our attention, and our good will. So he carefully insinuated into our excitement a new suggestion for The Caretakers. "Now boys, as you all know, in this business today, all the bands that are making it big are the ones that dress up in outfits that are all the same, like The Beatles did, you know?" He paused. "This is a pretty important consideration and it's one of the reasons I wanted us to all meet tonight, to talk about what we want as our trademark outfits."

Byron took a few seconds to survey the troops and see what our reaction was. As far as I could remember, Johnny was the only one who ever mentioned the use of similar outfits for the band. Johnny looked around at everyone, nodding his head and I knew that he put the bug in Bob's ear. This was the first thing I had a problem with, in all the time Johnny and I had played together. After a couple moments of shocked silence, which proved to me Bobby and Tommy didn't like the idea any more than I did, Johnny finally spoke up.

"Yesssss, band outfits. Hm, I like the idea. What do you think guys?"

We didn't know what to say, so we all sat there dumbfounded. Who would be able to do anything about what Johnny and Byron had decided? Had they already talked it over, without consulting us? I had always felt that Johnny confided in me before the other guys, before Byron, until this uncomfortable turn of events. Was this the way it was going to be, more and more?

Finally the silence was too much and I decided that I would speak up, even though I expected it would do little good.

"Well, uh, I'm not quite sure right now that this is the kind of thing we would want to do. I mean we're supposed to be rebels, right? And the uniform thing is kind of going out now, anyway. And even if it was still as popular as the British Invasion thing, I just think people will think we're selling out."

After I had left this turd in the punchbowl of Johnny and Byron's plan, I could see that they were as unsure as I was of our ground. The band never had an internal problem and up to that point, we never had occasion to quibble with Byron, either. Byron paced around the room in deep thought. Johnny intently smoked. Bobby and Tommy looked down at the floor. They knew that they were not the driving force of the band but I would have appreciated their saying something. It was clear we were all being faced with the power structure of the group shifting in a new direction, to say nothing of the direction of our appearance, our identity. I hated that moment so much and tried to find a way to at least delay the decision.

"Look, even if we decide that we are going to have outfits, will we have time by this weekend to have them made up?"

Byron brightened, thinking I was trying to save face and find a new way to agree.

"Oh, yeah, sure. I got someone who can put them together in no time at all, no time!"

We all knew that Johnny was the unofficial official spokesman for the group. He rose up out of his seat and stubbed out his smoke.

"Look, guys," and here, his eyebrows did a v-type thing, indicating he was going to make a crucial point. "Eddie here, now he's got some good points to consider. We definitely represent a type of individualism to our fans and they like that. But, consider this too: if we choose carefully, we can find outfits that could make a real rebel statement."

"A real rebel statement by all dressing alike? What does that mean? Breaking the mold by conforming?" I had again silenced the room.

Johnny and Byron exchanged a look. Bobby and Tommy were worthless, refusing to say anything. I guess they always saw me and Johnny as the leaders and they figured they were just along for the ride, as long as it lasted.

"Look guys," said Johnny, but everyone knew his words were meant for only me. "Hell's Angels wear outfits that look similar. They've got their emblems, right? Nobody thinks any less of their rebel status, do they? Nobody walks up to them and says, hey, how come you all have to wear the same emblem?" We could all see that Johnny was going to pursue this until we agreed. Byron cheerfully suggested we take a vote on it and we all said we would at least give it a try.

Byron came alive, jumping up and heading toward a desk. "Well good, good, this is good, guys. I'm glad we can all agree on this. It makes it better if we have a unity of spirit. I happen to have done my homework on this one and have some ideas that I want to throw out in front of you."

We bent over the pictures that Byron cut from magazines and had even roughly sketched. We shared some ideas of our own. We finally came up with a look that everyone else liked and I didn't hate. It was kind of a cross between a pirate and a French dandy of the eighteenth century, only there were no eye patches or powdered wigs or any other lame props, thank God.

***

I was utterly exhausted by the time Johnny drove me home. The stress of trying not to tell them I thought they were selling us all out, coupled with agonizing over my family and school and leaving the farm had sucked the strength from me.

"You look pale," Johnny said. "You look like you've seen a ghost."

I decided then and there to tell him about the figure I saw in the hospital, the night my father died. I had told no one, not even my mother or sister, thinking it was just an emotional hallucination or sheer exhaustion, like I felt at that moment. And I didn't know if anyone would take it seriously or laugh at me.

I felt it was the right time. Johnny knew I was under a lot of pressure and in some way, I thought it might heal the rift that had occurred at the meeting at Byron's place. And to his credit, Johnny was very decent in his response. He rubbed his chin with one hand while steering with the other and we listened to the engine of the Eternal Energy Machine in silence for a while.

"Eddie, me boy," he finally said, "I believe you have something that very few people are blessed with. That is the ability to communicate with the spiritual world. Now, I've read the books of Edgar Cayce. He was a spiritualist. He had the ability to grab onto certain frequencies and see things that were going to happen. I also once read this Nostradamus guy. You ever hear of him?" I shook my head. Once again, Johnny was being my teacher, my guide. "Well, Nostradamus had the same kind of spiritual powers, but he was way back when. He imagined airplanes hundreds of years ago, and the Second World War. Hell, he predicted when Kennedy would be shot.

Now you tell me, who are we to say we know everything that goes on?"

I was reading Edgar Cayce on the way to the gig at the Silver Bell Hideaway. In fact, I had been reading him and Nostradamus every spare moment, so much so that the guys in the group started calling me "Professor." I didn't care. I longed for the ability to reach into the spirit world, the other side, learn answers about life after death. I felt it would help me decide what to do with my own life.

***

The Silver Bell was an old ski lodge that had long since been out of business, and because of that there were lots of windows everywhere, which helped with the sound. It was set in the hills and was pretty secluded. Anybody who was cool knew where it was, and it was the happening spot to hear in band in the countryside.

After a rehearsal, Byron directed us to go to the main banquet room and have a pre-party dinner. The press and promotional people would be there too. We wore our modified pirate get-ups for the dinner. I had to admit that Byron had a lot of industry people there.

It was all so very terrifying and unreal. When we entered the room, a number of flash bulbs went off and people started chattering all over the place. Someone asked me, "How does it feel to be only fifteen and be in a rock band?"

Chapter 11

Johnny knew I was not content with the idea of dropping out of school. He told me we were going to California to "find our pot o' gold and to sit around with gorgeous women by swimming pools." Because I was the only one who showed any ambivalence about the rapidly escalating lifestyle The Caretakers were experiencing, he spent a great deal of time, when we were alone, to try and reassure me.

I nodded, mumbled something representing agreement in those moments, knowing simultaneously that this was a chance of a lifetime and that it was also a potential personal disaster, ignoring the needs of my family. It wasn't that Johnny didn't realize this. He just felt if he maintained his attitude and energy, we would be a successful band and eliminate my worries, as well as those of the band and Byron.

Byron really sensed the possibilities, for none of his bands had gotten this far, going to Los Angeles to record an album and develop a national presence. Unlike Johnny, he did not inspire confidence. Byron wasn't incompetent. But knowing how crucial the next few weeks were, he went over everything with us, over and over, as if we were mentally retarded. No matter how many times we'd remind him he had told us where we were staying or how many hours we had booked in the recording studio or when we would start touring after the album was done, he went over it again.

The day before we were to catch the plane to California, we had a rehearsal and meeting at Johnny's house. Byron went into his repetitive lesson plan routine, about the studio in Burbank and the Best Western motel just outside of Beverly Hills. I got so tired of it, I threw a guitar pick at him and hit him in the head with it.

The guys laughed and Byron brushed off the insult. "Okay, Mister Songwriter, I know, you don't want to deal with the details."

"Not forty-two times I don't," I mumbled. I knew it was rude but the pressure was building up inside me and it had to come out.

Typically, Johnny was there to smooth things over. "Hey, Byron says he's working on us getting a spot at the Whiskey-A-Go-Go on the Sunset Strip. Man, if we get in there, and they like us, it is the gravy train from here on in."

Everyone, including me, feeling bad about my outburst, agreed that would be wonderful and we continued with our meeting.

***

After I said goodbye to Byron and Tommy and Bobby and got in the Eternal Energy Machine with the eternally optimistic Johnny, I felt better. We were ripping down the road at a brisk pace, the wind blasting me in the face and I paid careful attention to the scenery, thinking about where I came from and wondering if it would be long before I returned.

"Just think, Eddie," said Johnny, jabbering, smoking, steering the truck with two fingers, "tomorrow that big bird is going to take us across this country and drop us off in the Golden Land. We've come a long way, Eddie, and this is the final step. It's the Golden State. We're rock and rollers, man. We're the gold miners of this era, guy. After we take on California, after we succeed in California, then the whole world will be open to us."

When Johnny said that last phrase, it made me puzzled. I was previously grappling with the concept of being in Hollywood. Now, he wanted me to envision conquering the whole world. It seemed like an immense and impossible task. After all, I hadn't even been on an airplane before.

At home, I managed to take on Johnny's energy and be positive, if for no other reason than to not break the heart of my mother and my sister. I didn't want to show them my inner turmoil to go along with their sadness at my leaving. I talked of achieving dreams, making money, coming back and spending money on them both, asking them what luxury items they wanted.

Michelle played along and asked for her own recording studio. I loudly guaranteed she would have it. My mother quietly said that it didn't matter whether I bought her anything, only that she wanted me and Michelle to be happy.

Ironically, that was about the worst thing she could have said. Oh, she theoretically could have said I was a lousy son, leaving in a time of crisis and all that, but that was not who my mother was, that was not how she talked. Based on how she did talk, just wishing me to be happy had made me unhappier.

My mother made a cake and brought a bottle of champagne out of the cupboard, to toast my trip to Hollywood. I reminded her that I was only sixteen.

"Oh, I suppose this would be your first drink of alcohol," Michelle kidded.

I opened the bottle and poured three glasses.

"To my brother, the rock star," Michelle toasted, as we clinked glasses.

"To my wonderful son, who had to become a man before his time," my mother wistfully said.

I had a dream that night, the last night in Romeo. It was a dream that was utterly fanciful but the colors were remarkably vivid. In the dream, it was the near future and certain people had the gift of being able to fly without the aid of airplanes or anything else. Some people simply had the power to raise themselves off the ground and, by tilting their arms, fly in different directions. Others could not master the ability.

I was showing Johnny how to fly. We were already celebrities, our band had become enormously successful and we both lived in a huge house in Hollywood with servants and a big pool. There was a gathering and rather than trying to fly, Johnny watched me and then turned to the other guests. He distracted everyone from the fact he couldn't fly by telling stories and making jokes and having everyone in stitches.

He continued to entertain everyone at the pool until, suddenly, a big bird flew overhead and blocked out the sun.

Everyone looked up to see what had happened to the light. The bird came plummeting down and headed straight for Johnny. It had its claws out like it was ready to grab Johnny, tear him to shreds. I could see the creature's eyes and they were fiery pools of anger and vengeance.

Johnny did not cower or retreat, like some of the people present. He stared up into the sky at the bird coming down at him. He threw his hands in the air and giant flames came shooting out of his fingers. He hit the bird straight on. The bird let out a loud, screeching noise and immediately veered off, then flew away.

Johnny turned back to everyone at the party who he had been entertaining. But now, his eyes were like fiery pools themselves, and he looked demonic.

I sat up, awake, in my bedroom, the image of Johnny's burning eyes still lingering.

***

On the plane, the pilot's voice was heard throughout the cabin, announcing that the Grand Canyon could be seen on the left side of the plane. Johnny and I, seated together on that side, stared out and down at the immense chasm, which prompted from us a huge exhalation of air and no words. We looked over to tell the others. Bobby and Tommy were talking to each other and Byron was looking over some papers. We looked at each other and returned to studying the monumental split in the earth.

As we did, I took the opportunity to tell Johnny of the dream I had the night before. He stared out at the Grand Canyon, listening, until I was done. I thought he might be annoyed or angry, but he shrugged it off.

"Ah, Eddie, there you go with those visions of yours. I guess poets are supposed to have visions. And if you think about it, in your vision, we both have power. You have the power to fly and I have the power to ward off any harm that might come to us. Your dream is a good sign. It means that no harm will come to us, you see?"

I nodded but didn't ask him what he thought about his eyes becoming as fiery and terrifying as those of the bird

But instead of dwelling on this, I thought about being sixteen, on a plane, flying to Hollywood to sign a contract and record my first LP. Perhaps I was dampening the excitement of this event. I tried to imagine all the groups that went before us to a similar fate, to record that first album. How many had gone on to have major careers? How many were one-hit wonders? But there I was again, being negative. Why couldn't I be enthusiastic about everything, like Johnny?

I knew that George Harrison was just seventeen when he joined The Beatles. He had, like the others, come from a working class background. How did he handle all that? I remembered seeing The Beatles on TV when they first came to America, and how composed and witty and self-assured they seemed. Where did that come from? And would I ever have any of it?

Byron was rumbling through the papers and looking over everything to make sure it was all in place. I was glad we had a serious minded manager. We had a manager who pored over

details, the charismatic Johnny who never ran out of energy or confidence and Bobby and Tommy, who never complained or challenged us, were always there, rock steady, to back Johnny and me up.

"We're only about a half hour away from the Promised Land." Johnny's eyes were big as he broke my reverie.

"Hey, Johnny," I asked, truly not being my typical, doubting self but being philosophical. "There's no doubt that our lives in Hollywood will be more interesting, right?"

"You're damned right."

"And, by definition, they'll also be more complicated than living in Romeo."

"Of course."

"So, isn't it fair to say that our lives are going to get a whole lot stranger?"

Johnny looked at me oddly. "Well, Eddie, you're the prophet, not me."

Johnny got down on the ground and kissed it when we arrived. He acted like he had been a prisoner of war in another country and finally returned home. He was looking around the terminal at Los Angeles International Airport, occasionally belting out the phrase, "Yes, yes, yes!" This litany got especially loud when we got into the limo and the driver headed toward our hotel. We were all staring out through the windows at our new world, of stunningly bright sunshine, palm trees next to dry cleaners and butcher shops, of perfectly coiffed people in expensive cars, jamming the roads everywhere, their eyes and emotions shielded by dark glasses.

We got into a pleasant routine which did not grow tiresome: up in the morning, herded by Byron to a restaurant for breakfast, after which we headed for the Burbank recording studio in the sweltering San Fernando Valley, for a full day of recording. Then, when we got done, Byron doled out money from our advance and told us not to stay out too late.

Telling Johnny not to stay out too late in Hollywood was like putting an alcoholic to work in a liquor store at the cash register and telling him not to drink anything at lunch time. Byron sometimes accompanied us to the Whiskey, where we delighted in watching the girls dance in the glass cages above the floor, as well as eying the luscious girls we danced with on the floor. Byron helped me get into some of the clubs where I never would have gotten in, due to my age. And while The Caretakers spent a great deal of time finding women to get close with, Byron, to his credit, continued to work the business angle, handing out business cards, introducing us to anyone he could find who was remotely related to the music industry and might give a damn that we were recording our first record.

We started going out on the town on our own, leaving Byron to his own devices. Sometimes, we got lifts from other musicians or engineers at the recording studios or someone we met at the clubs. It spared us the money we'd spend on cabs and Byron made us beg for every bit of money we got from him.

"If I left it up to you," he often repeated, "you'd spend all your money in one night."

Luckily, because we were young, from a small town and Johnny was the expert at gabbing with anybody, we got a lot of free drinks, joints, hits of acid, invitations to parties and our share of sexual liaisons. Sometimes, the girls we slept with, who were older than we were, drove us back to the motel.

It was all quite enjoyable except for the time I called home. My mother had decided to move down to New Orleans with Michelle. I congratulated them but was unsure how to feel. Of course, if I was leaving Romeo, how could I complain about their doing the same? It was just another sudden change among many and in some way, I was learning to adapt to a life that was becoming consistently unpredictable.

We were in a celebratory mood the day we finished recording the last song for the album. We laid down the tracks for ten songs in just over a month, working five days a week and sometimes on Saturdays. The record label had already decided that "This Is Your Last Chance" would be the single and the B side was a song that Johnny liked more than I did, a rocker I wrote when I was particularly pissed off at my father. Of course, instead of telling the story of a son and his restrictive father, it was about clinging love, called "Heading Out the Door."

On that last session, Byron told us to come up into the booth of the studio. We listened to the take and agreed it was good.

"Well, guys, I think we can really celebrate tonight. All we've got to do is mix this baby and we're off and running."

We hooted and hollered, like the kids that we were. The engineer smiled, because he was used to musicians acting cool, laying back, mumbling their approval. We sounded like a bunch of drunken high school jocks who had just won the big game against their cross-town rival. We all shook his hand, another formality he was not used to with the glib bands that came and went.

Byron took us out to dinner at the Brown Derby, a restaurant we loved because it was in the shape of a hat. We didn't care about the food as much as the architecture.

"What'll we do tonight?" Johnny asked excitedly around the dinner table. "The Doors are playing. They're amazing. Can you get us in?"

"Sure," said Byron quietly.

"You've got to come with us," I said.

"Um, not tonight. I've got a meeting with the guys at the label after dinner."

We all protested, shouting, jeering, making other diners look over at us. We didn't care. We wanted to all celebrate it together.

But Byron was not about to be moved. "I've got important stuff to handle."

"Come on," Johnny protested. "What's more important than getting high with The Caretakers after we finished recording our first album?"

"Well," Byron began, "we're not finished. It has to be remixed and mastered and pressed and distributed and that'll take a few weeks. I have to see if the label will pay for a few more weeks of us staying out here."

"Speaking of paying," Johnny mentioned, "aren't we supposed to get another payment once we finished recording?"

"You're right on," Byron smiled. "So, I'll get you guys into The Doors while I get the money out of the label in my meeting tonight."

The Brown Derby was not the kind of place that would look the other way and serve minors alcohol. So we toasted Byron's work ethic with Cokes and Sprites.

I will never forget having my arm around a girl, backstage, having her holding a roach I was puffing happily on, when I saw The Doors perform on the Strip that night. Everyone had been talking about them, playing their first record. Women in the club went utterly insane when Jim Morrison performed, watching him writhing in that open shirt and tight leather pants. Johnny watched him very carefully, enjoying his music, certainly, but studying him, cheating glances out to the audience to see which songs, which gestures they enjoyed the most.

I was amazed by the quality of his lyrics, the sheer beauty and utter passion of his words. It gave me the feeling that the words I wrote, no matter how influenced by the Romantics, belonged in rock.

I told Suki, the girl I was with, that I wanted to meet him, to tell him how great his poetry was. She nodded in a noncommittal way.

But after they finished the show and came off the stage, with the crowd still roaring its approval, Suki tossed her mane of impossibly lustrous, thick, blonde hair and stuck out her hand, introducing herself to Morrison. He took her hand and put it on his sweaty chest, right above his heart. He began to pull her along with him and the group.

Suki turned back to me, quickly introducing me to Morrison. He eyed me warily and then looked back at Suki, wondering if she would leave me for him.

"I think your lyrics are amazing," I said, my heart pounding. "Pure poetry. I'm into the Romantics a lot, Keats, Shelley. They've really influenced my songs."

Jim Morrison smiled at me, put a hand on my shoulder and said, "Listen, man, the Romantics are nothing but sugar on top of canned pineapple. They'll rot the fucking teeth out of your head. Read Rimbaud."

And with that he gave Suki a smoldering look, a slight nod of his head in the direction of the rest of the band and Suki gave me a wan smile, put a joint in my pocket, gave me a respectable peck on the cheek and went off to have wild, unrelenting sex with the latest high priest of rock.

I was envious, disappointed and thrilled. Johnny and the girl he had found sidled over to me.

"What did he say?" Johnny asked.

"He took Suki away from me," I complained and then looked at Johnny and said, in a quiet, trusting voice, "You ever hear of a poet named Rambo?"

He hadn't but he assuaged my resentment by announcing that Sheila, the girl of the moment for him, knew of a big party, walking distance, above the Strip on Horn Avenue. We collected Bobby and Tommy and walked up to the house.

The wooden house pulsated with the sounds of Jimi Hendrix singing "Manic Depression," and as we stepped through the door, our nostrils were greeted by the combined odor of human sweat, beer, marijuana and incense. There were strobe lights and lava lamps and a girl wearing only leotards, with her torso decorated with fluorescent paint, had a tray with a variety of drugs on it. She described each one, as if the LSD, psilocybin, speed and the others were all exotic desserts.

Johnny, in typical Johnny mode, complimented her on her remarkable paint job. She was so impressed with his dazzling smile; she did not notice that he had quickly taken a fistful of drugs, without even looking, from her tray.

As we passed her, Johnny saw me shaking my head, in judgment. "What? This is for you. We're going to make you forget all about that Suki. I think her real name is Sucky."

He handed me a tab of the psilocybin and we both took some at the same time. We surfed through the ocean of lights and bodies, Jimi's screaming, crying guitar reassuring us, as we searched for beer to wash away the bitter taste in our throats.

***

I woke up the next morning and the feeling of unease could have been due to the lack of sleep, the drugs and alcohol, the let-down from no longer having to be at the studio by a certain time.

I glanced at the alarm clock in the room. It was already 11:30. I thought it was curious that Byron had not been by, banging on the door, getting us up for breakfast. I shook Johnny with one hand. He mumbled something into his pillow and tried to brush my hand away without looking at me.

I got washed and dressed and went outside. The sunlight made me cover my eyes. I stumbled next door to check on Tommy and Bobby. Their door was locked. I knocked and called their names.

"We're sleeping," yelled out Tommy.

I figured they deserved to sleep in, too. We had worked hard and played hard for about five weeks. I went down one more door to Byron's room. He had to be awake. There was a guy who worked hard and never played. I knocked. There was no reply. I knocked again and called his name. I tried the door and it opened.

I stepped into Byron's room. The bed was made. A few drawers were open here and there but the room was utterly, completely empty of his belongings.

I shook my head, trying to clear it. I had trouble getting air in my lungs. I went outside and hung my head over the railing of the motel, breathing deeply, trying to stay calm.

What did I remember from the night before, at the Brown Derby? He had said he was meeting the guys at the record label, to get the rest of our advance. I walked back to our room in a daze, sat heavily on Johnny's bed and picked up the phone and dialed the office of the president of our label, who we had met once. I went through two assistants and one exec, insisting that I had to talk to Simon Turtletaub.

The exec asked what was so important that I had to talk to Simon personally.

"Our manager has run off with all our money and we're stuck in this goddamn motel with no way to get home! Does that sound important enough to get him on the fucking phone?"

Johnny sat up in bed and looked at me.

"Just a second," said the exec. "Hold on. I'll find him. I know he's in the building."

I wound up having a conversation with Simon Turtletaub as Johnny angrily smashed up the room, tearing things off the wall, hurling anything he could get his hands on, cursing.

"Johnny, keep it down," I demanded. "I'm trying to work this out."

"What's going on over there?" Turtletaub asked.

"You fucking scumbag, Byron! I will kill you! I will find you and tear your goddamn throat out!" Johnny screamed. I had never seen him so out of control.

"We need to talk. Did you give the rest of our advance to Byron?" I asked.

"Yes. Last night. I can show you the paperwork. You're sure he's gone?"

"I'm sure," I said, cringing as I heard Johnny break some glass in the bathroom. "Johnny, stop breaking stuff!" I yelled. "We don't have any money to pay for it!"

"Piece of shit!" he yelled from the bathroom.

"Look, you come down to my office right away. We'll work this out," said Turtletaub.

"Can you send a car for us?" I asked humbly. "I've only got seven dollars on me."

Johnny insisted on coming with me and I told him he had to act calmly or not bother. He promised. The confidence, the bravado, the charisma, were all gone. As much as it shocked me to learn about Byron's treachery, it was even more shocking to see Johnny in such a depressed state after his rage.

We told Tommy and Bobby about the ugly development and that we would be back from Turtletaub's office as soon as we could manage. I remember their pale faces, their hair still matted and sticking out at odd angles, trying to fully comprehend what we were saying without their being fully awake.

On the drive over, I saw Johnny pull out some of the acid he had helped himself to the night before. He jammed a few tabs into his mouth.

"What are you doing?" I said. "We've got to deal with these people!"

"We don't have to do anything anymore," he said.

To his credit, as soon as the car dropped us off, Turtletaub immediately greeted us and ushered us into his office. He introduced us to a lawyer. No one shook hands. Turtletaub asked if we wanted anything to drink.

"A fucking beer," Johnny mumbled.

Turtletaub tried to chuckle but it came out like a cough. He apologized; he showed us the paperwork and the copy of the check that was issued to Byron. He brought out the contract and he and the lawyer kindly explained that the label had paid Byron, our representative, all monies due us until such time as the sales of the record earned back the advance.

"Can't you cancel the check?" I asked.

"We can try," the lawyer said, "but it's likely that Mr. Orr has already cashed it and short of finding him, there's nothing that can be done about it."

"So, what do we do now? What about the record?" Johnny asked, helplessly.

"Well, you finished the last song, so we'll mix it and release it and hope it does well and makes us all some money."

"Look," I tried to reason with them, "Byron controlled all our money. We don't have enough money to live beyond today. We can't pay for the motel or anything."

Johnny's anger flared again. He was up on his feet, pacing the huge office. "Byron Whore! We don't even have a fucking return ticket home."

Home. Johnny was talking about Michigan as home, and just weeks ago, he was saying we were in the Golden Land.

"We'll get you back home and take care of the motel," Turtletaub said, "but of course, we cannot advance you any more money on this contract."

The lawyer chimed in, "We don't even know how the album will do, whether it will sell enough to cover our costs."

A hideous silence descended on the office. "I don't think Byron ever mentioned the name of the album," Turtletaub said softly, carefully looking over at Johnny, wondering how out of control he was going to get. "Did you have a title? Or did you simply want it self-titled, The Caretakers?"

"How about 'The Colossal Rip-Off' as a title, huh?" Johnny smacked his palm against the wall, making some framed gold records jump. "Or let's change the name of the band to the fucking Gravediggers? How would that be?"

Turtletaub looked at me, and I understood that he expected me to make the decision. I walked over to Johnny and put a hand on his shoulder. He was trembling.

"Johnny," I said as privately as I could. "How do you like, 'The Road to Golden?'

"Like in The Golden State," he said bitterly.

"The Road to Golden," I repeated. "Like in Keats."

"Sure. It doesn't matter." Johnny walked out of the office. I quickly thanked Turtletaub and his lawyer, who apologized, said they would call later with flight arrangements. I rushed out to catch up to Johnny.

We rode in silence in the car furnished by the label. I looked over at Johnny. His eyes were wide open, his irises large, gleaming, but there was no excitement in them. They were the eyes of someone staring at a battlefield of corpses, after the adrenalin of victorious battle had worn off.

"Driver," he called out, "take me to the Sunset Strip."

"What are you doing?" I asked him.

"Take me to the Strip!" he shouted, pounding his fist into the ceiling of the car. The driver turned around, alarmed. I calmed Johnny and we said nothing for a long while.

As we approached the row of clubs on Sunset Boulevard in West Hollywood, I dared to ask again.

Now, Johnny simply looked crushed, neither angry nor confused. He directed the driver to pull over and stop near the Whiskey.

"Where are we going?" I asked.

"I'm going," he said. "San Francisco, Eddie. That's where it's happening, anyway. The Jefferson Airplane, man. The Grateful Dead. It's a whole new sound. Not this soulless bullshit down here. You look me up if you get out there."

Johnny got out of the car so swiftly, I couldn't follow him before he slammed the door shut. I rolled down the electronic window.

"Johnny, goddamn it. You're not running out on us. We're a band!"

"We *were* a band," Johnny said. "If you want to try it again, you come see me in San Francisco."

He walked away swiftly, and I instructed the driver to follow him. Johnny then broke into a run and darted between two buildings, disappearing down an alleyway. I ran after him but he quickly lost me. I returned to the car, closed the door and put my head in my hands.

"He'll probably show up, later," the driver said.

"I don't think so."

"Where to?"

"The motel. Then the airport."

"Heading home?" The driver tried to sound a little cheerful.

"Home," I said, in a way I had never said the word before. "Home. I wonder where that is."

Chapter 12

Deep inside, I had always known things could come apart. But I always felt that no matter what transpired, Johnny, the driving force of the band, Johnny, the Human Eternal Energy Machine, would be there to come up with a new idea, get a new manager, even new members of the band, if that was needed.

I knew there were no guarantees when we went to Hollywood. But what I didn't conceive of was the possibility that Johnny might break down, might desert us in an hour of reckoning. It was Johnny who was mostly responsible for our getting as far as we did. The idea that he would simply split, to leave us to wonder what had ever become of him seemed ludicrous after it happened.

I delivered the news to Bobby and Tommy, who kept shaking their heads, asking me to retell the story over and over, as if I was leaving out a crucial piece of information which would explain everything.

"How much acid did he take?" asked Bobby.

I didn't exactly know.

"Did he mix it with the other drugs?" Tommy wanted to know.

I couldn't be sure.

They both agreed that he would eventually come down and after they wore off, Johnny would come to his senses.

"He'll come back here, the old Johnny," Tommy told himself more than he was telling us. "He'll come through that door, saying, 'Come on, we got an album to promote. We're going to be fine.'"

Bobby nodded. "Yeah, probably he will. He just freaked out. That's all, Eddie. He just freaked out."

"Hell, we're still freaked out and we didn't take a handful of psychedelics like they were M&Ms," Tommy noted.

The label called. Turtletaub's secretary asked us what time we wanted to fly back and I suggested an early evening flight, to give Johnny time to come down to earth and call us. She assured us the bill was taken care of and asked for a contact number.

I turned to Tommy and Bobby. "They need a contact number."

"Give them your number," said Tommy.

I thought a moment and then returned my attention to the voice on the phone. "Listen, we need three tickets back to Michigan. And one to New Orleans and then to Michigan."

Johnny never appeared. Whatever made him decide to leave us and set out on his own, with almost no money in his pockets, it could not be attributed solely to a drug high. On the trip to the airport, I tried to reassure my band mates.

"Listen, we can still find Johnny and keep going." I looked at them, but they stared glumly out of the window of the car, the promise of California fading before their eyes.

"How do you even know Johnny went to San Francisco?" Bobby asked.

"I don't know about you," Tommy said, looking over at Bobby quickly, avoiding me entirely, "but I think this is it. It's over."

"Over? You don't even know how our album is going to do. It could be a hit."

"Yeah, and how much do you think the label is going to promote it with the lead singer missing?"

I had no answer. I couldn't prop up their hopes, at least in the present moment. We parted ways at the airport, as I promised to see them after I got back from New Orleans.

***

My mother was living in Michelle's small apartment on Toulouse Street in the French Quarter but out of respect, Michelle gave up her bed and slept on the couch. I was not impressed with Bourbon Street's brawling, drinking, free-wheeling atmosphere. After all, I had been drinking and playing in clubs since my early teens.

But I did love the music I heard there and the musicianship was tremendous. Whether it was in a club or on the street, the talent seeped out of doorways and windows, echoed from Jackson Square to Louis Armstrong Park.

I was happy for them and my mother and Michelle actually seemed happy. While my mother still looked frail, there was a peace in her expression that I had not seen since my father died. We sat outside at the French Market, eating *beignets* and drinking coffee, the third day I was there. Our conversation was punctuated by Michelle waving hello to some of the locals who passed by.

"You've really made a life down here," I said to Michelle.

"We've made a life," she corrected me, tilting her head toward our mother.

"I have to say," my mother admitted, "I thought it would be impossible to leave Michigan. But Michelle and I have actually played together, made some money, doing upscale jobs."

"And we have one tonight," Michelle reminded. "Eddie, you'll get to see us play together."

"That's great," I said, trying to muster enthusiasm, but part of me was still in California.

It was all to clear to them. My mother reached across the wooden table and took my hand.

"I know you're hurting about The Caretakers. But we're very proud of you."

"And we can't wait for the album to be released," Michelle added.

"If it's released at all," I said morosely.

And then, our thoughts were interrupted by Oliver, a middle-aged black man, wearing a straw hat, black pants, white shirt and pink, silk vest, as he sat down in front of a piano which sat near the market. Michelle and my mother applauded and called out his name, as Oliver began to play boogie-woogie and stride piano, the joy and syncopation of it, plus the looks of pleasure on my mother's and sister's faces lifting me, for the moment, out of my dark mood.

They had found a whole new world to live in and as surprised as I was, I couldn't help but feel grateful that it had worked out so well for them. They bought me some clothes from a thrift shop downtown and we went to a banquet where they were to play smooth, low-key jazz music while some company celebrated its sales force with dinners and dancing.

I sat at a table with a bunch of men in suits, ignoring their idle, drunken chatter, looking at something which had seemed as incomprehensible just weeks before as my going to Hollywood: my mother was playing piano again, playing wonderfully and being accompanied by Michelle, first on guitar and later, a duet on the same piano.

I filtered out the sounds of eating, shouting, talking, laughing, as I watched them play, background for the scores of people in the banquet hall but a concert unlike any other for me. The memory of my father's rages, his closing down his appreciation of music because of his disappointment in

Michelle, and later, in me, had been overcome, replaced by this new configuration of our family, this new location, this new spirit.

I had the sudden disaster of my own group still fresh in my mind yet at the same time, felt such joy and relief to see my mother and Michelle playing together, living together, making a living, getting to be close to one another again.

After they were done, they were paid in cash and given some cold cuts and salads to take home from the kitchen. I balanced the paper bag of food carefully on my knees as we took the St. Charles streetcar through the Garden District, back toward their apartment.

I marveled at the mansions we passed by, some protected by ornate iron gates, all perfectly landscaped and painted, so beautiful that it seemed unreal to me. Michelle caught my expression of wonder as I stared out the streetcar window.

"So, you're liking the Garden District, eh, little brother?"

"It's beautiful, all right. And so was your playing." They both thanked me at the same time. "I only wish we didn't have those drunken slobs to contend with."

My mother made a dismissive hand gesture and smiled. "Eddie, we play all kinds of places, at weddings, banquets, clubs, even on the street, like the other musicians."

"Sometimes, the crowds on the street are the most appreciative," Michelle explained.

"It's true," my mother agreed. "Oh, Eddie, this place is a second chance for me."

"I'm really glad about that," I said.

"It could be a second chance for you too." I saw the look of hopeful desperation in my mother's eyes and it was hard to bear it. I returned to staring at the huge, elegant, out-of-reach homes.

"I have to figure out what's going on with the band." I knew it was a delaying tactic, that I expected that the band was over forever, that it was unlikely that I would ever see my best friend again. But to say it would have been too much. By not saying it, I kept alive the possibility.

Michelle grabbed my attention by gripping my arm. "Eddie, Mom and I have talked about it, ever since you called us from L.A. We think you should move in with us and get work down here. You could easily find work. You could form your own band if you wanted."

"It's kind of crowded now," I said, "what with you on the couch and me in your sleeping bag on the floor."

"It's just to get you started," my mother offered. "You'll find your own place, your own way down here. But the music is everywhere, Eddie. This really is a good place for all of us to begin again."

There it was. The offer I knew was coming, the offer I hoped for and dreaded, the offer I couldn't say yes to without feeling I had given up, and couldn't say no to without feeling I had given up on them.

"Tell you what," I said in a mock cheerful manner, "the label gave me a ticket that goes on to Michigan. I want to see what's going on up there with the guys. I'll call you and let you know what my plans are."

Michelle's face sank. "It was years since I saw you and then it was Dad's funeral. We got to spend a little time together and then it was Hollywood. I don't know when we're going to see you again."

"Michelle, there is nothing and no one to stop me from seeing you and mom. I promise you, I'm not going to disappear. I just have to figure out what's going on with Johnny and the band. And I want to see some old friends up there. That's where most of my friends are."

Michelle was not about to accept this easily. "You were ready to make a new life in L.A. You could just as easily make a new life here with us."

My mother interjected, "Michelle, Eddie needs to figure some things out." She touched my face with her delicate, long, musical fingers. "We'll miss you, Eddie. You let us know where you are, wherever you go, okay?"

My throat tightened and I nodded my head vigorously.

"Here's our stop," my mother said and I welcomed the interruption, rising before they did.

***

I was glad when the bus finally left Detroit for the small Romeo depot. Detroit had been where we had recorded our demo and that was a pleasant memory in a way, but it was also a reminder of the failure of The Caretakers, the promise of creating in a big studio, where so many great recording artists had been, where the Motown sound had partly taken shape, only to have it all evaporate like mist.

We passed by sections of Detroit that looked tight, worn, volatile, ready to lash out. Cold stares came from the black kids who walked the street, resenting the white faces in a bus going somewhere else, people with the ability to go somewhere far away from their neighborhood. I thought about the Vietnam War on TV, the Watts riots I had seen on TV the year before, how the country was wrestling with itself, trying to grow, trying to find a new direction. Like the story in "Hyperion," I was seeing both beauty and wretchedness and seemed to pass through both sides, not at home in either one.

I searched through my backpack, through the clothes that my sister and mother had bought me, the food they had cooked and wrapped for me, through the sundries and notebooks with lyrics and ideas, to find the battered copy of the Keats poem. I opened it, beginning to re-read the words that I knew so well already, hoping, this time, to find some new truth that applied to my situation.

I did not look up from "Hyperion" until we were far out of the environs of the city and into the Michigan countryside again. I looked out to the fields, feeling the comfort and familiarity of the scenery, but wondering what changes I would find when I returned to Romeo, almost eight months after our last gig at The Mumps.

I had called from New Orleans and arranged for Bobby and Tommy to meet me at the depot and take me to the Janowski farm, where I would stay. In addition to the hurt of Johnny abandoning us, I had the further humiliation of telling a number of people, including Mrs. Janowski, who asked me a couple times why Johnny had disappeared. I had no answer.

The first omen I had that my life in Romeo was going to be very different came at the beginning, when I stepped off the bus. No one was there to pick me up. I paced back and forth, in front of the bench at the local grocery store. Finally, fifteen minutes later, Bobby drove up, without Tommy.

I got in and shook his hand but he was downhearted and made no attempt to hide it. "Sorry Tommy's not here. He's got a girlfriend now and he wanted to spend time with her tonight."

I thought about what that meant, that Tommy was not interested enough to meet me, after all we had been through. I was annoyed. I knew deep down I would have been there to meet him. But I said nothing about it, thinking of all the people and places of Romeo I wanted to revisit.

As if reading my mind, Bobby asked, "Where do you want to go?"

"Let's just drive around a bit. I'm staying at the Janowskis. Let's go by the farm."

"Which farm?" he asked in a concerned voice.

"The potato farm."

Bobby drove through the fading afternoon light. "It's kind of amazing, all the stuff that's been going on here since we were gone." Bobby did not specify.

"I know," I sighed. "Ever since my dad's accident, I can't seem to catch up to reality."

Bobby nodded and flipped on the radio, not knowing what to say. In mid-song, I heard Eric Burdon of The Animals wailing plaintively "Don't Bring Me Down." I smirked at the irony of it.

"Is Denise around?" I asked. "Have you seen her?"

"She split, Eddie. I heard she went east somewhere, to live on one of those communal farms, you know?" He looked over at me and saw the disappointment in my face. "They said she missed you. But I guess a lot of people here didn't know if we were coming back." He turned his attention back to the road. "We weren't supposed to come back," he said.

Bobby turned off the highway toward the familiar dirt road that Johnny had taken at breakneck speed so many times in the Eternal Energy Machine. But the farm house was closed up and there were no workers in the field.

I turned to Bobby, not comprehending. "What's going on? What happened to the potato farm?"

"I don't know. Maybe they know over there." Bobby indicated a farm house across the field.

"I'll be right back," I said and jumped out, striding angrily across the dirt I used to work with my hands.

Bobby could have driven me but I didn't want him to see the fear and confusion I was feeling. As my boots mashed the clods of dirt, I heard voices from the past, the Petersens wishing me a good weekend, handing me a check or Leonard teasing me when I first started working or the other workers, laughing and joking about my staying out late to play music with Johnny. And Johnny, asking, "So, Eddie, me boy, off to Missy's after work?" Ghosts in the fields. Ghosts in my head. They were all there, as real as anything else.

This farmhouse was illuminated, and it was dusk. I knocked on the door loudly. A skinny woman answered with a babushka on her head. It looked like she was doing the house cleaning and had patches of dust on her clothes.

"Yes, can I help you young man?" Her voice was weak and frail and she looked at me curiously.

I felt like I was intruding, even though she was cleaning. "Um, yes, um, I was wondering what happened to the Petersens who used to own the potato farm over there? I used to work there once."

A confused look came across her face but it finally shifted. "Oh, yes, the Petersens. Well, they sold the farm to some developers. They're going to put one of them new malls there. The Petersens went and moved to Florida. Sorry but that's all I know."

I thanked her and when I got back to Bobby's car, it wasdark outside.

"Can you drive me to the Janowskis?" I asked.

Bobby and I drove in silence to their house. When we arrived, Bobby finally spoke. "Listen, G Factor is touring and they're going to be at the Silver Bell next Friday. You could meet us there. Sort of get the gang together again. Tommy thought it would be a good idea.

I do too." "Sounds good," I agreed, grabbed my belongings and headed inside.

For Johnny's parents, I basically added details to the story of Johnny leaving, leaving out, of course, his swallowing the handful of psychedelics, which I thought would not bring much comfort to them.

"You think Johnny went to San Francisco?" Mrs. Janowski asked, her sweet doughy face stretched with concern. "I worry about him."

"He'll let us know where he is, mother," Mr. Janowski told his wife. "I'm sure he'll call, eventually."

"Johnny was just kind of in shock," I explained, vaguely. "Once he gets over the idea of Byron running off, he'll get back in touch. Probably come back, after a little time on the road."

There was nothing more to say and I declined Mrs. Janowski's kind offer to feed me some more, after feeding me too much. I went up to sleep in Johnny's room. But as I looked around at the posters and books and all things that meant something to him, I couldn't sleep. I took out my guitar and softly picked a sad, slow, bluesy line that came to mind.

"Come back, Johnny," I said aloud, put down the guitar and climbed into his bed.

I spent a great deal of time by myself, trying to figure out what to do, walking, reading, getting more than enough of Mrs. Janowski's great home cooking and helping around the house. In a way, I had not tried to contact others in Romeo because I felt like a failure and wasn't sure how they would greet me. I also was unsure about what life had to offer, now that Johnny was gone. I might be able to find another drummer who could sing, but the undeniable, uncomfortable truth was that Johnny was the driving force of the band. Could I become the leader of the band? Would it be as enjoyable? Would it work creatively? They were questions I did not want to confront just yet and I spent the week avoiding them. I knew that I would probably have to deal with them when I got to the Silver Bell.

If Johnny and I had been going, he would have put the word out himself, would have contacted someone and had our names placed on a guest list at the door. Instead, I borrowed Mr. Janowski's truck and showed up just before starting time.

I got in line to buy tickets and it wasn't long before Tommy and Bobby spotted me. Tommy introduced me to his girlfriend Jennifer. I didn't question why he didn't meet me.

"What are you doing in line for tickets? We're on a guest list." Tommy seemed to have gained a bit more confidence since the fiasco in Hollywood.

I followed them up to the door. Some of the faces in line noticed us and waved hello or called out our names. Tommy and Bobby waved back. I felt unsure of myself and just wanted to get inside and find a good place to stand and listen. I would find the right time to talk to them about the band.

When the lights went down and G Factor hit the stage, the old ski lodge rocked with applause. Rick Rosten walked up to the mike. "Hey, everybody, after we won that Battle of the Bands, we released our first album and went on tour."

The applause was controlled by Rick, who held his hands, palms down, looking for quiet. When he got it, he continued. "But we told them, no way we're going to do a national tour without coming back here to the good old Silver Bell!"

Now, the audience truly howled their appreciation. They launched into the music and as I listened and enjoyed it, I simultaneously felt an emptiness, preventing me from truly having a good time. What G Factor accomplished, we should have done as well. The Caretakers should have had a national tour and made a triumphant return to their hometown.

I didn't take my eyes off the stage until the end of the third song, when I felt a tug at my shoulder. I looked over to see Missy. She was holding The Caretakers album. Bobby and Tommy had already signed it for her. We looked at each other and hugged ferociously. Her sad eyes held me. She leaned over to me and whispered, before the next song started, "Can we talk outside for a minute?"

I nodded and told the others I'd be back in a little while. They nodded back.

Missy and I got our hands stamped, so we could reenter the hall and went outside. We stood under a light, so I could see the album cover better. There was a photo of us, standing together, Johnny with his arm around my shoulders. The art department had used a yellow background with flowers and psychedelic lettering for "The Caretakers" at the top and at the bottom, "The Road to Golden."

"Will you sign it for me?" Missy asked in a small voice and I took her pen and wrote my name on the golden background. I continued to look at Johnny and me on the cover.

"I got it in Ann Arbor," Missy said.

"I hadn't even seen it until now," I said, not looking up. "I didn't give the label an address so they never mailed me any."

"I heard he went to San Francisco," Missy said. I looked up from the smiling, confident face of Johnny. "Do you think he's all right?" She didn't wait for an answer. She wasn't sure she wanted the answer. "I wish I could see him again. I just don't understand why he ran off like that."

I handed her back the album and pen. "I don't know. I think Johnny is so powerful, so used to making things work just the way he wants, that he broke apart when Byron stole our money."

"But it's a great album," Missy said, her voice breaking. "You've got to find him, Eddie. You guys have to tour, to stay together." Her eyes became wet and she angrily brushed some tears away. "Going back in," she said.

She got a few steps away from me before I could call out, “Missy, you still dancing?”

“Afraid so. Come by soon.” She quickly retreated back into the Silver Bell, our album hugged to her chest but before she was out of sight, I could see her body convulsing from the tears.

I looked up to the stars in the sky for a while and then, made my way back inside. I rejoined Bobby and Tommy and Jennifer and watched the rest of the concert. At the end, amid the cheers, Rick Rosten held his guitar aloft with one arm and shouted, “No matter where we go, we’ll never forget you, Michigan!”

The lights came up and Jennifer had the good taste to say she had to go to the bathroom and would meet us out front. This left the three of us alone, looking at each other, as people filed out of the Silver Bell.

“So, what did you think?” I asked, just trying to break the silence among us.

“Good show,” Bobby stated.

“Yeah, G Factor is tight,” Tommy agreed.

Neither one of them was going to bring it up, so I had to. “So, what about The Caretakers?”

Bobby looked off into the crowd, milling toward the exits.

“It was fun while it lasted,” said Tommy.

"Hey, we have an album out," I said.

"Yeah, but Johnny's gone." Bobby looked pained to state the obvious.

"Well, we have two options, as I see it," I said. "We can find another singer and drummer or we can hope that Johnny comes back."

"You think Johnny's going to come back here?" Tommy snorted in derision. "Man, he couldn't wait to get out of here."

"He said he's going to San Francisco. That's probably where he is," Bobby ventured.

"Well, what if I can find him?" I suggested.

"Find him? He ditched us." I had never seen Tommy so demonstrative. The shock had obviously worn off and he was angry.

Bobby, on the other hand, had all the energy drained from him. "Eddie, I think you should just accept it."

"Accept what?"

"It's over," Tommy bitterly said. "The Caretakers is over. Do us a favor. Call the label and have them send us our copies of the record."

Tommy walked away. Bobby looked at me, the corner of his mouth drawn up in embarrassment. Before he could say anything, I heard a booming voice shout toward us, "Eddie, goddamn. I thought that was you."

I looked over. Gino, with his arm around a woman, was headed over to us.

"You got a ride?" asked Bobby.

"Yeah, thanks."

"I'm sorry, Eddie. We'll see you later."

As Gino got closer, I could see how he'd changed. He wore a beard and mustache now, his voice was more cheerful and he had a pronounced limp.

"Hey, man," he proclaimed, grabbing me and hugging me, pounding me on the back for friendly emphasis. "Hey, Sherry, this is Eddie Defoe from The Caretakers. I heard your album, Eddie. Good stuff."

"Thanks, Gino. I heard you joined up, went to war."

Gino sighed. "Yeah, nothing else to do here but get in gang fights. So, I went over to 'Nam after boot camp. And the reason I'm back so soon..." He leaned on Sherry and lifted up the right pants leg on his blue jeans, revealing a prosthetic limb. I winced. "Oh, yeah," he said. "Couple weeks in country, and I step on a land mine. Blew it off past the knee." He lowered the pants leg and winked lasciviously at me. "It doesn't stop me from doing anything I did before." He put his arm around Sherry again and we all began walking out of nearly empty hall. "Except driving. I leave that to her. So, Eddie, what the fuck went down with Johnny?"

I told him, including the details with the drugs. My story ended just as we reached his car in the lot.

Sherry started it up, that souped-up dragster still looking fine, and let it noisily idle as Gino opened the passenger side door and clumsily got in. He leaned out the window, grabbed my arm, and for a brief moment, the old intensity was there, the eyes that suggested he could hug you or slice your throat open.

"You know what you got to do, Eddie."

"Uh, no, actually, I don't, Gino."

"You got to go to Frisco and find Johnny, kick his ass for what he did to you guys. Then, you kick his punk ass again for me. And then, you guys record another record together and forget about it. See you around." He turned to Sherry.

"Let's roll, baby."

The car blasted away, leaving me standing alone between time periods, between locales, between destinies.

Chapter 13

I had all my possessions with me in the world, my guitar, my backpack with my clothes and not only Keats but a couple other books which meant a great deal to me. I left the rest of my belongings with the Janowskis and promised to stay in touch with them as I traveled. I was off to find Johnny, find out about my country, see how others lived, and by association, determine how I wanted to live. I had two hundred dollars, all that was left with my brush with fame, after Byron Orr finished with us.

As I stood alongside a highway, my thumb out in the crisp autumn air, the thought amused me. Instead of worrying what I would do when the money ran out, I was entertaining myself with scenarios of life on the road. Maybe I would explore some town, run into Byron, demand the money back, in fact, beat him senseless and take the money and then hook up with Johnny in San Francisco and start a new group. The power of youth is the willingness to suspend fear in favor of pursuing experience. It's the downfall, too.

My first ride dropped me off just outside of Toledo, which in terms of miles wasn't very far but at least it was out of Michigan and it gave me a bit more of a sense of excitement. I had brought a sleeping bag to save as much money on accommodations as I could and sleep out in nature in the cool but not yet cold nights.

My next long distance ride was from a salesman in the plastics industry and he carried on and on about the great future of plastic-dom, how it was going to revolutionize the way we lived. I thought about the civil rights movement, the protests against the war and wondered to myself if kids would soon be holding signs which read, "More Plastics Now!" His sales pitch, as if I was a potential client, was the most boring thing I had ever heard in my life, but as long as I was moving and comfortable he could talk all day about his utterly mindless profession. The only thing that caught my interest was when I was fiddling with his radio and caught a station playing "I Fought the Law" by the Bobby Fuller Four. I turned it up and fingered the guitar part as the Plastics King glanced over at me. To his credit, he let me listen to the entire song. But after it was over, he turned the volume down and began anew, asking me if I knew all the newest applications of his petroleum-based God.

On the superhighways of America, all the little towns blurred by in rapid succession. A majority of the interstate highway system had been built after World War Two, especially in the 1950s, when American prosperity was riding high. But then, the only people exploring the country were called hoboes and tramps and they hitched rides on trains rather than in the cars of traveling salespeople. There was no longer room for a Jack Kerouac hobo adventure in American literature. But it was a big country and even if I didn't find Johnny, I knew eventually, I'd find me.

Ohio eventually transformed out the window into the state of Indiana. The sign that announced our entry into Indiana reminded me of a fact I had not considered for a very long time: my father was born on an Indiana farm. We traveled there when I was only five, the four of us, for some purpose only my father could enunciate and he wasn't about to tell me now. The

memories of the trip to Indiana were vague to me, nothing more than like a half-remembered scene out of Erskine Caldwell's "Tobacco Road."

My father's family had been poor, and they lived off their land and the food they grew and sold for other essentials. But I was not interested in exploring his past and did not ask to be dropped off in that state and that state of mind. I was excited about making some headway south. My traveling salesman told me he was going to St. Louis, which was fine with me because I knew that was my gateway to the southwest.

It was about suppertime when we pulled into St. Louis and the Prince of Plastic took me right downtown into the business district. He had asked me if I wanted to have dinner with him and I knew that he was a lonely road warrior, but I had had enough, so I politely declined his invitation and looked for a friendly place to spend the night.

I spotted a little café called Louie's on one busy intersection. It had booths all along the window and people were engaged in lively conversation. There was also the long counter where all the singles would sit and read newspapers or talk to the counter person. I walked to the counter and sat down, noticing one booth full of "freaks," the cool term for hippies at the time, so I felt comfortable there.

I ordered a tuna sandwich with fries, a piece of apple pie and coffee. I noticed that the table of freaks was very animated in their conversation. There were three long-haired guys and one girl and while I was waiting for my sandwich, I decided to go over and talk to them.

I led off with conversation with the standard phrase, "What's happenin', man?" and they all shrugged and smiled and offered me a seat.

I waved to the counter server to have my food brought over to the booth. I grabbed a chair and sat with my new friends.

They asked where I was from and when I told them Detroit, they got all excited.

"Wow, what a scene up there, man," said one freak. "Like we went to that Grande Ballroom place a month or so ago and saw Cream, man. The next night they had a couple local bands play, The Stooges and MC5 and they just blew everyone away."

"What a great town," complimented another freak. "So what're you doing here, man?"

"Actually, I was in a band up there and we had this great gig going but drugs and bad deals went down and the whole thing came apart. So now I'm traveling to San Francisco to try and find my friend and maybe get things back together." They nodded their heads and wowed as I covered the basics.

When I told one of the guys who asked the name of the band, he said, reverently, "Wow, I bought that record, man. Definitely groovy."

I was part of a cultural fraternity, that of rock and roll brethren who admired both the music and those who made it. After the meal, they insisted I join them at a place called 'Webster's Last Word.'

"They're going to have music and poetry reading. It's going to be a total trip, man." The second long-haired freak was smiling widely in expectation. I told them I'd love to go but I had no place to sleep for the night.

"Hey, don't worry about that," the girl reassured me. "There are plenty of places to crash, we'll set you up."

Rod, freak number one, suggested that we go smoke some weed up in a friend's apartment, "in order to get our heads primed," as he put it. We walked about five blocks and then ducked into an alley, climbed a flight of stairs and entered a darkened apartment, illuminated only by lava lamps and black lights. A figure came from the back room and had a joint in his mouth. Without any hello or anything, as host of the party, he just handed the joint over to me in a welcoming gesture.

"It's killer weed, man," he sputtered and then started coughing. There was some strange music playing. I noticed the record, propped up against the brick and wood shelves holding the stereo. It was by Captain Beefheart and His Magic Band.

The apartment started filling up with more and more people and our host went in the back room and came out with a huge hookah pipe, the kind with about eight hoses attached. He motioned everyone to come around and partake of the ceremonial pipe. While others were frantically squirming to reach the hookah, I had noticed a shy, lovely girl standing over in the corner of the room. I wanted to go over and talk with her, but I was so high and felt awkward and so instead, asked somebody and found out that her name was Paula. I was about to make a move when all of a sudden our host announced,

"All right everyone, we're heading out to the party now. Come on, let's go."

With that, everybody started to head towards the door and I lost Paula in the sea of people. The walk down to the club was a mass of semi-controlled hysteria, people shouting, laughing, bumping into each other, changing places and talking with different people and I was swept up in the spontaneous tide, no longer worrying about annoying considerations like money and where one might sleep for the evening.. The club was only about six blocks from the apartment. It was a four-story brick building with a sign outside that read “Webster’s Last Word” in a tie-dye, Peter Max style. As we entered the building, we saw a series of signs with an eyeball and a finger pointing upward and the word “UP.”

The place took up the entire third floor. We joined about fifty or so that were already there. The club was laid out in three rooms, all about the same size, and there was activity in all three rooms. The smell of incense permeated the air. One room had just a dim red light with black light posters, another room had a strobe light in it and a third had twenty or so candles everywhere. I found out the room with the candles was where they read poetry. I couldn’t find Paula and there was a never-ending river of humanity coming in, so I went outside, fighting against the current, to get some air.

There in the back patio of the building was Paula.

“Hello there. Remember me?”

She turned her head ever so slightly and looked into my eyes. “Of course I do, silly. We all came over together, remember?” I didn’t care. The ice was broken, we introduced ourselves and I began to speak to her about how nice the place was and how wonderful everyone had been to me so far.

After I was finished, she nodded, agreed it was a great group of people and then asked, matter-of-factly, "Do you want to do some acid?" I paused and she asked if I had ever done it before.

"Sure, plenty of times. Yeah, acid would be, uh, very nice."

"Great I got one hit. We can split it."

She pulled out a little piece of tin foil and opened it. In it was a tiny dot. I wondered how we were ever going to split this. She reached in her bag and pulled out a tiny little knife and proceeded to dissect the tiny thing. I thought to myself, I'll be lucky if I feel anything after taking this tiny piece of LSD.

She wet a finger and touched the one half and put her finger in my mouth. I followed her lead.

"I hear you play guitar. Are you going to play something tonight?"

"I don't know, I guess so, if they want me to."

"Oh, cool. What will you play?"

"I don't know," I said, trying to be humble. "Maybe something by Dylan. He's a great poet."

"Something you wrote too," Paula said in a quiet but insistent voice. "I want to hear your words. Hear part of your soul."

"I hope you'll like it, Paula. I really want you to like it."

She smiled at me with a sweet, sad sensuousness I couldn't understand but was utterly entranced by and then she leaned over to me and very softly, pressed her lips against my left cheek.

"It's such a groovy night. I'm glad I met you, Eddie. Let's go back in now. "

As we made our way back upstairs, I had the sensation I could hear sounds so much more clearly, the laughter, the music floating down from the third floor, the sounds of our feet on the wooden stairs. Movement seemed labored and very slow, no matter how much energy I exerted. I moved my right arm and noticed I could see trails, like I was seeing in slow motion.

People speaking seemed to be loud and it made me want to whisper everything.

"Why are they talking so loud?" I said both to Paula and myself. She took my hand as a wave of partiers pushed us farther into the club. Paula led me to the candle-lit room where there was a poetry session taking place. Everyone listened to a woman poet, wearing a flowing gown and a lace shawl. I studied the patterns in the white linen shawl as her voice intoned, "Bombs, bombs, the burning of eyes/The scorching of earth, promulgation of lies..." Her voice went on, harsh, pained, creating horrifying images of war and disease. I saw the images clearly in my mind as she spoke them and I winced, feeling pain as the woman poet came up with more and more intense imagery.

Paula must have sensed my discomfort. She squeezed my hand and whispered in my ear, "Come on. I want to show you a secret spot." Paula led me through some hallways on the third floor, away from the club, into little rooms connected to one another. I felt like a male Alice in Wonderland, Allan in Wonderland, and wondered if I would ever get back to where I started this night. But I did feel totally comfortable with Paula. When we stopped at one door, Paula looked at me.

"This is the magic pillow room, where every movement is like floating in the clouds."

She opened the door and it was an entire room filled with pillows and people, most of them unclothed or partially clothed, gyrating this way and that. The walls had been painted as if they were blue sky and white, fluffy clouds. Paula closed the door and in the dim light, she stepped out of her clothes and fell into my arms. We kissed and my head swam with sensation. We fell down to the pillows. I took off one shoe as she took off the other and we both helped me out of my pants. Our arms, as we moved, came in contact with other bodies, and the moans and gasps of those making love excited us as finally, both unclothed, we attached ourselves to one another and joined the moving, evolving mass of sexual union, the acid swirling about in our brains, feeling disconnected from the world but enjoying a white hot sensation of passionate connectedness to each other.

After we had both satisfied each other, Paula, despite the LSD, seemed to be in total control of her senses. She then told me that it was time now to get back to the club and get into the music.

"I especially want to hear you, Eddie," she said as we struggled to find our clothes under the bodies of those either still making love or lying, dazed, recovering from the act. "I bet it will be like hearing the angels sing," she said and her gentleness amazed me. She took my hand after I was dressed and slowly pulled me to my feet. It felt like I was going fifty feet up in the air.

When we left the Cloud Room, straightening our clothes, I felt the rush of the world come back to me. "I don't know how I'm going to play in this condition," I admitted.

Paula rubbed my shoulders, encouraging me. "Don't worry about it Eddie, it'll come to you naturally, just like love making did in the clouds. You'll see."

If she had told me at that moment I would be able to walk on the shoulders of the people who jammed the rooms of "Webster's Last Word," I would have believed her.

When we entered the red-walled room with the candles, it was as though someone other than me was about to perform. I had never been on any drugs when we performed. Paula guided me through the people sitting on the floor and some chairs to a little podium and a mike. I heard some voices speaking but I couldn't tell what they were saying and then it dawned on me that they were asking me to play.

Paula started to speak for me. "Everyone, this is Eddie, and he used to be in a band called The Caretakers, and now he is on a quest to find freedom and his long lost band mate and friend in San Francisco." I spoke too close into the mike and it made a horrible, shrill sound. Everybody held their ears and I felt bad that I inflicted this on everyone. Paula pulled me back and handed me my guitar.

"Just play what you feel," she said, in a comforting tone. "Whatever you choose, it will be just right."

I sat back and having the guitar in my hand felt great. I began to tune the guitar but I drifted into improvising a sort of Indian raga. It sounded nice to my ear so I kept playing and to my surprise people started to move to it, including Paula. I reached a certain phrase that made me think of a Dylan song, so I just went right into "A Hard Rain Is Going to Fall." People were singing along to the chorus without my even uttering a word. Their applause, at the end, buoyed me. I played and sang a song Johnny and I had written, "In the Hardness of Time," because the title was similar to Dylan's.

Although it sounded strange to me to do it without the band, I really got into the song and ended up doing an extended version of it. It seemed like I was playing for an hour but I knew that it was just the acid making me think so.

I sang the final words, "And our mutual loss has neither reason nor rhyme/we'll make sense of it in the hardness of time." Over the applause, I wished everyone peace and happiness and lumbered away from the podium. Everyone was calling for more and Paula came up and gave me a hug. I told them I was too high to do another one that I just wanted to groove with everything and despite some good-natured moans of disappointment, everyone understood.

We made a last circuit around the club, going from room to room. I gathered my guitar and backpack as Paula held onto my arm. Some freaks patted me on the back and gave me an "All right, brother!" or a "Very heavy, man!"

Paula looked at me with great pleasure swimming across her eyes. "You are deeper than I ever hoped, Eddie. You're a great artist."

"Am I great enough," I asked, sounds and images still coming at me in delayed waves, "that I could spend the night with you?"

"Oh, I insist on it," she said and led me out into the night and stars, our breath twirling in clouds before us, as we walked to her apartment.

As if the night had not provided enough wild sensation, when I got to her room, I fell into her bed and the world turned to soft jelly. I felt myself sink, not met by firmness but the dizzying sensation of being swallowed up.

"It's a waterbed," she laughed, looking at my amazed expression.

We took off our clothes and got under the covers. "I have some hashish to mellow us out," she said and lit a bowl and held it for me as I inhaled. The sweet, pungent odor and unique taste of it was more exotic than the marijuana I had smoked.

"Everything about you is magic," I said. "What have you done to me?"

She set down the hash pipe and perched herself on top of me, moving unbelievably slowly, allowing me to grow hard and rise up into her with almost no effort.

"It's what you've done to me," Paula said. "You've taken hold of me. And I don't know how I'm going to be normal again."

"You don't have to be" I started to say, to reassure her, to try and put a smile on her mysteriously forlorn, delicate face. But she wouldn't let me speak. She lowered her mouth to mine, slipped her tongue between my lips, began rocking her hips down onto me and as the waterbed undulated at what seemed to be a miraculous pace, I was lost to all reason and enjoyably let go of all thought, succumbing to pleasure.

***

I awoke about noon and Paula was already up, completing a breakfast of pancakes and sausages. I was very hungry and ate voraciously, not really paying attention to her until I had finished.

"That was great. Thank you," I said but now, I could see that Paula was shrinking before my eyes, consumed again with a despondency I could not really penetrate. "I don't just mean breakfast. I mean thank you for last night, which was amazing to me."

"What do you want to do today?" she asked in a timid voice, afraid of my answer, knowing it would displease her and asking anyway.

"I'm going to keep moving, see what happens when I get to the West Coast again."

Now Paula turned her eyes to me, asking me plaintively, "You know, you could stay here a while if you wanted. You moved a lot of people last night with your singing and playing. Maybe we could find some clubs for you to play in here in St. Louis. I have a job and I could cover the rent for while until you start gigging. You know?"

For all the beauty and passion and free spiritedness of the night before, I wondered if it was worth the hurt of this moment, the disappointment I was causing Paula, the misery I was feeling in telling her I was going to go.

I apologized and she didn't try to convince me any longer to stay, except with her eyes, which did not seem on the verge of tears but had such a deep and abiding sadness in them, it was almost unbearable in the harsh light of the day.

When I told her I would write her and keep her informed of where I went and what happened with The Caretakers, she merely nodded and said, barely loud enough to hear, "Cool."

Paula walked with me down to the highway and when it was time to go down to the entrance and start hitching, we stood, looked each other in the eyes.

"Remember me and the Cloud Room," she said, kissed me ferociously and then turned and walked away.

"I'll remember," I whispered and then thought she could not hear me. "I'll remember!" I shouted after her. She never turned around.

***

Part of the beauty of the time was that in certain places, you could find a group of freaks sit down with them, eat a meal and wind up having a great adventure. The same held true for finding the right place, sticking out your thumb and, perhaps twenty minutes later, finding yourself in someone's car, experiencing their world as you traveled together. And it was about twenty minutes for me before I saw a funny-looking truck coming my way, about twenty miles an hour slower than the rest of the traffic. It was rust colored with bright yellow trim and had pictures of animals and clowns all over it. It slowly pulled off to the side of the road and I could read the huge letters on the side that read "Orvis Traveling Circus Show." Under that, in smaller letters, was "The Thrill of the Big Tent."

When I moved toward the passenger side door to hop in, I was greeted first by an angry roar of a wild animal that wasn't too happy about me climbing aboard.

"Precious, Precious, calm down and let the man come in." The door swung open. I saw a large, black animal with glittering teeth and I was rethinking the idea of taking this ride.

"Precious is okay used to people. No need worry and that."

The small Russian accented voice came from a man-child who appeared to weigh about 400 lbs and had hair all over his body. He was wearing a tank top shirt and hair was popping out of it like stuffing out of an old doll. He assured me that the baby panther next to him would be well-behaved and I climbed in and took a chance.

"You know, I take care of all the animals for circus," he said. "I could wrestle a bear, no sweating it."

"I'm Eddie. I play guitar and write songs."

"Da. Good. I am Tiny. I take care of big cats in back."

"You have other animals in the truck?" I guess I looked somewhat fearful and Tiny glanced at me, his broad face breaking into a grin. Apparently his name, Tiny, came from his high pitched voice, certainly not his size.

"I have some lion, tiger, oh yeah, Tiny has em all."

In my awe, I forgot to ask how far the not-so-tiny Tiny was going.

"Tiny goes all the way to Oglahoma City for next Big Top."

He looked me up and down and then his eyes returned to the highway. "Hey, maybe you need to make some money, ah? I have job for someone want to help me, scrub cages, feed animals, all dot."

I didn't want to seem ungrateful and possibly get deposited by the side of the road. But I was not about to commit right then and there to cleaning up the droppings of large wild animals who could take my head off with one swipe of a paw.

"How much do you think this job might pay, if it's available?" I asked cautiously.

"Tiny can't say for sure, but think it might be five dollar an hour, but got to ask boss first."

He saw me look outside at the cars zooming past us. "You get place to sleep and eating, too"

I thought about these added benefits, about the ride all the way to Oklahoma City, and that I could use the money to help pay for the next leg of my journey. I didn't have to commit to staying there for a long time.

"Tiny, it sounds very good. I'm eventually heading to San Francisco."

"San Francisco!" he interrupted enthusiastically. "Dot is one of the places we go."

"Well, great. Would it be possible to work for you for a few days, maybe a week, and then continue to California on my own?"

"You are like me, Eddie. Free spirit. I'm sure is okay."

"Well, I would be honored, Tiny, to come and join the Great Traveling Circus. You can count me in."

A big smile came over Tiny's face and showed proudly the few lower teeth that remained in his gums, for some unknown reason. "Da, dis is good," Tiny announced and he began to tell me all about the circus life, the people, the towns, the animals. It was like he was a refugee, not just from the Soviet Union, where he had been born, but from American society, part of this ark of people and animals that didn't "belong" anywhere in particular, but just traveled through life, entertaining, never taking root. I liked the idea of it. I would become one of them, I thought, even if it was only for a short while.

Chapter 14

Tiny drove and just talked the whole time with an occasional break here and there for gas and food and bathrooms. It seemed as though Tiny owned the road, not in the sense of driving all over it, thankfully, but in the comfort he displayed being on it. When we stopped, his chatter ceased, and he lowered his head and bulled ahead with whatever the task was. But as soon as we were back in the circus truck, his mood lightened.

He murmured lovingly to the panther known as Precious and checked on the other wild beasts, talking with them in a sweet tone, as if they were toy poodles, anxious to get out and romp around in the park.

As dusk approached and we entered the state of Oklahoma, I sleepily mentioned my concern about Tiny's generous offer. It was one thing to be accepted by other freaks, but I was not sure that those who worked in a traveling circus would not look upon me with some disdain. Tiny noted my lidded eyes, my look of concern and he let out a big belly laugh that literally shook the truck.

"These are circus peoples, my friend. We always are coming and going. Change is the only thing we know. That and pleasing audience. You understand both things, da?"

"Well I'll tell you, Tiny, I sure am glad you came along. This is the best ride I've ever had in my life. Thank you."

"Ah, well, you just go to sleep now. Tiny get us dere soon."

And with his permission and reassurance, I slept the deepest sleep, exhausted by hashish and LSD and lovemaking in the clouds with Paula amid others and baby panthers snarling at me. I was utterly depleted and the bouncing of the truck, the low moan of the engine, the occasional rumble of a wild cat displeased with its caged condition, the now low humming of a sad Russian folk tune from the voice box of the huge Tiny, none of these things could any longer keep me awake. The road either lulls you to sleep or excites you with the knowledge of going, of heading toward something new. I had absorbed all the newness I could for the while.

When I finally woke up, we were pulling into an open field and the jolting of the truck brought the wild animals to life, roaring their complaints. It was dark and except for stars dripping light down from the sky into my foggy eyes, and a few campfires and lanterns here and there, I could barely make out anything.

When we got out of the truck, Tiny pointed to a tent about fifty feet away.

"You go and put your stuffs over dere and come back to Tiny, da?"

On my way over to the tent, I noted the outline of people walking about on the grounds of the circus-to-be. An overly muscular man in tights, I assumed, was some kind of strongman or perhaps a gymnast. Another man carried a fright wig, bright orange and wildly colored clothes over his arm, a clown, I assumed, off duty and being serious.

I walked, still sleepy, not quite used to the darkness around me, until I found the tent Tiny had indicated. I put my belongings on top of a bench inside. I headed back to Tiny, wondering what acts the circus had, what I might be paid, whether I could play music or was just going to be stuck cleaning out disgusting animal cages.

And then I stopped in my tracks. I saw before me was the most beautiful girl I had ever seen, her dark, lustrous hair, deep eyes highlighted in the black night by the lantern she held. Her lips curved in a way so inviting, her long-lashed stare drew me in and I was frozen in place, just staring mindlessly at her. She looked at me and smiled and said "Hello." Her voice was like chocolate syrup cascading down a hill of ice cream. My knees sagged, just hearing her voice and my tongue was heavy, unable at first to form sounds. When she began to walk past me, the lantern revealing the lush eyelashes that framed her dark, almond shaped eyes, I was jolted into saying hello back to her. She was wearing a uniform, which to me looked like that for an acrobat, or maybe she rode an animal bareback. It was silvery, shaped like a one piece bathing suit and she had a long jacket over it. I glimpsed her curvaceous-ness and she smiled but then was past me and I shook my head, trying to comprehend the girl I had just seen. I couldn't tell how old she was but in the dimness, she appeared to be not much older than I was. I was no longer thinking about how much I was going to get paid.

When I asked Tiny about her, his eyes widened and he smiled in only the way that Tiny could. Then Tiny poked me in the ribs and proclaimed, "Oh, you like the little gypsy girl den, da?" He slapped me on the back and this time he made me buckle and fall over. It was like having someone slamming a canned ham against your back while you stood on one leg. He

extended a hand and easily yanked me to my feet and we silently walked to another tent, which had the sounds of snoring and breathing inside.

"Lie down before you are falled down," Tiny advised and I took off my shoes, crawled in, found a blanket and lay down, awaiting sleep.

So much had happened in the last few days but of all the images, all the memories, the only thing in my mind as I drifted away, was the image of the hauntingly stunning girl I had just seen.

***

The next day, I was shaken awake in the early dawn by Tiny, who advised me to get dressed.

"We go to meet the boss and he will say you are okay," Tiny promised in his peculiar way, and I only hoped he was right, for now, the gypsy girl was flooding back into my groggy consciousness and I could not bear the idea of having to leave the circus and her to hitchhike again.

At yet another tent, which was about the same size as all of them, save for the Big Top where the performances actually took place, Tiny and I trudged in through the dank, early morning light. Seated in a folding chair, like that of a film director, with canvas seat and backing, was the Boss, whose name I never learned. He was balding with strands of hair combed over his head. He sat in front of an old steamer trunk, with papers laid out in front of him, with the concentration of an archaeologist who had just found a new language and was disgusted he couldn't understand a word of it.

"Uh, boss," Tiny said, after lightly clearing his throat.

"What?" said the boss, more a complaint than a question.

"New guy I find to clean cages and like dot," Tiny explained.

The boss continued to try to understand the paperwork in front of him and after a long while, bothered to look up to evaluate me, as if the time meeting my eyes would be a major imposition. The boss looked at me and his scowl did not change. He then shifted his eyes to Tiny.

"Fine. Five bucks an hour plus grub and a tent to sleep in. If it works out, you travel with us. Mondays and Tuesdays off."

I said nothing and the boss just grunted, as if to indicate the legal wrangling, as it were, was over. He returned his attention to the paperwork.

"Okay, okay, now please, just get to work. We are the Big Top. People come to us to expecting the moon! So let's deliver. Go! Go!"

We left the boss man's tent.

"Is he always so friendly?" I asked Tiny, shielding my eyes from the new-rising sun.

"Trost me," Tiny said. "You don't want him getting to know you."

There was a tent for everything at the circus, including food for the company. Over breakfast, Tiny introduced me to a number of other people and I kept looking around, hoping I would find the gypsy girl.

"Tiny, last night when you told me about that gypsy girl, you didn't mention her name and what she does here at the circus?"

"Da. You pretty gaga over this girl, eh? Okay, Tiny will introduce you. Her name is Cybele. She work over in Big Tent riding horse and outside as fortune teller."

And with that, Tiny was off in a hurry, leading the way, and when Tiny was moving in a hurry, you didn't want to get in his way. It was evident by the way people were moving aside when he stormed past that they weren't about to have a head-on collision with this mountain of a man.

"Is custom for gypsy people when you meet girl that you must have blessing or it will be doomed. Cybele's father, he gypsy fortune teller too and I ask if you can talk to her."

"I have to ask permission just to talk?"

Actually, despite my surprise at this, I was getting to appreciate Tiny more and more. He was honorable, loyal and made things happen rather quickly. I would have blundered into that situation and ruined the whole thing. We were now at the tent of the gypsy family, with clothing and pots and utensils scattered about and a pot of soup slowly simmering over a fire.

Tiny with great pride rolled up to the wagon and announced our arrival. A few seconds later, a short stocky man appeared dressed in colorful shirt and trousers and boots, complete with a scarf around his neck and sash around his waist. Tiny and the man spoke quietly for a few moments and then Tiny turned to me.

"He is saying that maybe it is not good idea to have young American boy in love with Cybele. He says he doesn't want to do wrong in this country and make big mess." The gypsy father was wringing his hands, looking at me intensely.

"May I talk to you?" I asked Cybele's father, and learned his name was Tibor.

He said "Eddie," after I told him my name, trying to make the sound seem acceptable to his tongue. It did not seem to sound right, the way he said it. "It is our way in America to accept all people regardless of their beliefs, religion, or race and that is what makes us a strong country."

"But you are a boy. You are here to clean animal cages. This is not for Cybele." His thick Romanian accent did not hide the fact that, while he was not trying to be rude, he was proud, protective and a bit wary of me. I couldn't have looked too good, with the lack of sleep and rumpled clothes.

"I am doing this for money," I defended myself. "I am really a musician. I have been a professional musician and have a record that has been released."

"You? Musician? What do you play?"

"Guitar," I answered.

He turned and disappeared into his tent.

I turned to Tiny. "Guess he doesn't like guitar," I said.

Tiny held up a hand, indicating I should wait.

Tibor came back with a guitar, a battered acoustic with mother of pearl inlays, which I sensed he did not use for rock and roll. He handed it to me. "You play."

I strummed it and it was in tune, had a warm, mellow tone. I put my knee up on a rock and began to play a song I had never performed with The Caretakers, one that told of lost love and had a softer sound, a ballad I thought Tibor would respond to.

When I finished, Tibor took the guitar from me and began to play himself, a fiery instrumental tune, picking with a speed I could not begin to compete with. Tiny and I watched his fingers fly, and some of the other performers stopped as they were strolling by to watch him. Tibor finished with a flourish and received a small round of applause from us all. He quickly went back into his tent and came out, without the guitar.

"You play with much soul," he told me. And he marched off and bid us to follow him.

Tiny gave a slight shove and I followed, as we were off to the Big Tent.

When we entered the Big Top, it brought back my childhood trip with my family to a circus near Romeo. Here, all the performers were rehearsing their acts and it was like having my own private circus. I looked around for Cybele but didn't see her. Tibor led us to the dressing room.There, Tibor found the dark angel of my current dreams. He leaned down to her, whispered something in Romanian in her ear and then led Tiny out. But the huge Russian gave me a wink before leaving us alone.

Now, she stood in front of me, shy, demure, head bent to the ground. Amazingly, she stood again in a remarkable light, this time a shaft pouring down from a hole in the top of the tent. Her jet black hair and blue eyes devoured me. She had a tight-fitting, blue sequined outfit, her riding outfit.

"Hallo, I am happy to make your acquaintance," she said with a faint accent that I thought made her even more beautiful. Her shyness sent her right back to the pose she had before. A few seconds passed, which seemed like hours, and then finally I was able to untie my tongue.

"Cybele. Such a beautiful name. It's perfect for you."

"Thank you. What is your name again?" I told her and she said it, but it had a different ring to it and she said it again and smiled and I found it hard to breathe. How could I be in love with someone after exchanging a couple sentences?

"You are going to ride horseback tonight?" I asked, unable to think of anything else to say.

"I ride tonight. Today, when we open, I will tell fortunes."

"I'll come see you tell fortunes and then, after the show, I would enjoy it very much if you could join me for a walk?" I didn't have the courage to say it as a statement or invitation but only as a question.

"I would like that very much," she said in the softest tone and I parted from her, floating, moving backwards, my eyes on her for as long as I could manage.

All in all it was quite a long day. Circus people deserve a lot of credit. They do hard work and put in long hours every day just so they can give you a three hour show. And I was lugging food and water back and forth, helping others with whatever small chores they needed. But the time goes quickly when the workplace is that entertaining. I saw people go by on unicycles, horses, elephants and tiny motorized cars. One clown came by and shook my hand. While I did so, he squirted water in my face from a daisy on his lapel. Tiny almost fell over from laughter.

And then the gates were opened and the pre-show entertainment, wandering clowns and jugglers, worked the area, prior to the audience taking their seats in the Big Top. I hustled to help Tiny feed the animals and clean their cages, after, thankfully, they had been transferred to other cages. I liked the chimpanzees best of all because they were like little kids who followed you around. They could be very mischievous too. They would throw things at you, including droppings and would grab your behind and run away. But they made me laugh so many times during the day, I didn't mind.

It was deep into an afternoon reverie, and I was thinking of Cybele. I guess my expression, my dazed look, told Tiny everything he needed to know to read my mind.

"Hey, lover boy, you are thinking about Cybele again, da? Or did you even stop?"

"I'd like to watch her read fortunes, Tiny. Can I take a few minutes?"

Tiny couldn't deny me. "Okay but you come back soon. Or I make you clean cage with tiger still in it."

I patted one of his meaty arms happily, got cleaned up a bit, slicking back my hair, and found Cybele, now wearing a bandana, a frilly white blouse, low cut, and long, colorful skirt. I didn't want to disturb her so I watched from some distance, among the milling crowd. Tibor was to her other side, attracting potential customers with his guitar playing.

A plump woman, perhaps in her late forties, sat with her right hand being studied by Cybele. I kept one eye out for the Boss while I caught a piece of their conversation. Cybele held her hand and studied it carefully. She pointed out a line in the woman's hand.

"You want to know about love," said Cybele. The woman nodded.

"You want to know," Cybele said, pausing, "because there is someone you are very interested in. The love line in your hand says you have recently had a break in the flow of love in your life."

"Yes," gasped the woman. "That's right. A couple years back, my husband and I ended. I been by myself since then."

"Yes," Cybele confirmed, looking back at her hand. "There is a man but he does not know you care for him."

"What should I do?" asked the woman, her plea so full of hurt and fear.

"Sometimes, you must take a chance," Cybele said, looking at her and gently closing her hand. "I see that he might or might not respond. It is very hard to say. But, you must live, you must take a chance, invite him to something and let fate take its course."

The woman thanked Cybele profusely and got up and went on her way. Cybele immediately looked in my direction, as if she knew I had been there the whole time. I smiled widely and she returned it. Then, she turned and looked in the opposite direction. Her eyes went back to me and widened in concern. She nodded to her right. The Boss was wandering about the grounds. I saw and immediately fled back to the animal cages.

After a long and hard day, it was great to sit with other circus employees in the stands and watch our friends and co-workers perform, making us laugh, ooh and aah with concern for their safety as they worked with ferocious animals and challenged gravity on the trapeze and high wire.

But my favorite performance was one that was in the background, when Cybele, having changed her outfit from fortune teller to horseback rider, wore her blue sequins, which made her even more stunning, as a crude spotlight occasionally glanced off her impossible beauty. Despite the romping and roaring, the crowd noise, the multi-part hysteria, I locked onto Cybele's riding, with every fiber of my being, all other stimulation fading into the background.

After the show, I brought my guitar and walked with her, beyond the circus grounds, off into a grove of trees. We talked about her leaving Romania, her mother's death, my leaving Romeo, my father's death. She was not familiar with rock and roll, for her father, like my father, did not like it and prohibited her from listening in his presence.

Now, I felt like we were two halves that not just her beauty but her life and livelihood fit in a perfect meld with me. I told her so and played softly and gently on the guitar as we sat together under a tree with whispering leaves.

And so it was, for that week, my custom to always wait for Cybele until after the show. It was after a week of walks that we found ourselves under our usual tree at night, she with the lantern, me strumming out another tune, as lush and romantic as I could make it.

She asked me to play a song she could sing and I mentioned some of the most popular rock tunes. Cybele knew none of them. She mentioned some Romanian folk songs and gypsy tunes. I didn't know them but asked her to sing a little of one.

Her voice was smoky and sad, which surprised me, for her singing sounded like it came from the throat of a woman, a female singer who had lived a life of pained experience and now, getting older in life, had the emotional qualities to sing well.

"You sing like you've lived a lot of lives," I said.

"I want to sing with you, Eddie," she said, and the sound of her words made me so hungry for her, I almost threw myself upon her, then and there. But I didn't want to scare her away, not now, not when we both felt so close.

I wracked my brain, trying to think of lyrics we both would know.

"Do you know any American songs?"

She shook her head. "Nothing. I'm sorry."

"We'll find something," I offered hopefully. Then, I had the most peculiar thought.

"Do you celebrate Christmas?" I asked. She nodded. "Do you know Christmas songs?" She sat up straight and grabbed my arm with excitement.

"I know 'White Christmas.' Bing Crosby. 'White Christmas!'"

And she from Romania and I from Romeo, Michigan sat outside under the tree, warmed at night by lantern light, and sang "White Christmas" together, slow, with as much feeling as we could manage, staring at each other, our voices blending easily in the night.

And when we finished, I set the guitar aside and said, "Cybele, I have to tell you that I love you. I know this is sudden and all I'm saying is, when and if you feel that way toward me, I hope you will tell me. Because I am going to follow this circus everywhere it goes, to the four corners of the globe, if necessary, to be near you. I'll clean up filthy animal cages the rest of my life, if I have to, if there's a chance that you could one day feel something for me."

And in my young life, with wild shenanigans and drug-laced lunacy, I had still not experienced anything as breathtaking, as powerful as the kiss of Cybele, of the memory of her telling me how much she wanted me, of the image of her slipping out of her clothes and helping me out of mine and of the electricity in the air as we made love in the grove of trees.

And when we both felt the thrill of ecstasy course through our bodies, felt ourselves strain and buckle and gyrate and call out each other's names and collapse in each other's arms, I felt as if my life could not be happier, that this moment was so pure, so fulfilling, that no matter what happened next, that I had been luckier than anyone I knew.

Perhaps I shouldn't have had that thought. Perhaps thinking I was so lucky brought me bad luck. You can never know, especially with things like fate and luck and timing in life.

But as we lay there, the grass tickling our bodies, the sweat drying on us, listening to the far- off hooting of an owl, Cybele looked into my eyes.

"I haven't even told you your fortune, yet," she laughed a little.

"I already know. I am one of the luckiest people on earth because I have found you and you're perfect and some people wait their whole lives for that person."

She took my right palm and put it on her moist, heated thigh. Then, she brought the lantern over to better study the lines in my hand.

"A long life," she smiled and nodded, tracing the lifeline of my hand. "It will be healthy and you will have good things happen for you throughout."

"For us," I said, enraptured, giddy with adolescent joy and contentment.

And then, Cybele returned her dark, penetrating eyes to my hand and the smile melted away. She traced a line which branched off on my hand.

"This line," she said somberly. "This line is..." Her voice trailed off. I asked her, worried, to tell me the truth.

"This is change, something very soon. Many big changes, taking you to different places for a long time."

"No," I protested, a bit too loudly. "I'm not going anywhere, Cybele. Wherever you go, I'm going too."

She folded my hand and pushed it back away from her flesh and rose, getting dressed. I did the same but continued to ask her what her reading meant. She refused to talk to me and I couldn't stop asking, pleading, upset that she thought I would leave her. Cybele picked up the lantern and finally silenced me by placing a forefinger across my lips and then kissing them.

"Ssssh," Cybele murmured. "I don't doubt you." And she took my hand and we walked

slowly, wordlessly out of the grove of trees that had seemed so impossibly magical such a short time before.

***

Chapter 15

As it happens, many people feel suspicious when things are going very well in their lives. Maybe they think this because it is so rare when you're riding high in life. Maybe it is partly because we feel guilty that others are not doing as wonderfully well as we are at that time. Maybe it is because we simply know that life is generally about blandness and stress and disappointment.

But my life on the road had been about excitement and adventure and following my instinct and utter, pure unpredictability and sensation. It is rather odd to live life like that and the joy and energy of it, as I found out, can make you forget how most people live and the limitations of life.

Cybele and I knew that her father was not about to have me as his son-in-law, even though I would do anything to spend my life with Cybele. And while she was not as strong in her words as I was, her passion came across loud and clear when we would sneak off and make love in the grove near the circus. I felt I did not need to have her say the overly romantic and, I suppose, silly things I said to her all the time when we were alone, things like,

"I've been waiting for this moment, to meet you," and "Cybele, it's a miracle I found you."

Cybele would look at me, in those moments with a combination of sadness and love, and I did not want to mention to her the sadness I saw, only soak myself in the love she gave me, without holding anything back. I was willing to travel with the circus, to hide our love as long as necessary to be with her.

We never brought up again the reading she had done on my palm. I would on occasion watch her from afar, reading the palms of men and women, young and old, and I wondered what it would be like to see something unpleasant in another person's future. Would it be hard to lie, to ignore it, to not warn the person of some imminent and terrible event? Was there some rule among gypsies that you never tell anyone anything bad? I guess it would be bad for business.

But sometimes, it ate away at me, Cybele's moment of panic, after the first time we had made love, seeing my divergent path, worrying that I would not stay there long enough. I did my work, I stayed out of the boss' way, grew closer to Tiny and got along with everyone at the circus. I even played a duet one night with Tibor and put a big smile on his face at the end.

The time flowed so smoothly and the circus was like an extended family for me. We did good business in Oklahoma and it was just about three weeks of hard work and blissful love, before the boss announced to everyone that we were moving on to another location in the panhandle of Texas.

Two days before the end of our run in Oklahoma, Tiny and I were bringing meat back from a neighborhood market for the animals when we noticed a large crowd concentrated in one area. People were shoving and pushing each other, to see whatever it was that was taking place.

But I knew it was not a performance, for it involved both visitors and employees of the circus. There was loud shouting. Tiny, with two huge sacks of raw meat slung over his shoulders, barreled easily through the crowd, cutting a path for me to follow. I shuffled quickly as I dragged the heavy burlap sack of meat behind me, anxious to see what was happening in my traveling family.

And when Tiny finally bumped the last person out of his way with his big belly, he let out a loud, thick guttural sound, a sound all about pain and heartache. I bobbed this way and that until I could get a clear view.

The boss was shouting, as were a couple of other circus employees and a man who claimed he had been cheated out of his money. I looked to the right of them and Tibor and Cybele were both in handcuffs and two Oklahoma policemen, with a squad car, were trying to separate themselves from the circus employees.

"No!" I screamed and fought my way to Cybele. "You can't!"

"Were you in on this?" asked the man, enraged, looking at me. Then, he turned to one of the policemen. "I think he was their accomplice!"

I put my arms around Cybele, demanding to know what was going on.

One of the policemen said, "Fleecing people out of their hard-earned money is a crime. It may not be where you people were born but it is in the state of Oklahoma. These people are going to jail. And you are too if you don't get out of the way."

"You can't take them!" I roared, ready to gouge at the eyes of the police, of the man who had filed the charge, of anyone who tried to take away Tibor and the love of my life.

And had either of the policemen tried to pry me away from her, I am sure I would have lashed out with all the strength in my teenaged body. I would have gone to jail for her. I would have paid any price.

But the thing that stopped me was the only thing that could have stopped me.

Cybele, with silent tears, put one hand over my heart. I pressed her hand closer to me. Then, she took my hand, the one that she had peered so deeply into, and opened it. She glanced down at it and then back at me.

"We're going different ways, Eddie."

"No," I insisted. "I'll find out where you are and we'll get you out, somehow."

"Don't follow," Cybele said softly. "Your path is different."

The policemen, Tibor, everyone seemed to melt away in the moment. She drew my face to hers and kissed me tenderly, and despite the moistness of her eyes, they were not entirely sad. There was a glimmer of kindness and appreciation in them.

"I don't doubt you," she said again, and then she and Tibor were escorted to the squad car.

I followed them, stunned, as if I was going to get in with them. But the doors were slammed closed with resounding thuds and as they drove away, I felt two bags of meat hit the dust and two big, clammy hands settle, surprisingly gently, on my now trembling shoulders.

"Come," said Tiny quietly. "We drop off the meat. And then we get drunk. So drunk, we cannot feel our bones, our teeth. Especially, our hearts."

I sat in the dusk with him, drinking cooking sherry he had gotten from the cook for the circus and we drank and the only sounds for a long time were the crickets and my sniffling.

"Is a terrible thing," Tiny said, finally speaking, "to have your heart break. But is even worse if you never love so much to have heartbreak."

"I can't understand this," I said. "I can't believe this. I can't go on. I don't want to live without her."

"Ah, Eddie," Tiny said. "You love the beautiful gypsy Cybele. Your dream come true, then ended, poof, like that. Is terrible, terrible."

Tiny had drunk much more than me, being a lot bigger, but he was getting fairly sloshed himself, and his Russian accent was getting harder and harder to understand. He mumbled some things and I think some were in his Pidgin English and some in

Russian. Finally, I understood the last phrase, "Tomorrow, we go to Texas."

"Not me," I said, lying down but not about to fall asleep for a long, long time.

"Where you go?" Tiny asked, concerned.

"I don't know," I said, cradling my guitar case, as if it were a security blanket. "But I can't work one more day in the circus. Not now."

The next morning, Tiny accompanied me into the boss' tent. I told him I was quitting, that I appreciated his hiring me but I was too upset to continue traveling with them. The boss, who had been sharp, brutal, all business, every time I had seen or interacted with him, merely nodded. He opened a metal box and took out some bills and handed them to me.

"There, that's two extra weeks."

"Thanks," I mumbled. "Sorry, I just have to go."

And the boss truly surprised me then, for he showed the only vulnerability I ever saw in the next moment. "I like traveling, kid. I like the circus, the noise, the people who watch, the people who perform. I had my heart broken a lot of times. The circus never broke my heart. In fact, it mended it. You did a good job for us, kid. Anything else you need from us?"

I looked at him. I saw in his eyes a tough guy who had cried a long time ago over lost love. It erased everything else I had thought of him. "Just a ride to the highway, please."

Tiny knew his cue. “Boss, I drive him to highway, okay?”

“Sure, Tiny, sure.”

I shook the boss’ hand and Tiny and I took the same truck that had picked me up and brought me into their world and drove me to the highway so that I could leave it. Tiny drove me to a highway onramp, stopped the truck and left the engine idling.

“Maybe Tiny will see you in West, da?”

“Da,” I answered. “You’re a good friend and I won’t forget you.”

“Remember something for me, Eddie.”

I had opened the passenger side door and was ready to step out. I looked into his doughy face, his wide features which never seemed to show anger or fear or anything but bemused detachment.

“I tell you, Russian people have hearts broken a lot. The way they can live with dot, they respect sadness. Is part of life. You cannot pretend is not dere. Sadness, you make a partner in life.”

“I’m sad to be leaving and happy to have met you,” I said

“Dot’s right!” Tiny smiled widely and I slammed the door and set myself up to hitchhike as the circus truck ground gears, sent out a puff of smoke and chugged away.

It was a blessing in many ways that I did not wait long. An extended stay by the side of the highway would only have increased the sadness, whether I had made the sadness my partner or not, in leaving Oklahoma and the circus, Tiny and Cybele.

But as luck would have it, I stood there with my thumb out for only about forty minutes. There was a lulling roar of cars and trucks zooming by, none taking a chance on the young, long-haired, sad-eyed vagabond with the guitar and backpack, with no longing in his eyes, only the expression of vacancy.

Amid that continuous noise, came a high whine, like a distant, speeding bullet. It got my attention, because my musician ears had not heard the sound out there on the onramp. The sound materialized into the form of a motorcycle. It was gaining speed, now seen darting between two slower moving cars, building up to blasting onto the highway. But the driver of the bike turned his head ever so slightly as he zoomed by and again, it was a sound that captured me, the sound of the bike's engine decelerating, the brakes grabbing, the gravel spitting as the tires dug into the side of the road.

I saw he had come to a full stop, a few hundred feet ahead of me. He was not looking back but I was not about to hesitate. I ran as best as I could with my gear and as I got closer, I noticed he had an enormous load of belongings piled on his bike, taking up the back seat, strapped to the frame with bungee cords. I wondered if he was going to pick me up or just ask for directions.

When I stopped in front of him, I was surprised when he said, "Climb aboard," to which I replied there was no place to climb aboard.

He lifted up his dirt encrusted aviation goggles, and straightened his dirty bandana and smiled as he looked back at his bike. Two lower front teeth stuck out like a dental pitchfork as he evaluated his situation.

"Oh yeah. Hmmm, let me clear you a spot on the limo." He started to rearrange all the things on his bike. I hoped he would not get frustrated with his attempted rearranging and just take off, so I silently stood there, while he mumbled to himself, "Let's see, this could go there. Nope. That don't work. How about, mmm, not going to happen."

He did finally make room for everything. I kept my backpack on and cradled my guitar case on my lap, holding on tenuously to the frame of the bike for stability.

"You on?" he asked and before I could answer, he lurched forward, gaining speed on the highway. The rush of air pushed my head backwards a little but despite the blood pulsing through my body, I crouched down a bit behind him and the feeling of wind whipping my hair was a delicious sensation. I hadn't even asked him where he was going. He hadn't asked me. And it seemed neither one of us cared, for now.

I couldn't see much on the first leg of our journey, not only due to my hair lacerating my face and obscuring my view but due to the biker's buckskin cap, complete with raccoon tail which kept wagging in my face whenever my hair allowed me a view of the world zipping by. Underneath the coonskin cap was an aviator's leather helmet which went along with his matching goggles.

It was about an hour into the ride when the motorcycle pulled up at one of those roadside lunch places that is as much a piece of the landscape as any road sign or road kill. The long, shiny trailer with an awning coming down from the top had plenty of customers and he stopped the bike between two cars, had the stand in place and strode in ahead of me, confident I would catch up eventually.

Once seated at the counter, he never took off his coonskin cap or leather helmet, and he just rolled his goggles up on top of his head. When I sat down, he whirled his seat around, shoved his hand and proclaimed, "Freddie Bartholomew Hornblaster the third, but everyone that knows me calls me Blaster. Pleased to make your acquaintance."

He was from New Jersey and told me he was eventually heading to San Francisco. I got excited and started to tell him about Johnny and The Caretakers but didn't get very far, even when his tuna fish sandwich and milk arrived. He continued with food and drink in his mouth.

"Haight-Ashbury in Frisco. Man, this dude told me about it in Ohio. There's a girl for every guy, and sometimes two. They are all into the love thing, man, and they share everything. I mean everything, man." He poked me in the ribs when he made the last declaration, as if I needed the physical pain to get all the implications.

"But first I'm going to this way out commune in Arizona," Blaster went on, somehow enunciating with a pickle shoved into his mouth. "Over there, you don't even need any money, man. All you have to do is pitch in and help with all the chores and stuff. Doesn't it sound just like heaven on earth, man?"

Before I could manage a response, he was off and running again, so I continued with my apple pie and coffee, occasionally nodding or making a grunt of understanding.

"You see with me, it's all metaphysics, man. Everything moves with the laws of nature and there is an energy that is all one. We are, the motorcycle, this diner, that waitress, we're all connected to this greater energy, and some people realize it, but most don't, so they just go moping along, like that waitress. She doesn't know that everything is connected to her." I looked at the waitress, in her fifties with bleached blonde hair, too much makeup and steely eyes. She did not seem to be a conduit to the entire universe, from what I could see. "It all runs through her," Blaster narrated, as I studied her. "She doesn't want to receive it, or she does but she suppresses it. You dig it, man?"

I wasn't exactly clear on his concept so I thought I'd move on to slightly more familiar ground. "This, this commune you mentioned. Is it like a nudist colony or something?"

"A nudist colony?" he shouted and he began laughing, although it seemed like a choking noise more than laughter. "A nudist colony?" Then he actually fell off of his stool and was writhing around on the floor, laughing his peculiar laugh. Everyone was staring at us and the waitress who should have been connecting to all the energy came over to see what the problem was.

"Is your friend some kind of epileptic or something? Does he need help?"

I paid the bill and headed outside as Blaster stood up and headed outside, still chuckling, repeating "Nudist Colony.

That's a good one."

Blaster pulled into the barn on the vast desert property identified with a wooden sign, which appeared to be painted by children, which read "Cosmos Ranch." Immediately, we were surrounded by all kinds of people, in various stages of dress, from cover-alls to nothing at all. I began to wonder why Blaster had so laughed at my comment about it being a nudist colony.

You could tell from the start that these folks, who were living on this "commune," as it was called, were going to make your stay as comfortable as possible. As soon as Blaster mentioned the name of the guy from Ohio, they quickly fixed both of us up with sleeping accommodations, and gave us a nice lunch of rice and beans. There were no real leaders here as far as I could tell, although a red-haired guy in his early thirties, Kurt, spoke on behalf of all of Cosmos Ranch, welcoming us. Everybody seemed to be busy doing assigned tasks, cleaning, building, cooking, weaving, taking care of children. No one looked to be running out of things to do. We walked around with two escorts, Kurt and this lovely girl, Sarah. They looked to be very healthy and quite tan. They alternated, explaining to us that they combined a rigid work schedule with meditation and recreation at night. My thoughts quickly wandered as to what type of recreation would be in store.

As we were heading back to main house, Blaster was firing questions at Kurt, who was trying to keep up with his unceasing verbiage. Sarah and I watched them walking ahead of us, and then looked at each other at the same moment and smiled together, shyly. I had noticed that there was a group of folks gathered around a huge tub of some kind. I asked her what was happening.

Sarah informed me, "They're making wine over there. We have a small vineyard and we take the grapes and make our own."

This intrigued me so much that I asked if I could join in on the festivities. When we got to the vat, I realized that the people were unclothed, giggling and stamping on grapes, sometimes holding onto each other for support. Sarah introduced me as a new arrival and when they all called out to have us join them, Sarah didn't even look at me for a reaction. She removed her long skirt and peasant blouse, revealing her glowing, fit body, and was helped into the black-green muck being stamped underfoot.

Since I already had some experience with group nudity, although admittedly not dedicated to so useful a task, I quickly got out of my clothes, and Sarah and the others welcomed me in by hurling handfuls of crushed grapes at my body.

I felt a little light-headed, with the smashing of grapes, the sun beating down on me, the bronzed bodies gyrating, the laughter and relaxation of it. I stopped and held onto the edge of the vat to steady myself. Sarah immediately came over and put her arms on me, looking at me inquiringly. Her breasts were brushing against me and I suddenly was dealing with dizziness and the growing hardness I did not want to feel at that moment between my legs. I assured her I was okay.

But Sarah, being very solicitous, told the others I had traveled a long way and needed to rest. She insisted we continue the tour and we carried our clothes, still naked, as the other grape-covered members of the commune called out in a friendly manner, welcoming me again and advising me to take a nap.

As it was in any other spot at the Cosmos Ranch, the main house was a beehive of activity. Sarah toured me through and we ended up with a group of women in the kitchen preparing the meal for dinner. Sarah asked if I would help her knead the bread dough, which was her assigned task before dinner and I agreed. We washed the grape pulp off our hands and arms and she patiently explained to me all the details of bread kneading.

I was amazed at the way that Sarah so easily performed this task without any kind of break in her motion. I had already taken two breaks, in just fifteen minutes. She laughed and told me "You'll get stronger and better at it, the more you do it."

Now the late afternoon sun was pouring in through the window of the kitchen and it caught Sarah lovingly, outlining her body through the thin, cotton blouse with colorful embroidery. I watched her, so happy to be doing something so simple, humming as she hypnotized me with the strong, rapid motions of her arms.

Then, she looked up at me, suddenly and said, "Penny for your thoughts."

I suppose I was tired or just overwhelmed by the conglomeration of adventure and so, without thinking, without trying to censor myself, I said, "Sarah. I'm a musician and I write songs about a lot of different things. But watching you make the bread dough, I've just seen a new side of beauty."

She stopped kneading and smiled at me, put it aside and took my hand. "Come on, Eddie, we have to get cleaned up before dinner."

"Well, I think that's great," I replied, "but what about the bread?"

"Oh, don't worry about the bread. We're actually making surplus bread. We always have at least a week's worth." Sarah led me out of the kitchen. "You are a good soul, Eddie," she said, in a breathy voice and led me to the showers.

When we got there, I expected separate rooms for men and women, which, of course, was absurd, given what I had already seen of the Cosmos Ranch. A man finished showering, said hello to Sarah and made his way off to his room, a towel wrapped around him.

Sarah and I walked into the concrete floored shower area and removed our clothes, already stained purple here and there. She turned on the water, grabbed a bar of chamomile soap and got under the water, gasping with pleasure. I could only watch, fascinated.

"What are you waiting for?" she called and motioned to me.

I stepped under the warm jet of water and she began to soap me, first my back, which I could not reach, then my front, which I could have. She pressed against me and instinctively, our mouths came together and she continued to soap me, the suds surrounding my hard male excitement. She would increase the speed and when she sensed my breathing becoming faster, she would slow and stop.

Sarah turned her back to me and put her hands on the wall. “Your turn. I need you to wash me.”

I knew how to follow directions as good as anyone, and I gently played with her, using both the soap and the tips of my fingers as I massaged her. Just as she started to tense up, I slowed and stopped, as she had done.

Sarah turned, her wet hair flying, and looked at me briefly. “No,” she murmured, “I want you to keep going. Don’t stop.” And so, trying to show my appreciation to my guide, I placed my manhood between her legs and used the soap and my fingers to explore her, enjoying the cascade of water, the *shish* sound of soap on flesh and Sarah’s buckling, trembling orgasm, which required me to hold her so that she did not fall to the hard floor.

After she recuperated, I guided myself into her sudsy interior and we made love, the steam washing us clean, my running my fingers through her hair and our both crying out, as our voices bounced off the walls.

Back in Sarah’s room, filled with nothing more than a mattress, some flowers, books and papers, we lay together, our bodies drying. I lay my head in Sarah’s lap, nuzzling her femininity. She sighed and brushed my still wet hair with her fingers.

Finally, she got up and brought back a book that was published by the University of California, titled "The Teachings of Don Juan: A Yaqui Way of Knowledge." I mispronounced Yaqui as "Yah-kwee" and she laughed and told me that Carlos Castaneda, the author, had taught at UC Berkeley, where she had attended until recently.

"Why did you leave?" I asked.

"There was something called the Free Speech Movement, trying to let us express more what we wanted to do with our schooling. But the police came in and there was violence and I just decided to learn about life in other ways."

Sarah brushed a wet strand of hair out of her eyes and turned to a section of the book.

"Here," she pointed. "Castaneda talks about Don Juan using psychedelics to experience non-reality, to give us greater awareness. This is a section about one's power spot."

"Power spot?"

"Yes, the Indians believed that being in a specific position, and attuned to the spirit world, you can gain the most insight." She gave me the book again. "I want you to read this."

"Thank you," I said. "But I think I have already found my power spot." I kissed her deeply. She giggled.

"No, I really want you to read it."

"I will," I promised.

"Okay," she said, double-checking with a long look. "Now let's get dressed. It's time for the evening meal."

The dinner that night was as expected a very communal affair. Everyone had specific duties assigned to them. Kurt, who had welcomed us before, told the group at the long wooden tables, surrounding by about thirty people, sitting on pillows, that Blaster and I had joined them and would be given work to do for as long as we wished to stay.

Instead of a formal prayer, there was a chant that was performed by the group. Two of the people had little cymbals on their fingers that chimed along with the chant. There was the smell of incense floating through the room, and then it was time to eat.

The food was laid across the tables in pots and all was passed along the group. Sarah sat next to me and during the meal, I felt I wanted to touch her the whole time, brushing my leg against hers, asking her to pass me something and laying my hand on her arm. I found myself wishing that Sarah and I could eat alone together in her room, but I guess that was the wrong kind of attitude for someone planning to live in a commune.

Blaster had women on either side of him, and he was thrilled to turn to one and then the other and tell them of some of his exploits on the road. The food was bland but I didn't mind, so happy to be there, to have met Sarah instantly.

After dinner, we went to an area that was set up for a bonfire pit, a little walk from the main house. I was pretty tired from my day's activity and sat with Sarah as I strummed my guitar. Another member of the commune came over and a group sang songs around the crackling, jumping flames.

Kurt came over after an hour and said it was time for bed, which surprised me, for I figured people were free to spend their evenings as they wished.

He caught my surprised look. "We like to get to bed by a certain hour here," he explained. "It's a long day when you get up early. Let me show you and Blaster to your rooms."

Mine was even simpler than Sarah's, with no books but the Castaneda I had been given, nothing on the bare walls, and the omnipresent mattress, which was lumpier than the one Sarah had. I read the book for a while, with the illumination of a kerosene lamp. But I found myself unable to get Sarah out of my mind. I took the lamp and quietly sneaked down the hall to her room and carefully opened the door.

She was lying in bed, already asleep. The light of the lamp shone on her angelic face. I just watched her for a long while, sitting on the edge of her mattress. Finally, ever so slowly, she stirred awake.

"What are you doing here?" she smiled and asked sleepily.

"I can't sleep," I admitted. "I want to stay with you."

"I'm all worn out," Sarah said.

"I know. I just want to lie next to you. To sleep beside you."

“Oh, I don’t know–“she began but my look of need did not allow her to finish her sentence.

“Please, Sarah. I just want to be next to you.”

She pulled back the covers and I got in next to her, spooning her, wrapping my arms around her body. “But you have to leave before everybody gets up,” she whispered, her back to me.

“I promise,” I said, turning out the lamp and grabbing her tightly.

Chapter 16

I learned a great many things at the Cosmos Ranch, including how to knead bread, like Sarah, expertly, without taking any breaks. I did repairs on the buildings, which included painting, sanding, fixing holes and plastering. I was among those who planted and harvested the crops which helped feed us all.

What we did not grow on the commune, we would obtain in trade from a farmer's market as barter, so that a wide variety of food was available and plentiful. As beautiful and peaceful as it was at the ranch, I started to feel a sense of unease. Sarah insisted we be secretive about our relationship, which made me think she was, in some way, ashamed of me or perhaps, was involved with someone else.

The work was hard and sometimes, at the end of the day, I felt like I wanted to go to a bar, to hear music, other than the random plucking of one of the Cosmos Ranch hands, none of whom could really play well. I wondered, also, what was happening in the rest of the country, and, to some extent, the rest of the world, for there were no newspapers and no television at the Ranch.

I asked Sarah about this and she said that mass media, such as newspapers, magazines and television manipulated the thought of the masses and were not to be trusted. I responded to this by insisting that a complete withdrawal from information did not educate us either but she would not waver, saying reading books was the best education and that considering the war in Vietnam and the civil rights problems that hounded the country, there was not much worth hearing about.

But there weren't even radios to listen to stations in Phoenix or Flagstaff or Tucson and I knew that there was rock and roll being made and being played and I wanted to at least hear it, if I was not going to perform it.

One night, I asked Sarah, after the dinner hour, if Kurt was in charge of the Ranch.

"No one is in charge, really," she said. "He helps organize, but it takes all of us to make this work."

"I know," I said, getting a little annoyed at her Cosmos public relations, "but if I wanted to ask about, say, bringing some radios down here, who would I talk to?"

"We don't listen to radios," she said and I rolled my eyes, since her stating the obvious did not help answer my question.

"It's okay," I said. "I'll just have a talk with Kurt. Can I spend the night with you?"

"Not tonight," she said without explanation and went off to do some chore or just went off to avoid discussing being with me.

Feeling very frustrated, I went to Kurt's room in the big house, a room I had never entered before, and immediately upon knocking, I heard talking and laughing. I opened the door, without hearing anyone say enter. That was my first mistake.

"Did I say you could come in?" asked Kurt.

I looked at him, lying on his bed, which was queen sized, not the smaller mattresses that most rooms had. He had some furniture, mirrors and paintings that were made by members of the Ranch. In fact, he had more decor than all the rooms I had been in. And lying on either side of him were two girls, who shared a pipe of marijuana.

"Sorry, I heard talking and thought it would be okay–"

"What is it you want?" Kurt asked, obviously not in the mood to discuss much of anything.

I asked him about the radios, told him how much I missed the music and that it would be a welcome addition to the Ranch. We could sing to songs on the radio and keep up our spirits. Again, I had made a huge error.

"You're new here," Kurt said, "and you may not understand that this collective does not need to keep its spirit up with outside influences from a culture that is sick. Radios have music on them. Fine. But they also have newscasts and opinions from people who are antithetical to our growth, people who would convince us that the consumerist values of spending money all the time and ignoring the improvement of society is what being American is all about."

"Look, I just wanted to hear some music. I can buy the radios."

"You are not getting it." Kurt was now standing, his red hair sticking out in different directions, wearing nothing but beads and some boxer shorts. "If you want to stay here, then you have to understand what we represent and how we intend to live."

I looked over at the women, both of whom were also clad only in underwear, neither wearing a top. They looked at me as if I was an unwelcome guest to be barely tolerated.

"Tell you what," I said, getting the feeling that I was getting nowhere with Kurt and that the only result if I continued could be real trouble. "We play guitars anyway so I just think a radio for myself would be nice."

"And I'm telling you to forget it." Kurt now stood in front of me and jutted his jaw out, ready to do battle.

"Do I need your permission to buy myself a goddamn radio?" I asked. "I asked Sarah if you were in charge and she said we all run this place. So, I'll just buy a radio in town and play it in my room."

"You're spending a lot of time with Sarah, aren't you?" He looked at me cagily, sizing me up and I had the feeling that my stay at the Cosmos Ranch was about to get a bit more unpleasant. I stormed out of the room and wound up spending the night walking around with a kerosene lamp, looking up at the stars, feeling that I didn't belong anywhere.

After breakfast the next day, I caught Sarah, talking with another girl as they made their way into the fields to pick zucchini. I asked her if I could talk with her a minute and she tried to avoid me by saying she had to go to her work assignment. It was only when the other girl said she would see Sarah out in the field, and then left us, that I could get her alone.

I told Sarah what had happened and she nodded and stood silent.

"Well, what do you think?"

"I think Kurt is the person who holds all this together and you should do as he says."

"Do you think it's right that I shouldn't have a radio? And what business is it of Kurt's that I spend time with you?"

"Kurt," she started, obviously struggling with her words. "Kurt is someone special. You shouldn't question his decisions. He cares about all of us and he makes sure we're protected."

"But how free can you be if some guy makes all the decisions? Is this a democracy?"

"Is America?" she asked. "The poor always fight the wars and the rich get the best justice. This is the best world we can all create, as a group."

I thought about that and then took her in my arms. "Sarah, Sarah, I don't know. All I know is I want to spend more time with you and you keep avoiding me."

She nodded again and then turned to the girl who had been with her, walking in the distance.

"Do you like her? Her name is Annie. You could spend the night with her."

I shook my head, barely comprehending her words. "You're giving me that girl to sleep with? I haven't even met her."

She smiled sweetly and caressed my chest with her hands. "Oh, Eddie, you're so young. Here, everyone does what they want with everyone else."

"But I don't want Annie. I want you."

"Then, you have to be patient. This is a different way of living, here, Eddie. But I think once you get used to it, you'll see it's much better than what they offer us out there." She kissed my cheek and walked away, to do her work in the fields.

I needed to get away and found one of the members was going into town to buy some supplies. I told him I needed to buy some medicine and it was personal and asked if I could tag along. He agreed and we drove a battered, communal pickup truck, with gray primer paint in splotches on it and a loose back bumper, into the nearest town, which wasn't much more populated than the Cosmos Ranch.

While my companion went into a store to buy sundries, purchased with collective money, I went to a pay telephone, dialed the operator and made a collect call to my mother and sister in New Orleans.

My mother was delighted to hear my voice again and I instantly felt bad for having waited so long to tell her where I was and what I was doing.

"Michelle is out right now but I'll tell her everything. So, are you happy there on that ranch? I'll bet the weather is pretty warm there, even for winter."

"It's okay. I'm thinking of maybe heading back on the road and going to San Francisco, check out the music scene, Mom. I don't know, maybe I'll find Johnny up there and see if we're still a band or not."

There was an inhalation of breath that I heard my mother take. I knew her well enough to know it meant the subject of Johnny was something we had to talk more about. But the silence just hung there over the phone line.

"What is it, Mom? It's Johnny. Did something happen–"

"No, no," she quickly reassured me. "It's just that he sent a postcard to you in Romeo and it finally arrived here."

"Great!" I was truly excited. "Can you read it? What did he say?"

She asked me to hold on and got the card. She juggled the phone for a moment. I looked down the street of the small Arizona town, thinking that I was only one state away from California, which good luck in hitching could get me up there in two, perhaps three days.

"Well," my mother said, cheerfully, "the post card certainly is pretty. It's a picture of the Golden Gate Bridge and it's very lovely."

"Mom, please. Read it."

Again, there was a pause. "Eddie, I don't want you to be too disappointed."

"It's bad news?"

"In a way. He writes, 'Eddie, I've failed you, I've failed me and The Caretakers. Now, people in the Haight take care of me. This is the edge. There is nowhere else to go. I'm sorry.' Johnny."

The words sounded so desperate, so unlike the Johnny I had known, at least until the last time I had seen him. His transformation had been a shock and time, it seemed, had not lessened its impact. If he had written to say he was in another band, that he was doing okay, my anger and hurt would have let me release him, give up. But his card, if anything, was a call for help.

"Does he list an address on the card, Mom?"

"No, he mentions the Haight, the Haight-Ashbury, I guess. It's postmarked in San Francisco."

Okay. Mom, I'm going to try and find him. He needs my help."

"Oh, Eddie, please. Please come back. It's your birthday in a couple of weeks. We want to see you again."

"And I want to see you too. But I have to do this, have to find out. I'm worried about him. And his parents will want to know."

"I'll call them, Eddie. You're a good boy. I love you."

"I love you too. And Michelle. I'll call when I get there."

When I got back to the Cosmos Ranch, I found Blaster, who had been digging in the fields with a young girl who wore overalls but no shirt. I excused myself and took him aside.

"Do you believe this place?" Blaster asked me. "Free everything and especially sex."

"Yeah, well that can be a drawback," I replied.

"I don't see how," Blaster chuckled.

"Listen, I need to know something. When you picked me up, you said you were going to the Haight. Well, I have a friend up there in trouble and I'm going as soon as I can."

"Well," said Blaster, chewing on a blade of grass and thinking it over. "I'm not about to leave this place for good. Too much good loving for this guy to leave behind. But if you want a ride to the next town, catch a bus or something, I'm there for you, buddy."

"Thanks, Blaster. Can we do this tomorrow?"

"He must really be in trouble," Blaster guessed.

"He sounds suicidal."

“Okay, I’ll get you up at dawn. That way, I can be back in time for breakfast.”I clapped him on the shoulder and went to dinner.

Afterwards, I played some guitar and sang with some of the members, keeping an eye out for Sarah. She did not show up. I couldn’t leave without saying goodbye. Although they called for me to sing another song, I told them I had to get to bed. I told no one but Blaster about my departure.

When I got to Sarah’s room, I knocked quietly on the door. There was no answer and I carefully opened the door. The room was empty.

I saw someone in the hall and asked if he had seen Sarah but he had not. I figured I could say farewell in the morning. But there was one person I wanted to inform of my departure and I headed over to the room of Kurt.

I knocked on the door. There was no reply. I remembered my last interaction with him, so I pounded on the door with my fist.

“I’m busy,” was the response. “Tomorrow.”

Just the sound of his voice infuriated me. I had nothing to lose. I would be on a bus by the next afternoon. I opened the door, my voice booming even before I saw anything.

“No, tonight!” I strode in and saw Kurt lying on his back, a woman slowly, sensually grinding her pelvis on him, his head turning from side to side in great pleasure.

The woman was Sarah .I stood there until they saw me. Sarah slid off him and curled into a ball, anticipating a confrontation.

"You're not very good with following directions, are you?" Kurt asked and announced. "I don't think you fit in here."

"Well, it looks like you and I agree on something," I said. I turned to Sarah, who did not look at all guilty but sad, intuiting this would be the last time she would see me.

"Sarah, I want you to know how nice it was to be with you, to get to know you."

"Okay, kid," Kurt interrupted, "save your bourgeois sentimentality for another time and get out of my room."

"And I want ***you*** to know," I said, the blood rushing to my throat, "that your little kingdom here isn't that free. You have more belongings than everyone else. You tell them how to think by not letting them form their own opinions about the outside world."

"Get the fuck out of my room!" screamed Kurt.

"You can either shut up and let me finish talking or get out of that bed and try and make me stop."

Kurt looked at Sarah, furious at being humiliated in front of another member of the Ranch. He grabbed a statue of the Buddha, an odd choice, considering the peace and wisdom it represented, and hurled it at me. I ducked and it shattered against a concrete wall.

He rushed me, naked, and I waited, stood my ground and when his arms stretched out to grab me, I planted a kick to his chest and sent him staggering backward and right back into bed.

Sarah screeched and then looked at me with fear.

"That's your leader. He pretends everyone has a say but if you express another opinion, you see what happens. Good luck with your search for the truth."

I walked out and slammed the door. Some members of the Ranch were standing in the hall, having heard the noise.

"What's going on?" someone asked.

I stood there, looking at them, for a moment.

"Kurt says you're all a bunch of mindless sheep and that's the way he likes it."

I stormed back to my room to try and sleep, but I couldn't.

***

Blaster was good to his word, dropping me off at a bus station. I didn't try and convince him to leave the Cosmos Ranch. If it felt right for him, then I couldn't talk him out of being happy. I slept most of the bus trip and when we arrived at the Greyhound Bus Station in downtown San Francisco, it was dark and the characters that inhabited the shadows of Seventh Street did not exactly boost my energy or confidence. I asked around and found out which Market Street bus to take to the Haight.

When I got off, the street was bathed in pale street lights and a misty fog. I wandered down the street, nodding hello to the young people I saw, even in the cool, damp evening, congregating here and there in front of, as well as in, the stores and establishments of Haight Street.

I noticed a place called The Psychedelic Shop, one address from the corner of Haight and Ashbury. The hand painted sign, with swirling letters, had, upon close study, some dripped paint which created small runs under the letters. I saw two guys and a girl out in front, talking. The music I heard from inside was from a band I had never heard before, but it included a sitar and a terrific fuzz tone guitar solo and it did a lot to lift my spirits. I had been without rock music for so long and now, I was in the epicenter of a movement, with the opportunity to recreate my life. I sniffed the air from the partially open door and the incense which burned inside, the unique sounds from their record player, soothed me. I closed my eyes a few seconds.

"You a musician?" one of them asked, noticing the guitar, and without waiting for the reply, "You got a band?"

"I just got here. Looking for my lead singer who got here before me. Any of you meet a guy in the last couple months named Johnny Janowski? He plays drums and sings."

They shook their heads no.

"What's the name of your band?" the girl asked.

"The Caretakers," I said.

"What a trip," said the guy who had first spoken. "I think I heard your album a couple days ago inside here. Come on." He led me and the others inside The Psychedelic Shop and among the posters and paraphernalia and clothes and jewelry, he asked my name and then announced me to the man behind the counter.

The counter man dug into a stack of opened records and after a brief search, found our record and put it on, rather loud, and it filled The Psychedelic Shop. We stood around and listened and after a few bars, their heads nodded slightly, indicating they liked the beat. The counter man turned the record down to allow for human interaction. "Good stuff," he said and went about his business.

But Tomas, the dark-skinned guy who had recognized my band name, Deirdre, his red-haired, pale-skinned girlfriend and the third in their group, who went by the name Scooter and generally said little but agreed with everything everyone said, were very enthusiastic.

"So, you play guitar?" Deirdre asked.

"Lead. And write songs."

"Very cool," said Tomas.

"Yeah, totally cool," agreed Scooter.

"Where you staying?" asked Tomas.

"I don't have a place. But I have some money, if you know of a place."

Deirdre looked at Tomas and then at me. "Lead guitarist of The Caretakers comes out here to hook up with his singer. We have to show him some hometown pride. Let's let him stay at our place for a while."

"Sure," agreed Tomas and when I offered to pay him for lodgings, he forced my hand, with some crumpled bills in it, back into my jeans pocket. "Don't worry about that. We'd like to hear the rest of the album, though."

I turned to the counter man and told him I wanted to buy it. He said he couldn't sell it, since it was already opened but when he saw the look on our four faces, he smiled, sheepishly, handed me the album and said, "Welcome to the Haight."

I shook his hand, Scooter headed another direction and we walked up Cole Street to their apartment. Their furnishings were beat up, covered with patches, caftans and pillows, but the flat had a comfortable and inviting feel to it. They sat me down at their kitchen table and gave me a bowl of granola, a slice of ham on multi-grain bread, a big glass of milk and some chocolate chip cookies with chopped walnuts and dates that were still soft from when Deirdre had baked them that afternoon.

In between mouthfuls of food, and with The Caretakers playing in the background, I told them of many of my exploits, with punctuations of "Cool" and "Weird" and "Bummer" and

"Whoa!" the only interruptions to the long flow of images and events that came pouring from me.The joint that Tomas passed also helped loosen my tongue and after we had played our album twice through, on Deirdre's suggestion, they went into their collection of music.

"Put on The Dead," Tomas called out and Deirdre turned up the volume on the first album from The Grateful Dead.

"This is my favorite," Deirdre called back, just before dropping the needle on a certain cut. "It's called 'The Golden Road to Unlimited Devotion."

I repeated the title a couple times, as if it was a mantra and it steered me back to Johnny, to the hopes of recreating our band despite the trauma in Hollywood. After an album of the Dead and more monologue from me, we all decided it was time for bed. I told them I had a sleeping bag but they insisted, even with two other roommates in their three bedroom apartment, it was no problem to have me on the living room couch as long as I wanted.

Tomas shook my hand, grabbing it in that way in which the thumbs interlock. "Welcome to our home, brother," he said. "Dee will get you fixed up with some sheets and blankets. And we'll help you find Johnny. You get some rest."

He wandered off, down the long hallway, entering their bedroom. Deirdre opened the door of a hall closet as I stood in the bay window of their living room, staring out down the street at the San Francisco night, feeling the exhaustion of my journey setting in, letting the kindness of these people wash over me.

"Here you go," Deirdre said warmly but she stopped short as I turned to look at her. "What's wrong?" she asked, moving toward me, setting the bedding down on the couch.

I wiped the tears from my eyes. "It's okay," I said softly. "You people are so nice. And so much has happened. I'm feeling so many things at once. I just couldn't contain it all."

She squeezed my hand. "Don't worry. We're happy to have you. And we're looking forward to seeing The Caretakers, live."

I tried to say thank you and all that came out was a light hiss of air. She read my lips, smiled and walked down the hallway toward her bedroom.

Chapter 17

Tomas and Deirdre went far beyond what I would have asked of them. They let me stay on their sofa, they fed me and only when I absolutely insisted would they take any of my money, to go toward their expenses.

In fact, even though I did not have work and I didn't find a lot of people who did, it was amazing the level at which people helped each other. Deirdre and Tomas asked their other friends to look for Johnny and in the meantime, they did find me a couple of gigs, playing guitar at coffeehouses, where I would pass the hat after.

I found a lot of the musicians felt they had permission to experiment, to try new things without the fear of failure. I was fascinated by one group, H.P. Lovecraft, named after the famous horror writer, a band who had recently arrived in San Francisco from Chicago. We went to see them perform with Tomas and Deirdre's roommate Shauna, who had the only full-time job in the household, working as a secretary in the financial district, which allowed her to buy grass and psychedelics in quantity for the weekends.

When we saw H.P. Lovecraft, it made me think how this was a great place to restart a musical career with Johnny, if I could only find him. The group had two lead singers, one who was trained in folk and the other in operatic singing. They mixed folk, rock, psychedelia, classical, jazz and pop in a remarkable way.

After their set, I told one of the singers how much I enjoyed their work and how Keats had influenced my own songwriting. He immediately talked about how he had studied the Romantics in college and then invited Tomas, Deirdre, Shauna and me to join them and their friends. We pushed a couple tables together and all sat around, talking well into the night about music, politics, San Francisco, our hopes for the year 1967. One of the singers mentioned they had a record deal and were going into a studio to record later that month, which then brought a new round of drinks and toasts to their success.

The bus dropped us off on Haight after the show and as we all tumbled out onto the street, the January rain had started to fall in earnest. Deirdre squealed and laughed, grabbed Tomas by the arm, looked back and shouted at Shauna and me, "We're going to run for it!" They disappeared up the street, running.

I took off my jacket and draped it over Shauna's and my head. She thanked me and put her arm around me, to stay close, to keep dry. We walked in silence, listening only to the sounds of rain and tires whooshing through the accumulated water on the street.

"That was such a great evening," Shauna said, tucking a wet strand of her long blonde hair back under the protection of my jacket. "It's great that you're a musician and could talk to them about music like that."

I merely nodded and Shauna studied my face.

"You're upset about something. What's bumming you?"

"I want to be in a group again. I feel like I live next door to the greatest party that has ever been thrown and I can't get an invitation."

"You'll find Johnny."

"What if I don't? What if I never find him?"

"I guess you'll start your own group, right?"

I stopped walking, looked up into the sky and let the rain pound down on my face. Then, I resumed walking and put my arm around Shauna.

"I'm sorry I sound so miserable. I'm very lucky to be here, to have met you and Tomas and Deirdre. I guess I'm tired and I want things to fall into place and they won't. I can't make life snap into place, I know that, but I'm just trying to get some sense of things. Maybe I wouldn't feel so bad if it wasn't my birthday tomorrow."

We had arrived in front of the stairs to the flat on Cole Street. Shauna did not let go of me.

"Why didn't you tell us?"

"You've all done a lot already for me."

Shauna pulled my face to hers and gently brushed her lips across mine as the jacket covered our already soaking heads from the torrent above that would not stop. We pressed our wet bodies against each other and the sliding of our mouths became urgent pressing, tongues, lips, darting, teasing. It took the sound of thunder to stop us. We both laughed.

"Come on inside," Shauna said. "I have a birthday present for you, in my bedroom."

The house was quiet when we entered and Shauna brought me, by the hand, into her room. She gave me a towel and told me to get out of my wet clothes and into her bed. I did as I was told. I was about to get a present and I didn't want to seem ungrateful.

When she finally came out of the bathroom, her hair was still damp but its elongated curls were beautiful. The Chinese kimono she wore was red with black characters from that language.

"What does the robe say?" I asked.

"It's Chinese. It says, 'Lie on your stomach so I can massage you with some oil.'"

Again, I didn't want to challenge her authority. She worked her oiled fingers into the muscles of my neck and back.

"Those clothes are going to take a while to dry," she said.

"I know. And I only have one other pair of pants and they're dirty."

"Tomorrow," Shauna said, "you have to go to The Diggers. They give out free food and clothing. You'll find them in the Panhandle." She explained the former as a benevolent group, based on an old English agrarian social movement, which provided free aid to those who were neediest. She explained the latter as the strip of park that was bordered by Oak and Fell Streets, where so many free concerts and events were held.

"Thank you," I said. "You're really so nice. I don't now how to thank you."

I heard her say "Roll over." As I did, I saw her kneel on the bed, and drop the kimono, revealing her body to me. "I think you do know how to say thank you," Shauna said in a husky voice as she lowered her body to mine. "And I think right now is the time."

***

I walked down to the Panhandle in the morning, during which the winter sun was hidden behind a bank of thick clouds and the pavement and grass were still slick. I thought about how much I was beginning to feel at home in San Francisco, even though I had no band, no home, no source of income.

I didn't even have a girlfriend in Shauna. She had made it clear in the morning, as I lay tucked under her still warm sheets and she dressed for work that she had had a wonderful time but she did have a guy she was regularly seeing. She asked, worried, if it was all right if we didn't make our liaison an exclusive thing but one which we entered into when both of us felt it was right.

If Deirdre and Tomas caught on that my status as a houseguest had changed, they did not mention it as we went about our ways in the flat in the morning. I couldn't have asked for more gracious hosts, but I knew I would eventually need a place where I paid rent, and therefore could invite people over when I felt like it and, depending upon the location, jam with other musicians, and feel fully human again.

As I crossed Oak Street, at Masonic, dodging the cars zooming one way toward their appointments, I could already see a crowd gathered. The Diggers had set up a twelve foot high, yellow frame, leaning against a tree, to help people spot them. Near the three-sided frame, I saw some tables set up and people, not only young but older, some living in the Haight, some vagrants with no home, being served food.

There was also a box with clothes and I began rummaging through it.

"Hope you can find something good," said a man with glasses and floppy blonde hair and mustache.

"Anything I find will be good," I answered. "They don't have these kinds of things in Romeo, Michigan."

We talked a bit and once again, I felt I had found a kindred spirit. He was poet, like me, and a prose writer, too. I explained my search for Johnny and my desire to find a band for myself.

"There are a lot of lost Johnny's in the Haight," he nodded. "That's why The Diggers is here. This movement has to take care of its own. The government won't support us. We have to do it. That's why we have Huckleberry's for Runaways. That's why we have our Free Store over on Frederick and Stanyan. Have you been there?"

"No. Thanks for telling me. What about that frame? Is that so people know you're here?"

The long-haired blonde man looked at it and smiled. "That's our Free Frame of Reference. If you look through it, say from this side, you'd see the park and the people. But if you stood on the other side, you'd be looking at the traffic on Oak Street. Exhaust. People stuck in their cars. You can move that frame of reference anywhere. And there is always the other side to look through."

I nodded. "Like they say. 'There are two sides to every story.'"

"At the very least!" he said with loud pleasure. "Look, take you and Johnny. Maybe you find him and you get your group together again. And it's better than ever. Or it falls apart. Because you've grown apart. Or, let's say you don't find Johnny. He's not here anymore. You're sad about that and you quit music. Or, one day, you find another guy who's not like Johnny but you get to develop even more as a musician with him and form a new group that lets you grow even more. You see what I mean about the Free Frame of Reference?"

I did, even though I was busy putting on a faded denim shirt which was only slightly long in the sleeves and fit me quite well across the shoulders.

"Turn around," the friendly Digger advised and I did. "It looks good. Keep it. What else do you need?"

"I don't know. Another pair of pants, maybe. Something in a size twenty-eight waist."

"I think we can help you there, too." We both rummaged through the box.

"Where do you get all this stuff?" I asked.

"Dumpsters. Private homes. The food comes from supermarkets which throw out a lot of perfectly edible food at the end of the day."

I lifted out a pair of purple bell bottoms, which had a tag inside indicating they were my size.

I held them up against me.

"I'm not used to wearing such bright colors," I admitted.

The Digger smiled and pointed to the yellow frame. "Remember what I said about the Free Frame of Reference?"

I held the purple pants out, as if they were being worn by the Digger. I squinted. "Of course, wearing a new style of clothes might improve my attitude and attract like-minded people to me," I offered, helpfully.

"Ah, now you've got it," he said. "Make sure you wear your new clothes to the Human Be-In."

"What is that?"

He smiled impishly and gave his long mustache a twirl on one end. “It’s going to be a great and spiritually cleansing event. Bands, poets, food, drink, drugs, dancing, divine worship, all in the Polo Field in Golden Gate Park. On the fourteenth. We’ll all be together. The radicals from Berkeley, the hippies here in the city. We’re all celebrating a new way of living.”

I shook his hand. “I’ll be there. Thanks for everything. Today’s my birthday.”

He pumped my arm vigorously. “Happy birthday.” I started to walk off with my new ensemble.

“What’s your name?” he called, as an afterthought.

“Eddie Defoe,” I shouted back. “What about you?”

“Richard. Richard Brautigan.”

There was a large group of us who headed into the Park for the Be-In, including Tomas, Deirdre, Shauna, her boyfriend Chip, and some other friends. They had brought food and grass and wine and soda in a picnic basket. We had stocked up, befitting a huge, outdoor celebration that looked like it spread over the field to the tune of ten to twenty thousand carefree souls.

People were getting high, blowing bubbles, dancing, juggling, playing frisbee with their dogs, letting their children run around. A young man with a bag of microdot LSD stopped near us and opened it for our inspection. “Ten thousand hits. One for every person here. Help yourself.”

Our group passed on the offer. I myself wanted to keep as level a head as possible. I had a feeling that if Johnny was really in San Francisco, or anywhere else in the Bay Area, he would be at this event.

"I know it sounds crazy," I told Tomas and Deirdre, "but I think I might be able to find him today, even in this crowd."

"Good luck," Tomas offered. "We'll be right here." They had settled to the right of the stage about a third of the way back into the burgeoning crowd.

Deirdre squeezed my arm and gave me an apple and a cream cheese and jam sandwich. "We all hope you find him," she smiled.

I thanked them and began by walking along the outside edge of the throng, slowly. My plan, although it wasn't much of one, was to walk around the perimeter of the crowd and then, if necessary, wander through it during the course of the day, hoping to find him.

The roar of the crowd distracted me from my roving, as a series of poets read their work, sitting on Oriental carpets which draped over the front of a makeshift stage. They were writers whose work I would come to read and appreciate more after that special morning: Jack Kerouac, John Holmes, Allen Ginsberg, Gary Snyder, Michael McClure, Philip Whalen, Robert Duncan, Diane di Prima, et al. The beauty and richness of their words comforted me as I continued my search. I was on the other side of the field, almost completing the circle, when, about noon, The Grateful Dead took the stage and began playing their music.

Having covered the outside of the group, with no luck, I decided to stand near the left side of the stage and enjoy The Dead. Hearing, now live, "The Golden Road to Unlimited Devotion," I rolled the lyrics around my tongue, silently.

I felt a confirmation of my having taken the trip, the chance that I could recreate The Caretakers, or even call it something else, but somehow retain the two people who had forged a creative bond. But as I thought about the title, as they sang, I realized it could apply to my devotion to making music, with anyone who seemed right. I was beginning to realize that this was to be a new start, a new home, and the music would be fine with any configuration. I felt the weight of needing to find him lift off my chest. I flowed with the music, with the thousands who seemed in total harmony. I felt light. I was no longer a searcher. I was part of the community of freaks, of lovers, of those who wanted new rules, new music, new dress, new consciousness, and preferably as free or low cost as possible.

When the Dead finished their set, the crowd rewarded them with a terrific applause that echoed through the Park. I wandered toward the back of the stage, where the performers mingled with some of the crowd. There were no guards, just those who were supposed to go up on the stage clustered in groups.

I recognized Jerry Garcia, his thick dark helmet of hair, as on the album, framing an easy-going face. He walked toward me, chatting with people, receiving pats on the back and compliments with grace.

A man standing next to me called to him, as if he knew him. "Hey, Jerry, great set. Everybody loved it. How are you feeling?"

Garcia smiled again. "Good. Good. A little hungry."

Without even thinking, I took a couple steps toward him and held in one hand the sandwich and in the other the apple. Garcia took the apple and thanked me. I told him, in a rush of words, while he took a loud, crunching bite, my name, why I had come to San Francisco, how "The Golden Road" especially moved me because of my love of Keats and "Hyperion" and its mention of "the road to golden."

"I didn't know Keats wrote that when we wrote the song," Garcia said and then joked, "I hope he won't sue me." He took another huge bite of the apple, enjoying it. As he chewed, he asked "What's the name of your band again?"

"The Caretakers."

"And the guy you're looking for?"

"Johnny Janowski. He was our drummer and lead singer."

"Wait a minute. I think he came by our house. One of our managers introduced me to him."

I was stunned. I was ready to give up on looking for him minutes ago and now; one of the biggest artists in San Francisco was claiming he might know how to put me in touch with him.

"Hold on, come with me." Garcia gently guided me with him and waved to a couple more people as we headed toward the rear of the stage. "Rock. Rock!"

The man he had been calling left a conversation and came over to us.

"This is Rock Scully, one of our managers. Rock, this is Eddie from this band The Caretakers, from Michigan. Didn't you introduce me to a guy from that group who just got here a few weeks ago. A guy named Johnny?"

I watched Rock Scully stare at Garcia, rub his chin for a moment, stare down at the ground and then suddenly burst forth with, "Yes, that's right. Sings and plays drums, right?"

"Yes," I said or rather hissed, because I was so surprised by this turn of events. I cleared my throat. "You wouldn't know how to get hold of him, would you? He didn't leave an address or phone number?"

Again, Rock Scully searched his memory. "No specific address. He said he was looking to find a new band. I think he said he was staying with some people on Ashbury and Fulton."

"Can you believe this guy?" Garcia beamed. "What a memory. That's why we keep you on."

"Thank you," I said, stunned. "Thanks very much."

"Hope you find him," Garcia said and he and Rock Scully wandered off to talk business. I floated around the back of the stage and finally found my way back to Tomas, Deirdre and the others and excitedly told them what had happened.

"That is so cool," Tomas agreed. "This day is turning into such a mellow happening."

"Isn't it great?" Deirdre asked and stated at the same time. "You get to meet Jerry Garcia and he helps you to find Johnny."

I didn't have an address but I had the greatest confidence that I would track Johnny down, that he would apologize for running away, and we would find a way to create music again, in a city that, for me, was starting to take on magical proportions.

I contentedly munched on the sandwich Deirdre had given me that I had been carrying around for hours, almost as if it was a reward for my efforts. Bands and speakers and poets followed. Doctor Timothy Leary told the crowd to "turn on, tune in and drop out" and toward the end of the day, as it began to get dark, four orange flares were shot into the air and a man parachuted onto the stage. I felt giddy, like it signaled the arrival of my life, of happiness, of a new direction for me and even the arrival of a place in time, where people could be whoever they wanted and do things people had never seriously considered before.

Chapter 18

The excitement I felt after the Human Be-In continued the next day, as I walked early in the morning drizzle to the corner of Ashbury, the beginning of that street, and Fulton Avenue. Of course, I did not know which of the pastel-colored flats contained Johnny as a houseguest. So, undaunted by the odds of randomly finding him, I began ringing doorbells. At first, I got no answer. I came to the conclusion that not everyone was unemployed in the area.

Finally, though, a door was answered, and then another, and my inquiry, "Excuse me, I think my friend Johnny may be staying at your place," received some very odd looks and some doors being closed a bit louder than was absolutely necessary.

I thought about how it sounded and tried to rephrase it so it would not sound so strange, so disconnected to reality. But at the same time, I didn't want to launch into a full explanation of The Caretakers, Michigan, Hollywood, my trek out to San Francisco and my need to be sure, one way or the other, whether my future musical plans should or should not include Johnny Janowski.

After spending the better part of the first morning ringing bells around the intersection, I returned back to the Cole Street apartment and made a note of those addresses where I had received a definitive "no' as a reply.

This hunting went on for a while and I brought the list, checking off address after address gradually. I realized I would have to try certain houses in the evening or on weekends and it simply would not do to sit outside in the misty air all day, shivering and waiting for Johnny to stroll up, casually, notice me sitting on a front step and ask, "Eddie, me boy, how long have you been out here?"

In fact, my energy waned, and not only because I met with failure as I rang doorbells around that intersection. I also called the Janowskis, collect, of course, back in Romeo, to ask if they had heard anything at all.

Mister Janowski answered the phone and sounded so down, he mumbled an apology and a thank you for my contacting them and simply passed the phone over to his wife. The usually jovial and warm Mrs. Janowski, for the first time, sounded old to me, as if much of the life and vivaciousness had been extracted, sucked out of her by the sad realization that her son had not only deserted his best friend but his own family, without even sending them a card.

She was not at all comforted by the fact that I had received his cryptically worded card, for it still brought up the question of why he had not written to his despairing parents, who had loved and taken care of him and now had nothing but the disjointed and morbid words he had written on that card to me to allay their fears.

"You are a good boy, Eddie," she said to me, as the conversation slowed to an uncomfortable and bleak crawl. "You stay in touch with us. Maybe you will visit us again soon. We miss you and Johnny so much."

"Everything in life takes time," I said, trying to comfort her, and myself. "When Johnny is ready, he'll come out of hiding, or whatever is going on with him. It's a struggle and he probably feels ashamed of what he's done. It'll take a lot of bravery but he'll reappear. He'll apologize. He'll explain."

"It's so funny," she said, in a voice choked with bitterness. "Johnny, here, he was so popular, always so confident and making things happen. And you, Eddie, quiet and thoughtful, you turn out to be the strong one, traveling on your own, not giving up. Who would have imagined?"

I promised to call her again and gently hung up the phone.

I made my next call to my mother and Michelle and it too was difficult. They were not pleased to hear that not only had I not found Johnny but that despite that fact, I liked San Francisco and intended to stay a while.

After those two calls, it was no surprise when Shauna saw me, distraught, and asked what was wrong. I asked her to wait and went and found Tomas and Deirdre in the kitchen, eating and talking. I asked them to come to the living room and told them all the news.

"I want to stay in San Francisco and I know I've stayed here quite a while." There were polite protests. "And I haven't financially contributed. So, I'll understand if you want me to go." More simultaneous exclamations. "If I stay, you've got to let me pay you. I'll get a job somewhere. Man, I haven't even met your other roommate. I have no idea what he thinks of this."

"Bruce is doing an internship at UC Med," Tomas explained. "None of us ever see him."

“He works day and night,” Deirdre amplified. “Don’t worry about him.”

“The important thing,” Shauna said, with her eyes wide with concern, “is that we have room for you and you don’t need to move out.” Here she paused, her voice becoming quieter, filled with a potential hurt. “Unless you feel you have to.”

It was soon settled. I’d continue to stay on the couch. Everyone would keep their eyes open for a job for me and when I found one, I would contribute whatever everyone thought was fair to the rent. I was almost unable to get the words “thank you” out into the air. Tomas and Deirdre went to bed. Shauna and I sat alone for a while and then she moved over and sat next to me on the sofa, on my bed, in my communal bedroom, office, den, safe harbor. She put her hand on my leg and I took her hand, lightly stroking the fingers.

“I don’t know how I could have dealt with all this if it wasn’t for you, and them.”

Shauna looked deeply into my eyes. “I want to you to sleep with me tonight.”

“Shauna,” I began, filled with an unbearable level of self-doubt, “you don’t have to...”

"I don’t have to do anything,” she interrupted me. She stood and pulled me on my arm, bringing me to a standing position. She turned out the living room light and we were illuminated only by the hall light.

She put her arms around me. My arms slid around her waist, effortlessly, magnetically.

"Do they know about this? Or your boyfriend?"

"Ssssh," she insisted, and silenced me with a kiss and we tiptoed down the hall to her bedroom.

I didn't find Johnny and I didn't find work. So, I helped with the cooking and cleaning, hung around some of the clubs and coffee houses and played in some late night jams, some parties. I wrote songs late at night when everyone was asleep and the only sounds were the whistling wind and pattering of rain on the glass of the living room bay window, the slushy sounds of tires on wet pavement.

Scooter, the virtually mute friend of Tomas and Deirdre's, who I had met my first fateful night in the Haight, in front of the Psychedelic Shop, ironically turned out to be so well-connected in the neighborhood that he heard when drug deals were going bad, when someone had the clap, when a band was going to cancel a gig and, very fortunately for me, when a job might be opening.

So, when Scooter, who was getting everyone stoned at the Cole Street house, told me one blustery March afternoon that they might need some part-time help at The Print Mint, a poster shop on Haight Street itself, I was so excited, I bear-hugged him.

Everyone laughed except Scooter, whose eyes got very wide and went back to being monosyllabic after I put him back down on the living room floor.

"Whoa," he said.

I went for my jacket. "I'm going right now. Okay?"

"Talk to Rex," he said in a pinched voice as he inhaled deeply on a joint.

Rex had greasy hair that constantly flopped in front of his eyes, which were guarded by thick lensed horn-rimmed glasses. I tried not to act too desperate, mentioned Scooter only once and simply acted like the job was already mine.

But after the interview, which took all of five minutes, he asked how many hours I was looking for and I told him, "Whatever you like."

Rex then said it sounded good and he'd let me know.

Apparently, sometimes, one's will or one's vibe, as they called it, can actually change a person's mind, force a person into a decision, without coercion. When Rex said he would let me know, part of my mind went into panic mode, thinking, "If I walk out of here without the promise of this job, I won't get it."

And part of my mind, which I admit was somewhat hazy from a number of hits of Scooter's Columbian, felt light and confident. This mixture of fear and irrational confidence combined oddly in the phrase that I did not intend but came tumbling out of my mouth:

"That's great, Rex. When do I start?"

I had a soapy grin on my face. Rex peered at me through those Coke bottle bottom specs, and I waited, smiling, nodding, as if the only thing he could say to me was something good. My brain anticipated a pleasantry, not a "Sorry, I'll let you know," or a "Did you hear what I said?"

I don't know if it was the recommendation from the tight-mouthed Scooter or the expression of dopey optimism on my face but Rex, after a long pause, smirked, then half-smiled and said,

"All right. We'll start at fifteen hours a week. Monday, Wednesday and Sunday, eleven to four. You eat lunch when nobody's in the store."

I would have agreed to eating dog food from a dish with no hands.

The chance to feel better about myself by having some work helped me a great deal. Bruce, the unseen roommate, had left word he was moving out and so, I got his bedroom and while most of my salary went toward the room, I was quite content.

I went to The Diggers' store on Stanyan and got myself some odds and ends and found some used, simple furniture at garage sales. I had a job and a place where I could close the door and be by myself, if I needed. It meant a great deal to me and made me more hopeful about my life.

So did the weather, which began improving in late April. I had not been haunting the corner of Ashbury and Fulton for a long while but one day, despite knowing deep down I would probably not find Johnny, I bought some index cards and wrote on all of them, in block letters:

"LOOKING FOR JOHNNY JANOWSKI, STAYING IN NEIGHBORHOOD OF ASHBURY AND FULTON. PLEASE CALL EDDIE. (415) 555-7953."

I took the index cards and inserted them in the mail slots of doors and through the gratings of smaller, joined, metallic mailboxes, under front doors, throughout the neighborhood. I decided, in good spirits, it would be the last attempt to reach him. If I did not hear from Johnny, after blanketing the area with the note cards, then either he was not there or he was and did not want to be in touch with me. Either way, I needed to accept the truth, as sad as it might be.

The Print Mint certainly provided a great diversion. I met a wide variety of people, not just the freaks who had lived in the Haight, or the new people who seemed to keep pouring in, day by day. I met others, so-called "straight people," who looked at the wild designs, who acted like they had wandered into some bordello and didn't know how to react. I enjoyed them all. I treated them all with respect. Who was I to raise an eyebrow?

One thing that did bother me was the influx of tourists and the media. While we felt free to call ourselves freaks, knowing we were different from the rest of society, I personally resented the tour busses that roamed the neighborhood. They often had a man on a microphone in the front of the bus, either next to the driver or driving. The warm weather that began descending upon the city would prompt them to leave the windows open, and you could hear the narration as the passengers stared out at the street life, as if we were animals who had busted out of a zoo, wandering the streets freely.

Of course, they didn't have a complete tour of the Haight. The drivers who cruised by The Print Mint would never be heard saying, "...and ladies and gentlemen, if you look east, on the right, you will see legendary Hippie Hill, commonly known as Buena Vista Park, where you can always score good grass and sometimes other drugs, where there are always kites flying, guitars being played, bongos being drummed, soap bubbles being blown, where people, often strangers to each other, take time out of their day to talk, to relax, to create new friendships, find new lovers and forget, for a while, about all the things they despise in this country and this world. Now, over on your left..."

The Summer of Love, as it was dubbed, was a bad name from the start. Love is not supposed to last for one season of the year, with the usual callous and hostile environment reverting back to form after it is over. In fact, I did not welcome the exodus of lost kids with sunken eyes, with nothing in their pockets, ready to beg, steal or do almost anything to afford something to get high on and keep them warm in the doorways they inhabited.

I knew the Hell's Angels motorcycle gang was not to be messed with, but they had been around the Haight for a while. I met some of them at poetry readings and music events in the Panhandle. How can you generalize that bikers are just ruthless, drugged outlaws, wanting to destroy everything in their path, when you have seen them read from a small pamphlet of published poems and have been moved by it?

And, at the same time, it was getting harder for me to reconcile my feelings about the kids who paraded down the streets, asking for joints, acid, speed, mushrooms, not wanting to pay for anything. They came into the Print Mint and on more than one occasion I had to ask them to leave the store, because panhandling inside the establishments was strictly forbidden. But their desperation made some of these young people brazen. They were high, they were hungry, they were disappointed, after taking a bus or hitchhiking, that the stories they had seen in the magazines and papers and on television, touting a new paradise, like Hyperion, had turned into a harsher reality.

But there I was, lucky to have a job and place to live and perhaps my luck had been getting there just before the Summer of Love, just before the tidal wave of truth, beauty and freedom seekers had busted the walls of the dam and had come pouring in. How could I look down on some guy, about the same age as me, guitar slung across his back, walking the streets, trying to figure out how to eat, how to make a living with his guitar, where to sleep for the night? I might have been that person, had I arrived during the Summer of Love, rather than in the winter, with a record out and some kind friends to take me in.

One afternoon, there was a crowd in the Print Mint, and I was trying to help a guy who had me taking out posters and then changing his mind as to which ones he was going to buy. I bounced back to other patrons who knew what they wanted and were accumulating near the cash register.

Another customer, a woman in her early thirties, asked to see a crystal hanging on a display tree near the front window. As I reached over to take it off one of the plastic branches and hand it to her, I glanced out the window at the passing wave of traffic, both human and automotive.

It was a reflex. I wanted to be out in the sunshine, playing guitar, writing, seeing who I would bump into at Hippie Hill or elsewhere. And as I started to pull my glance away from the street, I saw someone on the other side of Haight who looked familiar. I squinted. It looked like Johnny, wearing a green Army fatigue jacket and jeans.

I dropped the crystal. The woman gasped. I ran around the counter and headed out the door. Three people yelled at me in the store. I got out onto the street and ran right into someone, knocking them backwards but not down. I apologized, still on the run, weaving through the faces and bodies, trying to see past the cars going by to the other side of the street.

I ran some more until there was enough space between cars and I dashed, zigzagging across Haight Street, on the balls of my feet, fearful of the car horns that sounded, holding out my arms, almost as if straight-arming tacklers on a football field, until I got safely to the other side. I looked up the street. I saw no one with a green jacket on. Did I miss him so much that I was now hallucinating him?

The unending flow of people, the press, drug dealers and con artists out to hustle bucks out of a movement based on love and freedom removed the special-ness of the Haight from my early, wintry memories.

\

That summer, I jammed with a couple of informal groups, guys with a desire to form a band, but no name, no real songs, just the willingness to sit around, make some music, get high, talk about their favorite groups. When I sat in on these casual affairs, I partially welcomed the chance to perform but at the same time, it ate away at me. I wanted to be in front of others, associated with a functioning band, not noodling around in some garage or egg carton encased basement room, with no direction, no real motivation to create for an audience.

The satisfaction of playing for yourself and a couple of friends is perfectly fine, but to me, I had already done something exciting with The Caretakers and I didn't want to go backwards. As I saw people at The Print Mint with equipment or even carrying a stack of records, I'd ask if they knew of any groups looking for a songwriter and guitarist. I would mention it casually but I would bring it up, offhandedly, at every occasion I could.

As the summer turned a corner and started moving in the fall, I became more daring. I saw the vocalist from H.P. Lovecraft in the audience at a gig, and in between songs and the swirling, psychedelic lighting of the club, I asked if he knew of a band I could play in.

I even walked by the Dead's house at 710 Ashbury, up the hill, in Ashbury Heights, sometimes longingly staring at its multi-colored paint job, listening to the music emanating from the bay window painted black, feeling the promise of the day I met Garcia at the Be-In and being told that Johnny had contacted them. But when I now walked by their house, I was simply weighted down by the heavy burden of expectations and hopes gone aground.

And it was probably made worse by those around me, at parties, at the Cole Street flat, at the Print Mint, on street corners, who resented the encroachment, the marketing of a dream, the crass commercialization of tours and genuine "hippie" this and "hippie" that, as if we were nothing more than an art movement that would fade away, to be filed in a dusty history book for some scholars to muse over and arrogantly compare to primitive art.

It was October sixth, I remember, and always will, as the day my love affair with San Francisco ended. It became known as the Death of Hippy Day, as the people who had lived there spelled it. The Psychedelic Shop, where my stay had really started in the neighborhood, sick of the circus atmosphere, decided to close its doors.

To accompany the drippy, hand-lettered sign, the owner had posted a fake funeral notice. It was made out to "Hippy, Son of Beloved Media." I felt sick at heart as they simply gave away everything in the store, with no joy, just defeat, the sense that some force greater than them had crushed them and there was no point to continuing.

A coffin was built, filled with beads and flowers and other artifacts of our bygone dream. Haight Street was no longer able to be navigated by car, as scores of people, feeling like this was their last true moment together, in remembrance, filed down the middle of the street, happy at least to have defied the conventions of society one last time, to have shifted the unending flow of traffic, even for a half a day.

I wandered along with it, seeing familiar faces, including Tomas and Deirdre, but being too sad to join them, to talk with them, needing to be alone, but with the crowd, having nothing but my thoughts in my head, but still feeling part of that energy milling past the stores I had walked by so many times before.

The Death of Hippy funeral procession made its way into the Panhandle, where the coffin was lit on fire. The funeral pyre glowed orange and yellow and people shared food and music was played and we all tried to convince ourselves, but failed, it was another joyous celebration and that our lives there could not be touched.

I stayed very late in the Panhandle, not wanting to let go of the event, and then ran into some guys I had jammed with. We talked about how miserable the Haight's fate had been and it was decided we would go to one friend's house, drink, smoke, blast music and not let the Death of Hippy be the death of our own attitudes, our own willingness to live life on our terms.

There were shouts of agreement, gleeful screams and we hit a liquor store with the money we could pool and one of the guys had a lid of Acapulco Gold and we went to his house and played music loudly, and when it was a San Francisco band, we sang along to the songs, as a matter of pride.

It was very late at night, or very early in the morning, if you prefer, when we had reached such a level of intoxication and exhaustion that the party began to break up. One guy was passed out cold on the floor. I decided to walk home, even though I was wobbling seriously.

I veered down the quiet, wind-whipped streets, pretending the breeze was the reason I was walking in such a haphazard way. A San Francisco police cruiser sidled up to me, watching me struggle to walk straight.

"Hey," called out the cop on the passenger's side front seat.

I stopped, squinted at him, shook my head and looking down, shouted, "What do you want from me? I'm just walking home."

"Just come here for a second," he said.

I teetered up to the cop car and leaned on it for support.

"Where you going at this hour?"

"Home. Cole Street. Although, I don't know if it feels like home any more. You know what I'm saying? You, you're a cop. That's fine. We need you. But I'm trying to find out how to be happy, to decide what to do with my life. And, and, don't you feel it? Whatever was good about the Haight, it's just over? Even though you're a cop, can't you feel something is missing, is wrong, isn't fun anymore? Remember when you were my age? Remember how important having fun was?"

Both cops looked at each other. The driver murmured, "Let him go."

The cop on the passenger side nodded and then turned to me. "Dreams die hard, kid. But they die for everybody. Just a different time of life. You live on Cole Street?"

"Yup."

"Go home. Get some sleep. Tomorrow, you'll feel better."

“Somehow,” I said, pushing myself off the car and upright, straightening up as best as I could, “I don’t think so. But thanks.”

They followed me for a while and when they saw me turn to walk up Cole, they turned off and headed elsewhere.

I clambered sloppily up the steps, struggled forever to get the key into the lock and stumbled inside. I made my way to my room and found a note taped to the door. I pulled it off, turned on the light to my room and struggled to focus my eyes.

The note, in bold, capital letters, read, “Eddie, Johnny called tonight. Said to meet him tomorrow at dawn at Golden Gate Bridge. Urgent!”

I shook my head, to clear it. It looked like Shauna’s handwriting. I banged on her door with my fist, the anger welling in me. This was the ugliest joke I could think of and it came after a very low day.

I didn’t wait but whipped open her door and turned on the light. I heard gasps from her and her boyfriend as they sat up in bed and shaded their eyes from the overhead light.

“Eddie, what the hell is your problem?” she shouted.

“My problem?” I asked, dumbfounded. I waved the note in the air. “You think this is funny? This note about Johnny? And don’t tell me you didn’t write it. I know your handwriting!”

She sat up, her eyes blazing, pulling the covers up to her armpits. “You poor misguided boy! It’s no joke! He called. He said he was Johnny. And that's what he said. The Golden Gate at dawn. I don't know if it was him or not. I'm sorry."

Doubt crept into my mind and I turned out her light and closed the door quietly, standing in the dark hall, still high, still drunk and wishing I could make my thoughts cohere.

Chapter 19

I had told myself that I would give up trying to find Johnny if I heard a response from one of the note cards I had left in the vicinity of Ashbury and Fulton. Now, I couldn't be sure if someone was playing a cruel joke, and, if it was Johnny, whether he was seriously at the Golden Gate Bridge, about to leap to his death.

I had to think and I dashed back outside, into the cold air of the middle of the night, walking furiously, my breath forming clouds, not knowing what to do.

I walked toward Haight Street again, wondering what I would do if Johnny did intend to go to the bridge and I did nothing to get there. I had no idea how to get there quickly. I saw from a clock in a store window it was three thirty in the morning. Taking two buses at this hour might take more than two hours and I didn't know what time dawn was.

No one at the Cole Street flat had a car. I couldn't call people I barely knew at three thirty and say, "Wake up! I need to borrow your car. My long lost friend may be committing suicide at dawn at the Golden Gate Bridge!"

I decided to jog back to the house where we had celebrated and mourned the Death of Hippy Day. I didn't care if the cops or anyone else tried to stop me. I would know, once and for all, if Johnny was in San Francisco and if it was real, finish, finally, the cruel and unbearable labyrinth of loyalty I was caught up in for all this time.

I rang the bell over and over and finally, one of the partygoers popped his head out a window.

I desperately explained why I needed a car, right that moment, and when I was greeted with confusion, I had to repeat myself. Someone from a neighboring window shouted out, "Go to sleep!"

My friend refused to let me in and further informed me I shouldn't be driving in my current condition. He closed the window and disappeared. I cursed at him and when the neighbor opened his window to say something, I told him to drop dead.

I stormed down the sidewalk, wide awake now, furious at the lack of help, angry at Johnny for putting me in this position and never having contacted me directly to this point. I knew I didn't have enough money to call a cab to take me there and it was very unlikely I would find anyone I knew to drive me.

Back on Haight Street, it was now after four a.m. and no one was in sight. I decided to run. I ran toward Fulton Street, not to the intersection which had seemed a blessing when I learned about it and now felt like a curse, but a few blocks away. I looked for westbound traffic, hoping to flag down one of the few cars on the road, perhaps convincing them to take a right on Funston and drive me toward the Bridge.

I was a sidewalk confined toreador, waving futilely at a couple cars which zoomed by with no interest in slowing. Between their appearances, I had time to ponder my situation, consider new and unpleasant possibilities. Was I being played for a fool because Johnny had been driven mad? What if he was insane but really planning to kill himself? I wondered, if I even got there in time, if I could convince him to struggle on. And perhaps he would not even wait until dawn. It was possible, in his misery; he had already done what he had threatened, in his last vain attempt to communicate with me.

I saw a car coming and now, barely able to breathe, so filled with fear, I stepped into the street, waving my arms. The car honked its horn and I refused to budge. It continued honking and started to change to the far left lane. I saw it shift its direction and I moved slightly in that direction, not in the middle of Fulton but edging toward it.

The car swerved even farther left when it went by me and its left side tires banged against the median. The car skidded slightly and then veered to the right where it came to a stop. I ran again, not knowing whether I would meet with someone armed with a knife or gun or bat, ready to do battle with a crazed man who was ready to lay down his life on a dark thoroughfare.

I caught up to the stopped car, a big four-door metallic monster, its left turn signal blinking, just sitting there. Panting from the sprint, I rested my hands on my knees, wondering if the driver would peel out, come after me or perhaps would do nothing, injured.

The door swung open and a middle-aged man put one leg on the pavement and looked back at me, his eyes wide. I didn't let him have the first word. This was important and I had to make it count.

"Sir, I'm desperate. I have a friend who is mentally unstable who left a message he is going to jump off the Golden

Gate Bridge at dawn. This is not a joke. I risked my life back there to try and help him. Please, help me. Just give me a ride to the last exit before you get on the bridge."

The man looked at me a long while, saying nothing.

"Please, I'm serious. I have no money for a cab and I can't wait for the bus."

"You know, you almost got yourself killed back there."

"I know. I'm sorry." I walked closer to him, wanting him to get a good look at my face. "It's my best friend."

That did it. "Get in," he said and I ran around the car and leaped inside.

We drove rapidly in silence for a while. "My name is Eddie," I said. "Thank you so much for helping me."

He gave me a quick glance and then returned his eyes to the road, zooming by. "I'm John. You want to tell me about this friend?"

I gave him the barest details. He took the corner at Funston so sharply, his tires squealed.

"You sure he's going to be there, to do this?" John asked.

I thought if I voiced my doubt he might stop, insist I get out, try and talk me out of going. So, I changed the subject. "What time is it?"

John turned on the interior light in his car and took a look at his wristwatch. "About a quarter to five?"

"What time do you think it will be at dawn?"

"I don't know, Eddie."

We rushed down the tree lined drive and John cut around cars in his way. We had to stop at a couple of red lights and he felt the tension in the car each time he did so. "Have to stop at the lights."

"There's no one coming. Please go."

I talked him into running the second red light we came to but as we rounded a curve of trees, all of a sudden, we hit a massive traffic jam, less than half a mile from the bridge.

"Oh, God, no!" I shouted.

"What the hell?" John was perplexed by the situation. "Why is there so much traffic at this hour?"

I opened the door of his car.

"What are you doing?" he demanded to know.

"The traffic. It's because of Johnny. He must be there."

"Stay in the car," demanded John. "We'll still get there faster than if you go on foot."

"No, I can't wait. I'm sorry. Thank you, John."

I jumped out of the car and slammed the door closed, running again, not even waiting to hear his reply. I cut across the lanes of traffic and got to the side of the road, my legs pumping, not wanting to look at the sky getting lighter.

I ran with all my might and in my oxygen-starved mind, I tried to think positively, to remember moments, things that I might remind him about, the nights of sex at Missy's parents, the gigs we enjoyed the most, the all-night party at Don Miller's estate, before the Battle of the Bands. If I could just get to him, talk to him, I believed I could get him down. They might take him away to jail or to a hospital, but if I could just talk to him, to be the embodiment of the things that had previously made him so alive, so a force of nature, he could recover, become something of what he was.

I didn't fool myself, as my legs pounded on asphalt, into thinking Johnny was going to be the old Johnny. I knew something was broken in him, and it was unlikely he would ever be the same. But I was willing to trade what little I had just to have, in a devil's bargain, some kind of Johnny, some kind of friendship, not even for the music, just for the closeness of two people who had grown up together, developed their voices as artists together, and were not supposed to be separated forever, so early, so unfairly soon.

The dawn was just breaking as I got to the toll booths at the Golden Gate and ran between the unmoving cars, closer to the booths, where the workers were all staring back behind them. I saw a huge group of people jamming the right side of the bridge and knew I could not penetrate the obstacle.

I squeezed past a car at one of the tollbooths, pushing past people, seeing police, firemen, photographers, reporters, early morning joggers, motorists who had left their cars. I shoved them, calling out, "Get out of my way! Move! I know him!"

One cop grabbed my arm to stop my progress and I ferociously ripped my jacket from his grasp, ducked under some legs, pushed another person to the ground and I was near the front of the crowd.

A ring of cops prevented people from approaching but I could see him, standing on the cement, holding firm the railing. It was dark, muddy orange, not gold. I had never actually been to the Bridge in the time I was in San Francisco and now, with Johnny standing solemnly, the wind whipping his hair, as he stared out to the bay, like a lost sailor desperate to find a horizon, I was thinking how wrong it was that he was up there and on a bridge that was not even gold colored.

"Johnny!" I screamed. He did not hear me. I stepped forward and two cops moved up to meet me. "I'm his best friend! He left me a note! Let him see me, for God's sake."

The cops took a moment to size me up and I screamed again his name, waving my arms. This time, as if in slow motion, he turned, caught sight of a small commotion and then his eyes, sunken, with dark circles where there had never been any, even after the longest night of revelry, his eyes narrowed and then widened again in recognition. He looked at me and gave a pained smile, so filled with longing despair, it almost didn't seem to be a smile at all. He raised one hand to belt height and gave a small wave, as if embarrassed to be seen by me, although he had called for me.

A police captain noted this and then turned to me. "You know him, huh? What's your name?"

"Eddie."

He firmly took me by my arm and drew me out of the crowd. He gave a quick look toward Johnny and then leaned in to me, speaking confidentially. "Eddie, listen to me. Do not rush up to him. Walk slowly toward him. Ask him to come down and talk to you. Don't threaten him. Just act like the friend you are and don't panic him."

I nodded and agreed. The captain stepped away. It was just Johnny and me, up on another stage, everybody looking at us. I walked as delicately toward him as I would a wounded bear, hindered but able to strike, to lash out at any minute, to cause injury to untold numbers in one rash, enraged moment.

As I moved closer, he moved toward the rail. A shout or two was heard from the crowd and murmurings. I stopped, looked back at the captain. He held out his hand, for me to stop my advance.

I was now fifteen feet away from Johnny and could see him well, as the morning light was fighting through the clouds. His boyish, good looks were obscured by his hair, now very long. It was clear he had not cut it since he left Hollywood. He was considerably thinner and his clothes hung on his frame.

But the most important detail was his eyes. There was no hope in them. A thin film of tears developed over them. The boy-man who seemingly could work magic with his own will, creating lovers and business opportunities as easily as he steered the Eternal Energy Machine, while sipping a beer or smoking a cigarette, that person was no longer there.

And there were no words from me, because I knew that anything I said, any faint expression of hope from me, any attempt to recall the times we had, or dream up new ideas for our future together, those would seem as absurd to him as they would sound hollow to me as I said them. I felt sickened in the moment, having made it in time only to see a skeletal Johnny, the life drained from him, even though he still, for the moment, lived.

"Johnny," I began, knowing I had to say something, that I couldn't watch him leap away from me, from this whole world, with nothing said. But when the word escaped my lips, he shook his head vigorously from side to side, splaying the tears that sat in his ducts across his cheeks at odd angles. He didn't want me to try. He just wanted to look on me, to pay homage to the life we had had. It was as if he only needed a moment of connecting to the past to convince him that life could not change for him, was not worth living, that what had transpired from Romeo to Detroit to Hollywood to the Haight-Ashbury to the crowd holding its breath for his final performance had not been real.

I had the horrible thought, as we were frozen there, our eyes locked on one another, that Johnny had not contacted me before because he feared, yes, feared, that if we sat around talking

about the good old days, if he heard my forgiveness, my encouragements about trying again in San Francisco, he knew I could talk him out of ending his life. And he knew the only way he could have a goodbye from me and not be saved, not dragged back to a life that he now found so unacceptable, was to invite me to this moment.

It seems impossible to assure anyone that all this happened in that period of time, this understanding I had, and to insist that I was right in my suspicions of what went on in Johnny's mind. But the reason I will never, ever doubt it for myself was the next moment in that series of disembodied seconds on the Bridge, when he gave me another wan smile and nodded, a nod not of goodbye, I don't think. It was a nod saying,

"You understood before. And you understand now. Thank you, of all people, for that."

And he was gone. The athleticism, the easy grace of leaping out of a truck thrown into park in a lot next to a nightclub while the truck still rolled, that fluidity, was what he showed me. Time was so warped that though I heard screams and shouts, it took me a while to register them, to turn and look at the crowd, the cops and firemen who wanted nothing more than to put a blanket around his shoulders and drive him somewhere safe and sedate him and give him some hot soup. I looked at the faces, sad, horrified, shocked, and repulsed.

"Eddie," I heard my name called, by the captain, but I did not even look in his direction. I walked to the rail and looked down at the grey-green swirling mass below. It just rolled and rolled, as if nothing had just entered it, as if nothing could disturb it and I stared into it, my focus dimming.

I heard no sounds, I saw no motion. But the words near the end of Keats's "Hyperion" came to me, insinuated themselves into my mind:

"Mute thou remainest–Mute! Yet I can read
A wondrous lesson in thy silent face.
Knowledge enormous makes a God of me.
Names, deeds, gray legends, dire events, rebellions,
Majesties, sovran voices, agonies,
Creations and destroyings, all at once,
Pour into the wide hollows of my brain,
And deify me, as if some blithe wine
Or bright elixir peerless I had drunk,
And so become immortal."

"Eddie," again I heard, and this time the gentle, burly hand of the captain was on my arm and I pulled away, could not look him in the eye. I walked away, walking through the cars, weaving, as if drunk, as I heard shouting, horns honking, questions from angry motorists asking, "What are you doing?" and "What's happening?"

I walked toward the Marin County side, through three lanes of immobile pieces of machinery that should have been moving a mile a minute but were helpless to do anything at all.

I moved over to and walked the center line of the Bridge, the lines of cars stretched in either direction, inching along with me, and past me. There were idling cars on either side, dark orange spans and grey cables overheard, with a sky that was as bottomless and featureless as the ocean that had just absorbed him.

I had the music we had created in my mind, and Keats's words, and curses and horns, radios blaring news and music from open windows, even in the early morning rush hour mist.

And again, unrelenting, I heard "Eddie! Eddie!" It was not the captain. I was alone among the sea of cars. It wasn't Johnny's voice. All that I had of that was on a twelve inch piece of vinyl, something that would make me feel proud and haunted always. This voice was odd, thick, somehow familiar.

"Over here, Eddie!"

I looked up. At first, all that registered, in the drab wash of car colors were incongruous colors. Then, the shape. An old, hump-backed bus. Then, over to the driver behind the wheel, and the pudgy, drooping, naturally sad face of Tiny.

"What, what you are doing?" he asked, incredulously.

I walked over to him, as someone seeing a mirage in the desert. I opened the passenger's side door and got in and slammed it. Tiny grasped my shoulder and shook me in hearty greeting.

"Eddie! So good to see you. But why are you walking in middle of the bridge?"

I stared at him and couldn't speak for a few moments. But I knew he deserved a reply.

"Tiny," I said. "Tiny."

"Are you okay?" he asked and looking at me, he knew the answer.

We sat quietly, staring straight ahead at the cars barely moving in front of us.

"Where are we going?" I finally asked.

"We? Well, I am going to next place for circus. In San Jose. Where are you living?"

"I have a room in San Francisco," I said. "I have some belongings to pick up."

Tiny thought a moment. "You want a job. Not just animals. This circus has music. You could play music, Eddie."

I looked at him, smiled and turned on his radio, found a station playing rock and roll. And we sat there, gently nodding our heads to the songs which we liked, sitting still during the ones we didn't care for, together, going somewhere, painfully slowly, but going.

Printed in the USA
CPSIA information can be obtained
at www.ICGtesting.com
CBHW020507060724
11187CB00032BB/345

9 781601 452702